FREE FALL

wilde boys · book two

USA TODAY BESTSELLING AUTHOR

SARA CATE

www.saracatebooks.com

Photographer: Michelle Lancaster

Model: JJ Michaels

Editing: Amy Briggs of Briggs Consulting

For my readers

PROLOGUE

AMSTERDAM

"CHOKE ME, NASH."

Squeezing my fingers around her throat, I press firmly for a moment on the spot under her ears, and she moans in response. I'm glad she's having fun, because I'm already bored. It's like watching a porn I've seen a million times. It's fine. Gets the job done, and if I could stop watching it I would, but I can't—because I need this.

Her hand slams against the wall. It's a little too fucking dramatic if you ask me. Lotte's friends are always like this. *Choke me, Nash. Punish me. I'll be a good girl.*

Over and over again, it's always the fucking same.

None of it is real. They want me to lose control on them, but I don't give a shit about them enough to do it.

We're in a dark back room of the party, and I guess this is what the rooms are for, but I can still hear the music and chatter from the crowd through the door. It's not my first time at one of Lotte's parties. I started coming to them a few weeks ago after a lot of persuasion on her part. Not that I was turned off by the idea of a party, but I knew through work gossip they were an easy way to get laid, and it felt too soon. I should have rushed my ass over the minute she told me about it the first time at work. I should have wanted to cleanse out any and all residual feelings for Zara, but I didn't. I can't explain why, but I wasn't ready.

Until I was. And then I never looked back.

My mind is wandering too much, and my arousal is moving in the wrong fucking direction. I'm supposed to be moving toward coming, but it's like a standstill.

"Harder," she pants, her lithe British accent not sounding so proper now as she begs me to stick my dick so far inside her it feels like I'm rearranging her guts.

The problem is I know she wants it harder because my cock is slowly deflating. What is wrong with me? This girl is hot. I've had my eye on her for a few weeks now. I like how she looks almost innocent and normal, and she's never with anyone except maybe a couple of girls. But maybe that's the problem. There is no ring on her finger or man over her shoulder. There's no fucking conflict. It was too easy to talk her into a private room and a quick fuck.

She's not fucking your dad, the voice in my head reminds me, so I squeeze my eyes shut.

A quick memory flashes through my mind. A dark night, a warm body in my hands, a cock down her throat that wasn't mine.

I don't get off on Zara anymore. But sometimes that

little flashback resurfaces, and it's like a secret key in my pocket, and as fucked up as I know it is, it gets me off easily because within seconds, I'm filling up the condom around my dick and the girl almost seems relieved. She probably thought it was going to end sooner.

We're both panting for a while before we start cleaning ourselves up and I discard the rubber in the trash in the corner by the door. It's a simple guest bedroom and it's bigger than the other room I've ended up in, which is a glorified broom closet.

"That was fun," she says before handing me a card. Looking down at it, I see her name scribbled on the paper with a phone number. Britta—British Britta. That should be easy to remember, if I wanted to remember it.

"Yeah, thanks," I reply.

Then, she steps closer to me, and I notice her eyes are two different colors. I know someone else with two different colored eyes, but I can't seem to remember who. The thought distracts me for a moment as she leans up to kiss my cheek, the most contact our faces have made through this whole interaction.

"You lived up to your reputation, Nash," she says with a mischievous smile. "I'd still like to see what you're like when you really let go."

She turns to leave the room, letting the door hang open after she passes through. The noise from the party is deafening now, but I'm not ready to rejoin it. I almost feel bad, like British Britta was probably worth more than a quickie in a dark room, and I shouldn't have had to think about a fucked up threesome to get off while I was with her.

I drop into a chair in the corner, pulling out the flask in my pocket and guzzling down half of it and letting the harsh burn of vodka singe my insides. It's better than letting my thoughts go where I know they're going.

I miss her, and it burns worse than the vodka. It's the regret, really. All the shoulda, woulda, coulda thoughts that haunt me at night. I should have stayed on Del Rey. We could have kept up the messy little arrangement we had, and everyone would have been happy.

But I didn't. I handed Zara to my dad because he gets everything. He's the superior version of me, and she chose him so easily. I mean, why wouldn't she? I treated her like shit, but in some fucked up way, she liked it. She wanted me to treat her like shit, and I didn't have to feel bad for how fucked up I was or explain why I liked the way she looked with my hand around her throat. It was easy and I wasn't alone.

Now I'm alone, and I jerk off to fantasies about fucking her while he watches. And every night I convince myself I never really loved her.

There's a knock on the open door, and two guys poke their heads in, both flinching when they notice me sitting in the chair in the dark.

"Oh, sorry," one of them mumbles. His hand rests possessively on the other guy's shoulder as he pulls him out of the room.

"I'm done in here. It's all yours," I say as I get up to leave.

They're blocking the doorway, so I shuffle awkwardly waiting for them to move and I get the distinct feeling they're both checking me out.

"You're welcome to stay," the man in the back says in a flat tone. The guy in front of him bites his lip, and I give them both a polite smile as I move closer to the exit.

"Uh, maybe next time," I stammer as my skin starts to flush with heat.

"Suit yourself," he says again, pushing his partner toward the bed against the opposite wall.

Clearing my throat, I pass them by. Once back in the party, the sudden pang of anxiety claws at my insides when I realize everyone I came here with is either gone or busy, and I'm in a crowd of strangers alone.

Time to go home, then.

I fish my phone out of my pocket and stare down at the screen as I move through the crowd and text Lotte to thank her for inviting me. I barely notice the tall black wall of man that steps in front of me, but I absentmindedly stop as I hit send.

"Nash Wilde."

It's a familiar deep voice pulled from a memory that has been locked deep down, like an echo from my past. My head flips up as I stare at the face paired with the voice, and it takes me two, three, four seconds before my brain catches up with itself.

Ellis Prior.

"What the—"

He laughs, a silky dark timbre that hums from his chest as his face cracks a cool, effortless smile.

Ellis Prior is standing in front of me. At a party in Amsterdam.

"I thought I saw you earlier. You remember me, right?" he says.

My mouth is hanging open like a fucking idiot as I nod. You don't forget Ellis Prior. Least of all me.

He worked with my dad for years when I was a kid, spending weekends on Del Rey, casting shadows with his larger-than-life personality. Or at least that's how it looks in my memory. And while I remember him as the young, twenty-something business executive with thick light brown hair and a smile as bright as his commanding presence, the man who stands before me now is about fifteen years older but no less intimidating.

"Of course," I stammer. "Ellis Prior."

"That's right. How are you?" He extends a hand, and I blink before reaching out to shake it. My eyes linger on the golden, tan skin of his arm under the black button-up shirt rolled to the elbows. After the handshake, he folds his arms in front of him, posturing with his shoulders back and chest out. It's a power stance, and I do my best to match him.

I know he asked me a question, but my mind is too warped by this sudden onslaught of past and present colliding.

"I'm good, thanks. You?"

Before he replies, he touches my elbow gesturing to the patio where there are only a handful of people congregating.

"Looks more suitable for conversation out there."

I'm following him through the crowd toward an empty spot on the large, covered patio. There are no more seats out here, but Lotte told me her neighbors hate her parties, so she doesn't encourage people to party outside.

The fresh night air does help to clear the fog from my head. Brushing my sweat-moist hair from my face, I stare at Ellis and laugh.

"This is fucking crazy, right? What are you doing here?"

There's that heavy chuckle of his again.

"I'm working on a two-year contract with a software company here in Amsterdam. I've been here for about a year now." He leans his elbows back on the railing, staring out at the party, where the crowd is starting to dwindle now as people head home with their partners—new and old. "What about you, Nash Wilde? All grown up and at a dirty party in the Netherlands."

His heavy stare lands on my face as he scrutinizes me, and I realize this is probably a lot more fucking weird for him. The last time he saw me I was about ten years old. While I looked up to him, he saw me as nothing more than a bratty kid who occasionally crashed the party.

I bite the inside of my cheek just thinking about it. He thinks this party is kinky and he has no idea what the last year has been like for me. He knows my dad. What would he think about what we did?

"So, what are you doing here, Nash?"

"I'm in an internship at Schiller Industries. I got here in January."

He leans toward me, a subtle smirk lifting the corners of his mouth. "What are you doing here at this party, Nash?"

I laugh, feeling like an idiot, but try to hide it. "Lotte is my friend. She's been trying to get me out of my apartment since I got here. What about you?"

"I get bored easily," he says in a dark, ominous tone like there's more meaning there than he's giving me now. In my memory, Ellis never seemed like the kind of guy who handled boredom well. He was younger than my dad and definitely had a wild streak. Apparently, he still does.

"I guess I do too," I reply, and he laughs again.

"You're not ten anymore," he says like it's an observation, but there's something about the way he's looking at me as if he's sizing me up, and I fidget under his stare. "So, how is your dad?"

My smile fades and I let out a heavy sigh.

"Uh-oh," he says as he pulls a rolled cigarette from his pocket. I watch his fingers as he lifts it to his mouth and flicks a lighter, the flame illuminating his dark brown, almost black irises. Once he lights it, the smell hits my nose and I bite my lip to hide my smile and look away.

Ellis Prior is smoking pot at a party in Amsterdam.

When I look back at him, he holds the joint out to me,

and I take it with a small shake of my head. "This is fucking crazy."

It's quiet for a moment, and I'm grateful he didn't ask me to expand on the dad question. I don't even fucking know what I would say about it. How I'm not mad at my dad, but I don't *not* hate my dad right now either. Ellis was present at a time of my life when I looked up to Alistair Wilde, worshipped the ground he walked on, wanted to live my life in his image. In that world, I still had a brother.

"Hey," he says after a moment, and maybe it's inspired by the fact I'm staring blankly ahead. "I heard about Preston. I'm sorry, Nash."

"Thanks," I reply, looking up at him. Whenever people apologize for Preston's death, I look at them to see if they're giving me pouty condescending bullshit or if they really are sorry. I've never known Ellis to be fake, so it's no surprise his expression is genuine.

"I talked to Alistair shortly after it happened. I never got to talk to you though."

His gaze is fixed on my face, and I start to feel a strange *thud-thud* in my ears. The pot hits my system, and the tension in my shoulders melts like wax.

Two girls walk up to us, and it takes me a moment to realize one of them is Britta, but she's not staring at me even though she announces herself by saying, "Hey, Nash." Both her and her friend are staring at Ellis.

"Hello, ladies," he says.

Ellis is only about an inch taller than me, but it does feel like we all have to look up to see him.

"I didn't know you were friends with him," Britta whispers toward me, but I shake my head because I have no fucking clue what she's talking about. Does Ellis have a reputation around here I didn't know about? I can't exactly say I'm surprised, but I'm still reeling from him being here and all this is a little bit too much to process.

"Nash and I are old friends," he says to her as he curls a piece of her hair behind her ear. She licks her lips in response. "I don't believe we've met yet." He takes Britta's hand, running his thumb over her knuckles. Then he does the same to her friend as the two girls stammer out their names, crowding close to each other.

"We were just about to get something to drink. Can I get you something?" Britta asks with a saccharine sweet smile.

"I'd love a beer," Ellis replies. "I think Nash needs one too."

"Okay," she says as she loops her arm through her friends. The two of them dash into the party, and Ellis takes another hit off his joint, offering it to me, but I put up my hand. My head is having a hard enough time keeping up as it is. There's something about how he spoke to them, the way he gently persuaded them without being harsh that fucking strikes a nerve. I'm pretty sure they would have dropped to their knees before he could utter the first syllable of "suck my dick".

My eyes track over to him again, and I fight the urge to pinch myself. I try to remember the last time I saw my father's old friend, and how it felt back then to stand next to him compared to how it feels now. As a kid, I looked up to him, figuratively and literally. Now...it's the same, except I'm supposed to be his equal. I'm a grown man now. I'm not supposed to gaze up at him like a God.

We make small talk for a while, him asking me more about the program I'm in, my plans for the future and what I intend to do with my life now I'm all grown up, as he continues to remind me. The entire time it feels like he is controlling the conversation. It's strangely comfortable.

"You got a girlfriend, Nash?"

Suddenly, there's a sharp bolt of pain in my chest, and her face comes to mind. Like there's a string draped across the ocean still connecting her to me even though she hasn't been mine in months. She never really was.

"Nope."

He's looking at me now, expressionless and unassuming.

"Do you?" I ask to fill the silence. The air feels charged now. Am I missing something?

He doesn't answer, just lets out a low, gravelly chuckle.

Just then, the girls come back with two Heinekens and hand them to us, but they're both still looking at Ellis. They're each sipping on their iced cocktails, bouncing lightly on the balls of their feet expectantly.

"So, the spare room is empty. Do you guys want to go back there?" Britta asks, and beer almost comes out of my nose.

Jesus, I don't know if I'll ever get over the forwardness of Lotte's friends. I had Britta bent over the bed within the first five minutes of the party, but suddenly as I'm standing in front of a family friend and a man who knew me as a child, it's jarring.

Then I feel Ellis's eyes on me for a moment. There's not a hint of nerves in his stance but calm confidence as he takes in my demeanor and shakes his head at the girls.

"Not tonight."

"But—" the other girl stammers.

"Nash and I are catching up," he says, placing a hand on my shoulder. "Thanks for the drinks though." And as he puts the bottle to his lips, he adds, "Maybe next time."

They both pout for a moment before nodding their heads and saying their goodbyes.

Once they're out of earshot, he mumbles over his beer

bottle, "So...you're not going to tell your dad we almost had an orgy at a party, right?"

What starts as a small laugh escalates until we're both red faced and biting back the sudden marijuana-induced hysteria. I don't answer him, but Ellis doesn't need to know my dad has done some way kinkier shit than he knows about, and he doesn't need to know how I know that.

1

"*Aufrecht sitzen*," my mother snaps while I browse the menu. On impulse my spine straightens obediently.

"What can I get for you?" the waitress asks, and before I can say a word, my mother orders a salad with grilled chicken and the dressing on the side for both of us.

Then it's silent at our table. Keeping a blank expression on my face, I stare longingly out the window. She browses through emails on her phone while I write verses in my head. Things I can never write down. Not so much words but images I want to commit to memory, feelings I want to assign names to.

The strange orange hue of empty pill bottles in the sun.

The sound piano keys make when you slam on them.

Things that cannot be unbroken and the way skin scars but is never truly uncut.

"Marina Vestenberg said she will see you next week for an audition."

I nod. "Okay."

"You're only twenty-nine, Hanna. Still a few years left if you don't waste them, but you have lost so much strength since you were sick. It's such a waste. Finish your lunch and then go to the studio."

"Okay."

When our food comes, I peek up at her periodically over my bland salad. I'd murder her for a cheeseburger, and it may sound cliche or harsh, but I would literally wring her neck at this table for a basket of fries. I'm not quite sure when this happened. When I stopped making decisions for myself and I started accepting my fate as my mother's puppet.

"You're pouting," she says flatly as I pick at my lunch.

"I'm tired."

"Get more sleep then."

"It's not that easy."

"Why not? You stay up too late, doing God knows what, and then you wake up with what, four hours of sleep. Of course, you're tired."

I don't respond because there is no arguing with her. She knows everything and is always right. She lacks the empathy to understand that at night I don't sleep because I lay awake wondering where my life went wrong. How eleven months ago I lost my spot in the ballet company—a spot I had to work twice as hard as every other girl to get. How I lost my apartment. How I ended up back under her roof, in her house, hating myself.

She likes to say I was "sick" but really, I was over-worked, under-nourished, and so depressed that one day I showed up to the studio so panicked out of my mind, I blacked out in the middle of a run through. I didn't even know someone could be hospitalized for three days for a nervous breakdown, but according to the press and my mother, it was nothing but low blood sugar.

"You don't like your contacts?" she asks after catching me blinking my eyes, fighting against the foreign objects shoved under the lids.

"I don't need them." There is nothing wrong with my eyesight, but the colored contacts hide my heterochromia. My blue and brown eyes are another one of my physical traits she wants me to hide. Right along with the three shades of melanin I have on her. I am a walking reminder my mother fucked up in the nineties and could never face going back to Germany with a curly-haired, father-less baby. She's never stopped making me pay for that.

At twenty-two, I was accepted into my first professional ballet company, and that night we celebrated. After two glasses of champagne, she confessed pushing me in ballet was her way of making the best of a bad situation. It wasn't until I woke up the next morning did it register how *I* was the bad situation she was referring to.

"Why can't we just have a nice lunch?" she asks through clenched teeth in response to my complaining about the contacts I don't need.

Ignoring her, I focus instead on more things without names, writing meaningless poetry in my head until the waitress clears our table and hands my mother the check, even though I'll be the one paying.

As promised, I go to the studio. It's an empty dance

space we rent from a German woman who owns the building and leases it out for sparsely attended yoga classes on the weekends. My mother will say she's a friend, but it was a form of manipulation, weaseling the woman out of her rentable space by befriending her and only occasionally inviting her over for *schaufele* dinner on Sundays.

It's dustier than ever now, and even though I play the music through the speakers, I never put on my shoes. Instead, I spend the next two hours lying on the dirty floor, scrolling through my phone.

I could go see Zara at her studio, but I feel like a virus in her happy life now. Married, with a new baby, in a perfect house in the suburbs. She runs the studio effortlessly and never looks tired or complains. It's exhausting to watch. She's a year younger than me, and I already resent her for how much more she was handed the day a billionaire showed up on her doorstep to change her life. Where the fuck is my billionaire?

I'm being a petty bitch. She's been trying to get me to teach a class at the studio since the incident last summer, but I don't have the heart to tell her the last thing I want to do is fill the shoes of my dementors. Even if I never worked them to the point of exhaustion, starved them, slapped them across the backs of their legs with wooden canes when their arabesques weren't straight, I'd still feel that abuse every day of my life.

Fuck this. I need to get out of this studio. The walls are closing in. I could use some actual food, but I'd prefer a drink instead. Changing quickly back into my dress I wore to lunch, I skip the leggings and shawl and dig a pair of high heels out of my messy locker in the storage room behind the studio.

The evening is cool as I step out into the dusk, quickly ordering an Uber as I walk toward the city center. For a moment, I feel free. She'll think I'm still practicing, and she won't bother checking up on me. For fuck's sake, I'm twenty-nine years old. I don't need to check in with my mother, and I can do whatever the fuck I want, but there's still a hint of guilt in my chest as I climb into the white SUV and head toward the nearest club so I can get drunk as fast as possible in hopes someone will strike my interest and make me feel something.

For a Saturday, the bar is quiet, but it's only seven-thirty. After a couple dry martinis, I get a few come-ons, mostly from older men which is fine. I have nothing against a sugar daddy—worked out great for Zara, but there's no real zing with any of them, so after short, stiff introductions, they all leave with their tails between their legs.

Finally, a group of four women sidle up to the bar next to me. They're already drunk from presumably day drinking because they also have sunburns, but they're still coherent enough to order.

"Oh my god, you're gorgeous!" one of the girls announces next to me, and I feel a soft hand drift down from my shoulder to my elbow.

"Jesus, Mia, you're cut off," the woman next to her says. Mia is short, blonde and straight as a board, but the woman who pulls her away from me is not. And how I can tell that is the level of confidence she exhibits as she checks me out not once, but twice.

I've been with a woman before. It was fun, nothing serious, and right now I'm in the middle of such a dry spell *fun and nothing serious* sounds like exactly what I need.

Plus, *dry spell* is putting it lightly. Ever since my breakdown, the state of things downstairs has been far worse than dry. It's like the whole system is dead. Even by myself with the kinkiest porn playing on my phone, I can't seem to work out the weakest of orgasms. Nothing.

"You need a drink?" she asks, putting herself where Mia once stood.

I hold up my nearly empty martini glass. "Good timing."

The next thirty minutes crawl by in basic pleasantries between two people who obviously want to fuck but need to know the basics first—name, status, confirmation the other person isn't a total psychopath. Her name is Ally. She's thirty, a retail manager, bold, tall with shoulder-length brown hair, and presumably single since she made a questionable face when I asked if she had a girlfriend. If she does, her girlfriend isn't here tonight, so I don't give a shit.

When she rests her arm along the back of my chair, I swivel my knees toward her. The gin is hitting me hard, and I'm feeling more bold than usual. And a good deal less patient. That's when I notice we're getting dubious glances from her friends she has neglected to spend time with since I stole her attention.

I don't have time for this shit. I need to get laid, and it's about that time of the night.

I glance down at my phone. Fuck, it's only eight-forty-five.

"It's getting crowded. Want to get out of here?" I say after I feel her hand land on my bare knee.

"Where did you have in mind?" she asks, her eyes trailing down to my low-cut neckline.

"Your place." Her eyes shift quickly up to meet my gaze.

"I wish I could," she replies, biting her lip. She does have a girlfriend, then. Or a boyfriend, who knows. I know I don't care, especially when a low, subtle warmth starts to build between my legs. It's the most action my body has seen in months, and I'm not about to waste it now.

I spot someone coming out of the bathroom in the back, and I get an idea. Standing from my barstool, I let my hand graze over Ally's waistline as I walk away toward the dark, back corner of the bar. At least this place is clean and upscale. I would never do this in a hole in the wall.

What am I saying? Yes, I would.

It only takes one "come fuck me" glance at Ally before I disappear through heavy, black swinging door. She's on my heels in seconds.

I know the gin's behind the wheel now because I don't remember kissing her for the first time. I remember her shoving me against the tiled wall and the way it fired up a mini arousal in my belly, enough so by the time she reaches up my dress, there's at least some moisture there. Then she's pounding two fingers into me, and I'm too busy searching my body for the heat and arousal that's only a memory now I don't think to do anything for her, and I feel bad for it. Well, almost.

She's kissing my neck, kneading my breasts aggressively, and the roughness helps.

"Harder," I gasp, latching onto her neck and rubbing my leg between hers. It's working. There's a slow build of heat at the base of my spine, and for a moment I'm relieved I won't have to fake it.

But the black swinging door of the bathroom hits the wall so hard, it makes me jump. Ally and I are hidden inside the handicap stall, which is a futile defense against the angry woman who shouts, "Ally!" as soon as she enters.

She tears herself away from my body, and I slump in defeat. I was so fucking close.

I assume it's her angry girlfriend who is violently jostling the stall door enough it finally pops open. The girl who appears on the other side is as tall as Ally with long blonde hair pulled into a tight ponytail, an athletic build, and a strikingly gorgeous face. *Fuck, Ally. Why are you messing with me when you have this girl at home?*

Ready to make my exit and let these two work it out, I realize I'm not getting away that easy when the blonde stops screaming at her girlfriend to focus her rage-filled expression on me.

"You fucking bitch!" she screams as her open hand comes flying across my cheek. I'm stunned for a moment. Between the gin, the hit, and their nonstop arguing, I'm disoriented. The room is spinning, and my brain is lost in a fog—a fog much like the one I drifted off into last summer when they had to sedate me during my maniacal fit. It's a welcome fog where I don't feel useless, worthless, nothing.

Then, the fog clears as quickly as it came, and I'm still stuck between these two fighting women. Something in me snaps. *Everything* in me snaps. The next thing I know, I have blondie's hair in my hands while I swing at her with the other. Ally is holding me back, yelling in my face, and I'm lost in the rage. I barely register being carried out by the security guards and deposited on the street.

Fifteen to twenty minutes later, I'm walking alone down a busy city street and shivering from the cold. Ally and her girlfriend are gone. My head is pounding. My face stings, and my hand aches from where it ricocheted off the stall door as I pounded a girl I don't even know and will never see again.

What is wrong with me? When did this happen? One year ago, I had my shit together. I was working full-time which is a blessing for a dancer in her late twenties. Every night I closed each show with roses and applause. I had my own apartment, and my mother's control existed only in the footnotes of my life.

Then, whatever had been holding me up all those years

just...crumbled. I withstood the pressure and trauma for so long one day, the foundation cracked, and the structure imploded. I don't remember much about that day, only that I was so hysterical, I had to be put in a medically induced coma.

When the gin wears off, I pull out my phone and instead of calling an Uber, I call Zara. I don't know why. I need to hear her voice. Someone who likes me, who is my friend because she wants to be. Fuck, I remember when we first met the night Alistair brought her to the ballet. She actually looked up to me. I hate to think what she thinks of me now.

"Hey," she answers after the first ring. I hear the baby crying in the background and Alistair's voice before the clear sound of a door closing and silence on the line. "What's up? Are you okay?"

She's at home with her perfect little family and I'm drunk-calling her from a dark street in need of a ride. I want to hang up immediately.

"I shouldn't have called," I mumble.

"Fuck that. What's up? Tell me now." Ever since the incident, Zara's friendship has taken on a new edge, a protective one with a hint of meanness. Like she knows I am my own worst enemy and she has to protect me from myself.

"I just need a ride and a place to crash."

"Drop me a pin. I'm on my way."

"What about the baby?"

"She's fine. Alistair's here."

This vision of Alistair Wilde changing diapers and holding a baby still doesn't fit right in my head, and I've seen them all together hundreds of times. But somehow it works.

"Thank you," I mutter as I reach a dark intersection, so

I turn around and head back toward the crowd and lights of the busy street. Quickly, I drop a pin and send it to Zara. Then, I pocket my phone and try to look natural as I pace back and forth, waiting for her to get here. The house isn't far from the city, and it shouldn't take her more than twenty minutes, but it's only been about ten when a familiar black sports car pulls up next to me.

I stiffen, moving away from the road as I wait for the window to roll down before I open it and get in. It doesn't roll down, but the driver's side opens, and Nash Wilde pops out, glaring at me over the top of the car.

"Zara said you needed a ride. I happened to be in the area."

My heart plummets. Why? Why did she have to tell Nash? Of all fucking people.

I try to paste on a casual, sober smile and act like everything is fine as I walk toward the passenger side. "Are you sure you don't mind?

"Of course not," he answers flatly.

"I could take an Uber, really."

"Just get in, Hanna."

He disappears into the car, and I let a deep exhale melt down my spine before I open the door and fall into the seat. The inside of the car is immaculate, high-tech, and expensive as hell.

"How's your night?" he asks nonchalantly as I try to pull down the hem of my dress to hide my thighs, so I don't look like a cheap hooker.

"Uneventful," I answer, squaring my shoulders and trying my best to appear as if I have my shit together as much as he does. It's impossible not to steal a glance at Nash in the driver's seat. How in only three years has he grown into an even more handsome, mature version of the reckless kid I first met? Back then I was the one with my shit together. And it grates my nerves to see how far he's come in such a short time, and how far I've fallen.

I don't know the specifics, but I do know from what Zara tells me, Nash took Wilde Aviation to the next level, expanding and adding so much to the company he's now in a place to expand to airplanes as well as helicopters. Which means he's rich as fuck.

"I'm taking you to Zar's, right?"

"Yes, please." I pick at the hem of my dress and add, "She and I have some serious catching up to do since Harper came along. Easier to just kill a bottle of wine at her house."

He doesn't respond. I feel like an idiot. It's clearly an excuse for not wanting to go back to my mother's house because I lost my apartment. Am I twenty-nine or nineteen?

It's a quiet ride until we get to their large brick home on a quiet road with houses scattered far enough apart it has privacy but not so far we can't tease them about moving to the suburbs. Zara is standing outside as Nash coasts up the circular drive to deposit me at the front door.

"Thank you for the ride," I say with false confidence and a fake smile.

Finally he looks at me, his expression harsh and cold like he's scrutinizing me, looking right through me, seeing right through the bullshit facade I put up.

"Good night, Hanna," he replies coolly before looking forward.

When I climb out, Zara is there with her arms around my waist and holding me up without even knowing why. She just knows. Maybe this is something she learned from growing up with a sister, knowing when your best friend needs a hug and someone to keep them upright, but it's my favorite thing about Zara. She doesn't make being me any more exhausting than it already is. I didn't grow up with best friends and affectionate women.

After Nash drives away, Zara and I tip-toe inside. It's not super late, but I'm sure the baby is already asleep. I can only assume Alistair is too. We move straight for the wine rack and she pours us both a glass of something red before we head for the patio.

There is a cozy chenille throw blanket draped over the back of each chair, and I cocoon myself in it as I tell Zara all about my evening. I see the interest pique on her face when I tell her I dragged a woman to the stall instead of a man.

"I didn't know you…"

I point a finger in her direction. "You don't get to judge me."

"Why would I judge you for that?" She sets down her glass and looks at me again. "The only part that concerns me is you're being reckless, Hanna. Pulling anyone into a bathroom stall while you're drunk and alone at a bar is a red flag."

I don't respond because I don't disagree. I'm not just waving a red flag; I'm practically leading a parade with it. Then she hits me with the truth.

"I'm worried about you." This is where the conversation gets heavy. Where I have to face reality and unleash every gross and toxic thought in my head. I haven't exactly been honest with Zara, or anyone, about how things are with my mother. How they've always been.

When you grow up in toxicity, live in it every day of your life, you can't see past the tidal waves that drown you in it again and again. Zara knows the pressure of dance became too much, I had a nervous breakdown, and was let go from the company for health reasons. As far as she knows I've been in a state of rehab for the past eleven months, living at my mother's house while I rest and recuperate. She has no clue things have only progressively gotten worse.

And I'm not going to tell her now. It's too much. If I open that box, we're going to need a lot more than this bottle of red to get through it.

"I need to get away," I mumble, not exactly knowing what it means.

"No more auditions?"

Zara is under the impression I've been auditioning and actively trying to get rehired, but the truth is I haven't even been rehearsing. Even if I did show up to an audition, the chances of me getting picked up are nonexistent.

I simply shake my head.

She watches me for a moment. "What are you not telling me?" Zara's level of intuition is unmatched, but I'm also not a discreet hot mess.

"I just wish I could escape everything for a while. Dancing, rehearsing, the constant reminder I fucked up, my *mother*."

Her eyebrows pinch together, and she leans toward me. I know she's scared I mean escape as in the permanent kind, but I settle her worries with a smile. "You don't have to worry about me, Zara. I'm not going to do that."

"I'm still going to worry about you. You know..." she says, her voice trailing, which tells me she's about to say something risky. "You could always stay at Del Rey for as long as you need."

My eyes dance up to her face, trying to gauge how serious she is. Del Rey is a dream land, and I've stayed there plenty of times with Zara. And if I wanted an escape, there is no place better. It's a secluded island without much contact with the real world. If I wanted to be far from my mother, it would be a great option.

There's one problem. Del Rey is where Nash Wilde now lives. And I can't be around Nash, not that much.

"You wouldn't have to worry about anyone bothering you. Nash works out there, but he works so much you'd never see him. You'd practically have the island to yourself. Except for Nash and the staff, you'd be alone."

Fuck, it's tempting. It could be the fresh start I need to get away from my mother and make a real plan for my future. Or maybe never come back at all.

But can I stand being around Mr. Perfect, even if I never see him? Because I can't tell Zara how Nash scares me. She's told me how he was with her, and I can't quite describe how that makes me feel. That I want to be as far from him as possible, but also can't seem to avoid the pull of curiosity.

Some nights I lie awake thinking about him losing control on me, and as much as I know he and I would never make a good pair because we're both too hot-headed and reckless, I still crave the chance to find out.

But I couldn't do that to her. It's crossing a line best friends don't cross. She may have chosen Alistair, but I know a part of her still belongs to Nash. And seeing how he has never moved on, I'm assuming a part of him still belongs to her too.

2

"Don't you two have a baby to take care of now?" I grumble, coming out of my office and crossing the helipad toward the hangar.

Zara gives me a harsh glare. "She's with Astrid. Your dad just wants to help." He's already in the hangar. I can see him looking over the new model that came in from the shop two days ago. It still needs work, but my palms are already sweating with the way he's scrutinizing it. This is my model, and he doesn't need to be looking at it yet.

She grabs my arm, and I flinch. "He's being support-ive. Don't start with him."

"He's breathing down my fucking neck." It comes out

too harsh. But the more I try to get out of her grasp to get him the fuck out of my hangar, the tighter she squeezes.

"Nash," she says with a warning. "You have a lot going on. It's too much for one person."

"I thought you liked him being retired. Take him home." I point angrily at my father now sitting in the cockpit, looking at everything.

"You need help out here. You can't work yourself to death." She puts herself in front of me, and I know what she's doing. I'm wound up, and if I go in there, he and I are going to fight. She's simply defusing the bomb before it goes off.

"I have help." I gesture to the new staff moving around the hangar and the new office building set up next to it.

"Those are employees. He's worried you're carrying all of this stress alone. This acquisition is a lot to handle. Let him help."

"Is this why you came? As a buffer?"

She scowls at me, and I pinch her on the hip to make her swat me away. Old habits die hard, and even though things between her and I are dead, I still love to fuck with her. I want her to think I'm still in control, at least a little bit.

In a pair of cut-off shorts and a loose-fitting white top, Zara still looks like the lost girl who started coming to the island all those years ago. She's an outsider, even now, and fuck if I know why she chose to spend her life around a couple of rich assholes like us. She's changed my dad, but he can still be the same cold prick with me.

Lord knows I haven't changed.

"Actually, no. I have a favor to ask."

This stops me in my tracks, and I turn to look at her with an eyebrow peaked. "I'm not babysitting."

She rolls her eyes. I know that's not what she's about to

ask, but I have to hold firmly to the reminder I hate kids. I love my new baby sister—a little unsettling how much I do considering I did not see that coming. Harper's only three months, and I'm wrapped around her finger, but I still have no desire to ever have any of my own. Especially when I'm fifty-fucking-three years old. I don't know what the fuck these two were thinking.

"So, what is it?" I ask through gritted teeth as I finally get to the hangar. Dad is keeping quiet, looking over the new model, and I'm itching to hear what he thinks, while also dreading it.

"It's about Hanna." My head spins in Zara's direction. Hanna?

"What about her?"

"She's going through a really hard time. I think she needs to get away for a few days. Maybe longer. I told her she can stay on Del Rey for a while."

Turning around, I glare at her. "So, you offered up my home?"

"Don't be like that."

"This is where I live and do business. It's not some rehab facility for your girlfriends."

"Nash," my dad barks at me. "Hanna is like family to us. Stop acting like that."

Now it's my turn to roll my eyes. "Fine. She can take the guest house. I'm not going to bother her."

"Thank you," Zara replies.

"I thought you were rearranging the dash on this model?"

I clench my jaw, turning toward my dad as he climbs across the new two seat model and moves the collective to the side to inspect the spot where the additional instruments should be. "It didn't work with the electrical layout," I answer curtly, hoping he'll fucking drop it.

"How are things going with the acquisition? Did you get the lawyers to look it over again?"

"I have everything under control. Will you stop harping on me?" I run my hands through my hair. It's getting too long, and I catch a glimpse of myself in the mirror. My beard is growing thick too, more from neglect than a fashion choice.

"I'm just helping, Nash. It's a lot for one person."

"I tried to tell him," Zara adds in, and I snap.

"That's it. Will you two get the fuck out of here?"

She gives me a worried look as she ruffles my unkempt hair. I watch his reaction, wondering if these little touches between us bother him, but he doesn't care; he doesn't even look as he passes by.

"I called ahead to have lunch ready. Come relax, Nash," Zara says, looping an arm through mine to pull me toward the house.

SITTING around the patio by the pool, the housekeeper brings us a pitcher of tea to go with our lunch. Feeling restless in my chair, I fight the itch to check my email again. I can't sit here and do nothing, but I don't want them to see this side of me. It's a hard pass on the same old rhetoric about being a workaholic.

The manufacturer we're buying out isn't huge, but it's still a big deal. I can't tell them I don't fucking sleep anymore because they're right. It is a lot for one person, and I know he was better at this, delegating tasks and utilizing the team of assistants and managers, but I can't seem to hand over control. Every time I want to relax, my brain pipes up with some reminder about a document I didn't get signed or some clause I didn't check. There's too much to keep track of, and as much as I hate to admit it. I do need help. I just don't want his.

My dad will take over. He'll be all over it, ready to make it his own again. This is my goddamn company now. We've managed to patch things up fine since everything went to shit after Preston died. By some miracle, his plan to bring Zara in to help bring the two of us back from the brink of self-destruction actually worked. He actually started living his life, and I pulled myself out of my brother's grave.

Leaning back in his chair, he assesses me through his dark aviators. His hand reaches mindlessly for Zara who laces her fingers with his. She's scrolling through her phone, probably working on something for her dance studio.

It's quiet until my dad finally starts talking, giving me all of his sage advice he's so goddamn convinced I need. "I brought in a business consultant when we went through a similar acquisition a few years back. He was a huge help. You could do something like that."

Fuck that. The idea of some asshole coming in and putting his hands all over my company makes me sick to even think about.

"No, thanks. I'm fine."

"Nash, think about it. I bet Prior is still available if you want me to call him."

The fork I'm holding drops with a clang against the porcelain plate. Bits of orzo salad scatter across the glass table, and I move to clean it before Zara can. Clearing my throat, I shove the plate aside and try to act natural. After taking a sip of my tea, I ask, "Who is it?"

"Ellis Prior. Do you remember him? You were just a kid when he worked with me."

I turn away, focusing on the movement of clouds gently rolling across the sky. "I remember him."

"You do?"

I exhale, keeping my calm. "Yeah. I wasn't that young."

"Well, he's still in business. He does shit like this all the time. He'll come out and help you through the whole—"

"I said I've got this."

I can feel my father's eyes on me, and it grates on my nerves. Downing the rest of my tea, I stand up, ready to get back to the office and away from the scrutiny of the two people I'd rather not hate, so it's easier if I'm not around them.

My dad's idea is not an option. There's zero fucking chance I'm calling Ellis Prior, not after what went down in Amsterdam, but my dad doesn't know about that, and he never will.

3

"Good girl," I purr to the pretty little blonde at my feet.

I stroke her chin as she licks up the leftover drops on her bottom lip, staring up at me with a look of adoration on her face.

"I have a meeting to get to now."

"You're welcome," she whispers even though I never actually thanked her. I zip up my pants and lean down to lick at her pink pouty lips, tasting the saltiness there. She jolts toward me trying to deepen the kiss, and I let her for a moment before pulling away.

My meeting is a video call, and I was tempted to keep

Valerie between my legs for the duration, but it's an old friend, and it didn't seem quite right to do that to him.

"Let me know if you need anything, Mr. Prior," Valerie chirps, standing and straightening her pencil skirt. She calls me Mr. Prior because she loves to play the part.

"A coffee would be perfect."

She smiles sweetly and scurries out of my office to the kitchen where I hear her preparing my latte the way I like it. The beauty of owning my own business and working from home is I can hire a secretary to do whatever I like, under whatever terms we can both agree to. When she brings my coffee in on a tray, I admire the way her skirt hugs her hips and decide after my call I will pull it up to her waist and fuck her over my desk. But not until after my meeting.

Reclining in my office chair, I wait for the call to come in and stare out at the city view through the large windows. Business has been quiet this week, so I hope he has something new for me to work on. I miss having new projects. Everything lately has been follow-ups and old clients.

Right on time, the call comes in, and I tap the green button to open up my camera. My face stretches into a smile when I see a much older version of Alistair Wilde taking up my computer screen. He's still a good-looking man, but his hair has grayed and the crow's feet around his eyes have deepened.

"Jesus, you look old," I say with a laugh, and he grins at me before holding up his middle finger on the screen.

"So, do you," he replies.

"It's good to see you. Congrats again on the new arrival. My secretary showed me the announcement a couple weeks ago."

Alistair stiffens, looking uncomfortable, and I laugh. This isn't our normal conversation. We don't talk about babies and weddings and wives. The last time I saw Alistair Wilde, we were in a much different phase of our lives, a couple of bachelors, impressing women with expensive wine and private islands.

"Thank you," he mutters. "How are you?"

"I'm good. Are we talking shop yet? I thought you were in retirement."

"I am, but Wilde Aviation is about to buy out a small fixed-wing manufacturer, and I'd like Nash to bring you on for consultation through the process."

Beneath the desk, I squeeze the cap of my knee to keep my face from portraying my reaction to his name. I know Nash would never tell his dad what happened between us in Amsterdam. Fuck, I don't think Alistair even knows we saw each other, let alone spent nine months together. So, he certainly doesn't know how it ended.

I knew Nash took over the company after his father properly retired. I know Nash has done well with the business—only because I have stocks in the company, and I watch it closely.

"So, are you open to new clients? I assume the job would take six weeks? Maybe less. You're always welcome on Del Rey, you know."

"Does Nash know you're asking me this?"

Alistair grimaces. That's what I thought. Nash would never ask me this. First, because it's me and he hates me. And second because Nash is no doubt the same stubborn prick he was three years ago, and he doesn't ask for or accept help. Fuck, he doesn't even take suggestions.

"You know I can't do anything until he hires me, Alistair."

"I know, but I think if you two had a conversation, he'd consider it. He always looked up to you, Ellis."

It's like needles under my skin, bringing enough pain to

the surface to make me choke on it. Nash did look up to me.

"I can tell you'd like a new project. This has your name written all over it. Consider it. Give him a call."

I *would* love a new project. And I'm enough of a curious fool I will contact Nash about this. Alistair and I spend the next fifteen minutes catching up, talking about his new projects even though he's supposed to be enjoying his new life with his beautiful, young wife and baby. He asks me what is new, and I have to fight the guilt because there is nothing new for me. I've been content with that for a long time, but now it's giving me a sour feeling in my gut. Finally, we say our goodbyes, and I stare at the view out of my window, jaw clenched.

"Valerie, whiskey neat."

"Yes, sir," she calls, her heels clicking against the marble floor.

When she comes in a moment later, holding the golden liquor in her hand, I stand up and nod my head toward the desk, already unbuckling my trousers. Her eyes light up and she bites her lip. She sits on the desk facing me and runs her hands down my chest with an apologetic look on her face.

Sometimes I wish this thing between us was real and that she cared more than a secretary or casual fuck would care.

"Bad meeting?" she asks, and I stroke my hand down her neck, pulling her toward me to nibble on her ear. There is nothing emotional tying us together, and I know Valerie likes it that way. She has her own life, and unless it's a weekday between nine and five, I don't care much about what that is.

But fuck, is she a great secretary.

"No, it wasn't a bad meeting," I groan, trying not to

think about anything Alistair said and especially not about Nash.

"You seem tense," she replies as I pull her off the desk and spin her around so she's facing it. She lets out a satisfied sigh as I pull her skirt up, letting it bunch around her waist.

"I'm fine," I reply tightly. Then, I pull a condom out of my top drawer and put it on quickly because like I said, what Valerie does on her own time is her business, but sticking my dick in her is mine. She keeps quiet, letting out only a soft cry while I plunge myself in, fucking her fast and hard. I try in vain to shrug off the anxiety the call with Alistair has caused.

But it's no use. Nash is back in my head, and I know from experience it's going to take a while before it's clear of him.

And I was having such a nice day.

4

"You called him?" I snap, shooting out of bed. It's not even six in the morning, but the email that just popped into my inbox had me calling my dad pretty fucking fast.

"Jesus, Nash. Do you know what time it is?" His voice is like gravel on the other line. He never used to sleep past six. I don't know why the fact he's changed so much in the past few years bugs the shit out of me.

"I can't believe you called a business consultant behind my back."

"Calm the fuck down. Ellis is an old friend. I was just checking up on him and mentioned the acquisition. You should consider it. He made a world of difference for us before."

"It's my fucking company, Dad. You don't run it anymore, so stay the fuck out of it!"

He lets out a frustrated groan. "You sound like a teenager throwing a fit, Nash. God dammit, will you grow the fuck up?" This time I do throw my phone across the room. I didn't even hit end before it lands with a thud against the plush carpet and slides to the wall. It's probably not broken, but right now I don't give a shit.

Ignoring his voice calling for me from the floor, I throw on a pair of basketball shorts and socks and run down to the gym. Pounding out a few miles on the treadmill should help me get his voice out of my head. I'll never stop feeling like a bratty teenager until he stops treating me like one. I said I didn't want a consultant, but he refuses to believe I can handle this on my own.

After mile number two I realize I can blame my dad as much as I want for putting me in a shit mood, but I know it's really the email that started it.

FROM: ellisprior@priorconsulting.com

NASH. This is strictly a business email. I hope you know, regardless, my services are still available to Wilde Aviation.

Ellis

.   .   .

So, fucking formal. Regardless. Regardless of what? Regardless of the shit that went down in Amsterdam. So much meaning in one fucking word.

The second I opened that email, I knew Alistair couldn't keep his fucking nose out of my business. He had to do something.

The jog does nothing to calm my nerves. I need to get back to work. After a quick shower, I get dressed and pick up my phone off the floor. It's covered in notifications, mostly notes and messages from my assistants. Nothing super pressing, which irks me. I need something important to work on.

As I cross the grounds toward the office building, movement in the guest house catches my eye. What the fuck? I've told the housekeeping staff to stay out of there unless I give them instructions to clean it. I've been in the habit of taking girls there when I can bring someone back from the city. Sometimes it involves kinky shit I don't need everyone seeing. I always clean it up myself, but I can't remember if I put everything away after my last time in there.

Fuck, when was my last time in there? Too goddamn long.

Before I head to the office, I make a detour and head toward the guest house. The door is closed, but I toss it open and hear scrambling in the bedroom. What the fuck? Is someone snooping through my shit?

Quietly, I creep across the living area and into the one bedroom. A blur of copper-colored skin and black hair flashes by, and I quickly reach out, grabbing onto the curls, pulling the girl out of the bathroom before she can shut herself in there. People are sneaking into my guest house, using my bathroom, getting naked on my property.

I'm more pissed than I should be, but there is something gratifying about the way she screams.

"Nash!" I catch sight of her face in the mirror and immediately let go of her hair.

Jesus Christ. Hanna Thurber is standing naked in my guest house bathroom looking fucking terrified, and rightfully so.

"Oh fuck, Hanna. I'm sorry." It feels like a full minute goes by while I stand there, stunned and staring at her naked body in the mirror. One hand hovers over the apex of her thighs, hiding herself from me, but my eyes go there anyway. The warm clean scent of her soap fills the steamy bathroom, so she obviously just got out of the shower.

It all comes back in a flash, racing through my head. Zara asked if Hanna could stay in the guest house. She literally told me a couple of days ago she would be here because she was going through a hard time.

What have I done to this poor girl?

Quickly, I grab a towel off the counter and cover her. "I'm so sorry. Did I hurt you?"

She avoids my eyes as she hides her body. "I'm fine. You just scared me."

"I'm sorry." How many times have I said it now?

"Can you leave, please?"

"Of course," I stutter. "I'll be in my office if you need anything. The housekeeper will help you."

"She already did."

Fuck, right. Of course, she did.

"Again, I'm sorry."

Turning, I rush out of the guest house and walk toward the office, but my mind is racing. Her hair in my hands. The feel of her backside pressed against me. The way her wet body looked in the mirror, so thin, so fragile. The way her hip bones protruded like her ribs against her perfect flesh. I'm torn between being turned on and mortified.

I've never so much as touched Hanna before outside of

a cordial hug when we greet each other. Not that I haven't wanted to. Fuck, I've definitely wanted to. I am a living, breathing man after all, and she's a goddess. Those long legs, the lush curve of her ass, and the bright blue and gold of her different colored eyes.

But Hanna Thurber is not my type. She's too...I don't know...graceful. Fragile. Regal. Like a princess I would only break if I had a chance to play with her. She wouldn't like my style at all. Plus, she's Zara's best friend, and that's just weird.

In my office, I try to focus on work instead of Hanna, and it takes opening up the email from Ellis to do it. I stare at it for I don't know how long. It's an email consisting of twenty words, and it's enough to shatter my day. Like a ball thrown through the glass of a fish tank, everything I've been holding in for the past three years is pouring out, and there's no way to repair it now. I can't push it back in and forget this email ever came.

Why would he send me this? Does he want to reach out? Want me to hire him?

It's business. Nothing more. I don't mean anything to Ellis anymore. Our friendship is over, and he probably doesn't even think twice about me. I'm the one sitting here dwelling on it, picking at the scab of our broken relationship.

Next to me my phone is vibrating itself to death, and I know there are a hundred emails waiting to be answered. Press releases to approve with PR, budgets to sign, business plans to update, and contracts to look over for the fifteenth time. If I fuck this up, miss one thing, screw up one part of this deal, I will have to live with it forever. How many of these did my dad do? And he never fucked them up. If I can't handle it, then I am the screwed-up Wilde. The worst of Wilde Aviation's CEOs. A poor man's Alistair Wilde.

There are probably a hundred other business consultants like Ellis I could hire. Ones without baggage from the past. Consultants that haven't seen me naked and how horribly I behave in bed with a woman. And so much more.

And yet, my curiosity has the better of me here. If I hire Ellis, we can finally bury the hatchet, put Amsterdam behind us, form a new relationship built firmly in business. He is the best at what he does. I know that. I know him well enough to know Ellis doesn't fail. He is perfection personified.

Next thing I know, I'm hitting reply to his email. Then I stare at the blank cursor wondering how the hell I'm going to respond to this.

FROM: nashwilde@wildeaviation.com
When can you start?

5

My hands won't stop shaking. Even after getting dressed and heading toward the house, I can't stop thinking about how it felt to have Nash grab me so violently. My head nearly snapped with the way he stopped me in my tracks. Then he saw me naked.

Not just saw me naked, he *looked at me.* Like he couldn't stop looking. And I covered myself, but I almost felt more naked the more I tried to hide my body.

I wanted to tell Zara about it immediately, but it didn't feel quite right. She'd yell at him, maybe even be mad at me for whatever reason, and I can't ruin this opportunity to be here right now. I need this.

Yesterday, I packed my bags and told my mother I was going to stay with a friend. Even when she bombarded me with questions, threw a fit about missing my auditions, played every card in her deck from gas lighting to guilt tripping, I still managed to get on the helicopter with Zara. It took a lot of reminding myself I am twenty-nine, a grown woman.

Her voice is still with me though. She's still in my head, reminding me I'm throwing everything away, fucking up my own life. I'm not good enough, so I have to work ten times harder than everyone else to keep up. Nothing I do will ever be enough. The thoughts have etched themselves into my brain the way water carves through stone over time.

The new head housekeeper, Thalia, said she would bring me my meals to the guest house, but I was always welcome to eat in the main house. I tell myself that's why I'm going over there now. I hate to have her deliver me food like I'm royalty or something. I'm perfectly capable of going to the house to get my own dinner.

It's a little after five when I walk into the house. It's silent except for the sound of someone in the kitchen. Expecting to walk in and find Thalia making dinner, I stop in my tracks when I pass through the dining room and see Nash shoving greens into a blender. He's in the same business attire he had on earlier when he practically attacked me in the guest house. His dark gray slacks are tight around his backside with a black snug-fitting T-shirt tucked into them.

When I first met Nash, he still seemed like a kid. We're the same age, but he was in such a low place at that time. Now he's a man, and it almost feels like we switched places. His life got substantially better while mine got so much worse.

For a moment I watch him fill the blender with yogurt and berries, trying not to gaze too long at the sculpted muscles of his back or the way he fills out those pants. He still doesn't even know I'm standing here, so I clear my throat and make my presence known.

He does a double take after first looking at me, probably thinking I'm one of the housekeepers. Keeping my eyes averted, I walk straight to the fridge to get something to drink.

"Oh, Hanna...hi."

I respond with a small smile. Nash and I have been acquaintances for years, but now suddenly things feel weird.

"Are you getting settled okay?" he asks after a moment.

"Yep. I'm fine."

"Good."

It's awkwardly quiet for a moment, and I'm tempted to leave but it would be rude to just walk in and out so quickly. Instead, I linger at the kitchen island.

"Would you like some?" He holds out his smoothie toward me.

"Aren't you going to eat dinner?" I ask after shaking my head at his offer.

"I eat late. I usually work until eight or nine."

His eyes linger on my face for a moment as the silence absorbs us, and I find myself biting my lip because I have nothing to say.

"I'm sorry again," he mutters before turning back to the blender. "For what I did today."

"Who exactly did you think I was?"

There's a quick glance in my direction before he answers. "I had no clue. Maybe a housekeeper or employee."

"And that's how you would treat them? Grab them like that?"

When he finally looks up at me, there's a thin layer of shame on his expression. Like I opened a wound or made him face something he didn't want to face.

"You took me by surprise. That's all. I wouldn't...normally..."

Suddenly I see Nash, the boy. The one I met three years ago. And I wonder what he sees when he looks at me.

Instead of harping on him more about the incident, I brush past him and head for the refrigerator. Seeing a carton of eggs and some vegetables in the drawer, I pull them out and make my way for the kitchen island.

"Thalia will be making dinner soon," he says, eyeing me skeptically.

"You need to eat more than a smoothie, and you shouldn't wait until eight tonight to do it. Let me make you an omelette." He doesn't reply as I set to chopping up the spinach, red pepper, and onions. For a moment, it feels good, like I'm a part of this family, not such an outsider, and in the silence of the kitchen, I write poetry in my head. Something about the sizzle of the skillet and feeling so far removed from the real world. It needs work.

"Thank you," he mumbles quietly while I work. Then he sits on the bar stool and scrolls through his phone. Every few moments I feel his eyes on me.

"Do you ever take a break?" I ask.

"I like to work." His fingers are typing away frantically at his phone, and I notice the way his shoulders are tight against his ears. I have the urge to walk over and smooth my hands along them, forcing them to relax.

"You seem stressed."

"Well, it's a stressful job."

"All the more reason to take breaks. Take care of yourself." As if I have any right at all to preach about that.

His jaw is especially clenched, and I can see how he's flexing his hands into fists. "You know what, I'm not hungry." Suddenly, he's marching out of the kitchen, and I drop the knife to follow after him.

"Nash, I'm sorry. Wait a second."

"Did Zara tell you to say that? Did she ask you to talk me into getting help? Or was it my dad? Well, you can tell him I hired his fucking friend like he wanted, and he'll be out here tomorrow, so they can get the fuck off my case."

When I grab his arm to spin him around, he flinches violently, spinning toward me with a hand near my throat, and I yelp as he stops himself, holding his open hand near my neck. With another flex, he pulls away.

"I'm sorry."

"I'm only saying this because I've been there. I know what it's like to be so buried in work you can't breathe. But you'd rather suffocate than face reality."

His head tilts, his eyes fixed intently on my face as if I've surprised him. As if I've just verbalized exactly what he's been feeling. Oh yeah, I know the feeling. When work is life and everything else is an annoyance that just gets in the way. When you're so resentful toward yourself because nothing will ever be good enough, perfect enough, happy enough.

Touching his arm, I continue. "I've never seen you like this, Nash. It's like you're killing yourself. Your dad didn't tell me to say anything. I promise. It's just me…and I'm concerned about you."

There's warmth in his eyes as he looks back at me, squinting at me as if he's scrutinizing again.

"Why would you be concerned about me?"

"You're my friend, Nash."

"Yeah, but you're here to take care of yourself, not me."

Reaching out, I touch the buttons on his shirt for reasons I don't even know. "I guess this is how I relax, by taking care of others. Let me help you."

When I glance up at him, my breath gets caught in my chest not only because he's so fucking intense and gorgeous it's unsettling, but because he's looking at me with renewed interest, the way a man looks at a woman he wants to fuck…or fight. It's hard to tell with Nash. It's definitely not the look of a close family friend. That much is for sure.

"How can you help me?"

"I don't know..." I stammer. Shit, this sounds like I'm coming onto him right now. Am I?

No, I can't.

"What's wrong with your eyes?" he says, interrupting me.

I flinch, reaching up to my face. "What?"

"Your eyes used to be…different colors."

"Oh," I reply, looking away. "They're contacts to hide the heterochromia."

"Why would you hide that?"

"I don't know…it's just strange, I guess."

"It's not strange," he snaps back, and I look into his eyes, the moment growing tense between us. Before I can say another word about helping him and all the ways I'd love to help him, he walks away.

It's for the best, I tell myself. I cannot get involved with Nash Wilde, not physically or emotionally. Not only because it scares me how alike we truly are, but also because I'm here to fix myself, and getting in bed with a strung-out control freak with a mean streak is a very bad idea.

6

I don't need a woman to mother me. I've gone this long without one. I sure as fuck don't need one now. Plus, Hanna is too soft; she's fragile. Every time I think about the way she looked, wet and shivering in the bathroom mirror, I remember this ballerina is not built to handle me.

It's past ten when I finally close my laptop. The office is quiet. My two assistants, the housekeeping crew, and the mechanics all head back to the mainland at exactly six every day, and I like to keep it that way. It was the tradeoff for opening Del Rey to the company full-time. I want the evenings to myself. I need the island to be silent when the sun goes down, alone with the night sky.

But tonight, it's not just me. The light is on in the guest house when I head back across the grounds toward the house. I should stop in and see if she needs anything. I could bring her some wine or something, apologize for being such a dickhead earlier.

I don't, because I'm not as nice as I probably could be. When I get into the house, I find a plate left out for me where Thalia always leaves it. It's wrapped in foil on the stove top with reheating instructions. But like most nights, I leave it there and head for the bar instead.

Putting a little vodka on ice with soda water and a slice of lime, I check my phone again for the hundredth time. I'm feeling especially restless today. Ellis is coming tomorrow. And because Hanna is already in the guest house, they're setting him up in the master wing. I kept my side of the house after Dad and Zara moved out, and we made his office and bedroom into another space for guests. It hasn't been used in months. Except for the few parties we throw on the island, we never have guests.

Ellis will be in my house, sleeping down the hall. Maybe I should put Hanna in the house where I can keep an eye on her. I don't know if I trust him with her around. No, I'll keep him closer, making sure I'm the last one to go to bed at night so I know she's safe. Should I tell him she's off limits?

If he's anything like he was three years ago, he won't care about what's on or off limits. Ellis makes his own rules, lives by his own limits. When he sees something he wants, he takes it.

There's movement outside that catches my attention. Going to the patio door, I watch as Hanna dives headfirst into the pool. It's weird having someone else here now. When everyone goes home at night, I'm alone. Being secluded on this island gives me a sense of eerie calm, but it's also like being suspended in air, waiting for something bad to happen.

I watch her swim for a few minutes, and when she pops out and sees me standing there, drink in hand, she lifts a hand to wave for a moment before climbing out and drying herself with a towel.

Finally, I walk outside, the clink of ice in my glass the only sound between us.

"The stars are beautiful," she says as she reclines in one of the lounge chairs. Lying all the way back, she stares up at the sky. She's right. Without the light pollution from the city, the sky is remarkable out here. Tonight, there isn't a cloud in sight, so the view is perfect.

"Don't you ever get lonely here?" she asks as I sit down in the chair next to her. Leaning back, I stare up at the sky too.

"I'm too busy to feel lonely."

She turns to look at me. "I've been busy too, but I still get lonely all the time."

My eyes snap toward her, and my heart cracks a little at her admission. I don't know why this surprises me. Hanna is the girl you see with a man on her arm at all times. She's always surrounded by friends. There's no way she feels lonely.

Dropping the subject, she glances at me as she asks, "So, did you say there's someone coming here tomorrow?"

Turning away, I hide the tic in my jaw. "Yeah, just a business consultant."

"Oh…" her voice trails. "Are they staying on the island too?"

"Yes."

"I hope it's okay I'm in the guest house. Do you want me to—"

"No, you're fine. He'll stay in the house with me."

Her head snaps in my direction.

"Not *with* me," I correct myself quickly. "I mean in the guest room. It's fine. You don't need to move."

"Okay…" she says, and it's starting to feel uncomfortable again. It really shouldn't. With as long as Hanna and I have known each other, I hate to feel like we can't even hang out casually like this, but to be honest, I haven't casually hung out with a woman I wasn't trying to fuck in… well, forever.

Just then, as if she's reading my fucking mind, she says, "You know, if you need company..."

My heart starts to hammer in my chest. Even the vodka flowing through my veins can't calm the erratic beat. I risk a glance in her direction, but she's not looking at me. Her eyes are still glued on the stars. It's quiet for so long I start to wonder if I'm imagining the assumption in her statement.

"I'll be blunt, Nash. You scare me. You always have, but right now I'm in such a rut I think I'd like to be fucked up."

"Hanna..."

"We don't need to tell anyone. Just one time, no string attached sort of thing."

I have no clue what the fuck I'm supposed to say right now, but she's throwing a curve ball at me, and I'm at a loss for words. Is she asking me to fuck her? And be rough? How am I supposed to answer that?

Um, fucking yes please.

"Never mind. I'm an idiot," she says in a rush before standing up and marching toward the guest house. I'm out of my chair in a heartbeat, running after her. Why did I have to take so long to answer?

As my hand latches around her arm, she quickly snatches it away. "That was stupid of me to say. I don't know what's wrong with me. Please forget I said anything…"

"I can't forget you said that."

"Then, just let me go." There are thick tears brimming in her eyes waiting to spill over.

"It's just...we can't, Hanna. It's...off limits."

Finally, her gaze meets mine, and she looks pained. "Don't you think I understand that? She's my best friend, Nash. But she fucked your dad, so you're lying to yourself if you believe that off-limits bullshit."

"What's that supposed to mean?" I snap, grabbing her arm again, this time with a little more roughness.

"It means you're still stuck on her."

"I am not stuck on Zara," I reply, which is true.

"All of this..." she says, gesturing around at the buildings. "All of it is just a cover. You're not lonely because you're busy. You're lonely because you're hiding, Nash."

Well, fuck, she's not wrong about that, but it's not because of Zara.

"Who are you to talk? You're the one hiding. Isn't that why you came out here?"

"Yes," she bites back, the tears finally running down her face. "I am hiding, but at least I know what I'm hiding from."

Then, she snatches her arm out of my grasp and jogs away. Choosing not to follow her, I stand alone under the stars trying to figure out how the hell this happened. Why couldn't I just decline her offer? Why do I have to be such an asshole?

Because she pointed out something about myself I didn't need her pointing out. I am hiding, and tomorrow, the one memory I'm hiding from is about to land on this very fucking island.

. . .

SPEND enough time around aircrafts like I do, and you can pinpoint every single model by sound alone. And I know the sound of my dad's N-2 approaching, which sends a flood of anxiety to the surface of my skin. He's early. Of course, he is. They were supposed to come in after lunch, but it's only ten and he's already landing.

Shoving my laptop away, I quickly fix my hair and stand up from my office.

"Charlotte, can you please forward the edits on these specs to the design team before I get back?"

"Yes, Mr. Wilde."

Adjusting my shirt again, I walk out to the helipad, holding my head up as high as I can. He's not going to intimidate me. I'm not going to let him get into my head again.

First, I spot my dad climbing out of the helicopter. The sun glares against the windshield, and I cover my eyes against the brightness. Then, Ellis steps out and comes into view. Something in my stomach plummets at the sight of him. And it's like I'm standing at that party in Amsterdam again. He hasn't changed at all, still the larger than life man I remember, the man I idolized for my entire adult life. The sudden onslaught of memories hits me hard.

Especially when his eyes land on me. I become hyper aware of my inadequacies. My hair is too long. My beard isn't clean enough. My suit isn't expensive enough, and my walk isn't confident enough.

His eyes linger on mine for the eternity of a moment.

"Son, you remember Ellis," my dad says when they approach, framing it like a question. I nod and reach out to take his hand.

"Of course. Thank you for coming."

There's a spark of mischief in his eye as he reaches out to shake my hand. The sudden contact of our palms touching feels like ice in my veins. I'm living in Ellis Prior's shadow again.

My dad's phone rings, and he peers down skeptically. "It's Zara. Nash, show Ellis where he'll be staying. I'll be right back."

As he rushes off, leaving me alone with a ghost from my past, I let out a forced exhale.

"I was surprised when I got your email. I'll admit I never thought you would talk to me again."

I glance up in a rush, shock flooding my bloodstream, but I control the urge to show it. Walking toward the house, I turn back as he follows. "Of course. It's just business. What happened in Amsterdam...water under the bridge, really. It's in the past." I wave my hand, trying to act calm even though my gut is so tightly wound I feel like I might explode at any moment.

I glance his way and our eyes meet. His brow is furrowed and his lips are gently parted, seeming like he doesn't believe me. "Okay, then."

It's not until we reach the guest suite that I realize he's making it sound like he's the one to blame for what went down. It feels like manipulation. He's trying to get on my good side, to pretend it was his fault one day I flipped a fucking switch.

"Listen," I say as he drops his leather satchel on the desk. "I never told my dad—"

He puts up a hand. "Don't worry about it. I won't say a thing."

"I didn't even tell him we saw each other."

"For nine months," he replies like it's a question.

"The whole time. He has no idea."

Ellis nods, and I have to glance away because seeing him here, standing in my dad's old bedroom feels like a system overload. Suddenly, his eyes fixate on the window as he squints.

"Is that your girlfriend?"

"What?" Looking past him, I see Hanna walking toward the house in nothing but a pair of tight yoga shorts and a sports bra. Jesus, woman. Put some clothes on.

"No, she's not," I reply quickly, but then regret it. That's exactly what I should have said she was. Make it very fucking clear from the start she is off-limits…and so am I. "She's Zara's friend. And she'll be staying here for a few days."

He nods, then glances at me. I'm standing so close to him I can smell his cologne and the product in his hair, so I quickly shuffle away, moving toward the door.

"I'll let you get settled for a while. Thalia, the housekeeper, will be in shortly to get you anything you need. We can start this afternoon if you're ready. I'll be in the office all day." Everything comes out in a rush, and I do my best not to stammer as I talk, too afraid to look at him while I do.

"Yes, sir," he replies, and it grates on my nerves the second it comes out of his mouth.

He's definitely fucking with me, and I already regret inviting him here. The problem with Ellis is he knows me too well. He knows exactly who he's fucking with and he does it anyway. He loves to see me fired up.

7

AMSTERDAM

"SHE WAS SLEEPING with both of you at the same time?"

Ellis is sitting across from me at a small bar in the city center, and it only took three rounds of dry gin before everything started coming out. Every secret I told myself I would keep buried I just puked up to not just anyone, but my dad's old friend. But he's my friend now too, maybe even more than my dad's.

"Yeah, but it was fine. We made it clear it was okay."

"But you had her first?" There is a mischievous

smirk on his face that is making my cheeks flush hot. I don't talk to people about this. I certainly don't bring up how the girl I was fucking suddenly started fucking my dad and how I was okay with that, to the point where we actually shared her. But in my defense, I was not surprised when she chose him. I guess I could have stuck around and stayed in the equation, but it wasn't right.

"She and I were never serious."

"Uh-huh." He doesn't sound like he believes me.

"What?" I ask with a laugh.

With his pursed lips and raised brows, the skepticism is written all over his face. "Do you think it would have been serious if he hadn't stepped in?"

I stare down at the gin-soaked ice in my glass. I told Zara I loved her. I had never uttered those words to anyone, and I said them first. I remember that night pretty fucking vividly. It was my all-in move. My last ditch attempt to win her over, but by that point I had already lost.

"She's happy. He's happy. I'm…fine."

"Yeah, you look fine," he laughs.

"I'm serious. I'm not ready to settle down. Fuck that."

He's smiling again. Ellis and I have made a habit of coming out for drinks every Friday after work. We sit at one of the many pubs downtown and have a few casual drinks. It's never anything more than that. It feels like we're always on the brink of doing something crazy, but one of us usually calls it quits when the night is about to take a turn.

I, for one, am in the mood to go nuts tonight. We have testing all week at work and I need a release. I don't really know if Ellis is down for that. After our few meetups I've gotten the feeling there is more to him than he's letting on.

Like a Hyde under the Jekyll. And I'm waiting to see what he's like when he lets loose.

"Don't you know that girl?" he asks, and I turn to see a familiar British blonde at the bar with another girl.

"Barely. That's the girl at the party the night you and I first saw each other here."

"That's what I thought. Why don't you invite her over?" he asks. My gaze lingers on him for a moment. I can't tell if he's trying to wingman or if he wants her for himself. But the thought of trying to land this girl in front of him has me feeling inadequate again. *Don't fuck this up, Nash.*

Grabbing what's left of my drink and throwing it back, I feel the burn down my throat as I walk over to where Britta is sitting with her friend. Softly I rest a hand on her back before she notices me, and when she turns around, her eyes light up.

"Nash!" Her arm snakes its way around my waist before she introduces me to her friend whose name I don't even catch. After a short moment of small talk, I point toward the table where Ellis is sitting, and both of the girls freeze for a moment. Even I can appreciate how he looks like a god under the dim lighting with his arm resting against the back of the seat and looking as if he doesn't have a care in the world.

"Come join us," I tell them.

Britta looks at her friend with intensity and they seem to have a silent conversation with just their eyes before they both smile my way. As we make our way over, I notice the way Britta instantly takes the seat next to Ellis, leaving her friend to sit next to me.

Ellis is a smooth mother fucker. He puts his arm behind Britta, compliments her, finds ways to touch her without it being creepy and I'm too busy eating it all up to even pay her friend any attention. During a quiet moment I do have the good sense to catch her name, Alyssa, and she tells me a little bit about her job and how she's from Canada, but the conversation runs dry, and after a few more rounds of drinks, all of which she skips on, it becomes glaringly obvious she's not feeling it. A little after midnight she makes an excuse about needing to work in the morning and leaves.

Britta stays. None of us are really drunk, but we're far from sober. So, when Ellis suggests we take the party back to his apartment, a wave of nervous excitement manages to make its way past all of the beer and gin into my blood-stream. Should I bow out? Leave her for him? I don't exactly feel like a third wheel, and he did look at me as he asked it.

Fuck it. When we get up to leave, I stick with them, walking together to Ellis's place which isn't far.

Of course, Ellis lives in a beautiful fucking apartment outside the city center. It's not huge, and it's more of a row house squeezed between a collection of other apartments.

Once inside, he puts on some music and pours us all more drinks. I find myself staring out the window toward the canal in front of his house when Britta joins me. Ellis is somewhere else in the house for a moment when she whispers to me, "I can't believe I'm really here."

I laugh. "Why?"

When she looks at me, there's a hint of humor in her eyes. "You really don't know what he's like, do you?"

"Ellis? Yeah I've known him like my whole life."

This time she really laughs, looking behind her to make sure he's not within earshot. "He has quite a reputation, Nash. When Ellis brings you back to his apartment, there's usually a good story to go along with it."

I swallow. Maybe I am a third wheel.

"I won't get in your way."

Before I can turn away feeling like an idiot, she puts a hand on my arm. "I wasn't talking about me, Nash."

"What are you talking about then?" I ask, feeling very fucking lost.

She only laughs into her drink. Just then, he comes back into the room. "Am I interrupting something?" he asks.

"Not at all," I stammer quickly.

Ellis is holding a joint in his fingers, and he gestures to the back of the house. "The rooftop patio is lovely. Let's go up and have a smoke." Then he looks at me. As if he's specifically inviting me.

I'm getting a strange vibe, like something has changed. And instead of backing out or walking away, I follow him. I'll unpack that later.

There's an outdoor sofa and two chairs under a canopy on the rooftop, and Ellis was right, it is nice up here. Britta sits first, and Ellis gestures for me to sit next to her. I want to tell him she doesn't want me. She wants him, but I don't argue, taking my spot next to her. Immediately after sitting down, she cozies up next to me. Ellis takes the chair across from us, leaning back to light his joint.

Once he starts passing it, I only take a couple small hits. I'm already paranoid as it is. What the fuck did Britta mean downstairs? It's like she knows what's up and I have no fucking clue. Is Ellis trying to hook her and me up? Is he into some kinky orgy shit and that's what she's talking about?

Then the final thought, the one that has the hairs standing on my arms and neck: is he into me?

The patio grows quiet, and Britta scoots even closer until she's practically on my lap. Why is she fucking with me when she could have him?

He's staring at us, eyes hooded and dangerous looking.

"I think he likes to watch," she whispers, but not so quietly he can't hear. My mind races, and I stare at him, feeling a little confused.

"I think she wants you to kiss her, Nash. Why don't you?"

I can't *not* obey him. For one, I don't want to disappoint him. And two, I do want to kiss her. I'm already sporting a hard-on that appeared shortly after we got to the apartment. Just the quiet intimacy of being in Ellis's house is sending thrilling jolts of excitement through my body.

So, I turn toward Britta, putting my hands on her jaw and pulling her toward me. I lock onto her lips more gently than I normally would and she purrs in response. We kiss for a few moments, her climbing even closer until one of her knees is resting between my legs. My hands travel down her neck, over her shoulders until they're resting on her waist. I almost forget Ellis is watching until I open my eyes and see him staring at me. Our eyes lock for a moment, and I get suddenly self-conscious, so I gently pull away from the kiss.

Her lips don't stop, traveling down my neck and up to my ear.

Ellis is still watching.

Is this weird? I briefly wonder. He's my dad's friend. He knew me as a kid. It doesn't feel weird, not to me. But I'm fucked up. What if I humiliate myself by showing how fucked up I really am?

"What's Nash like in bed, Britta?" he asks, and I stare at him.

She laughs against the cool, wet skin of my neck. "Well, we never made it to a bed, but he likes it rough."

I swallow down my nerves.

"Was he good? Tell me."

"He was good," she replies, looking at me now. "I think he was holding back though."

"Is that so?" He takes another puff on his joint, and I can't tear my eyes away. "I wonder if we can get him to let go."

"I'd like to give it a try," she hums against my lips.

"Help him relax a little first."

I watch as Britta sinks down to her knees between my legs. As she tugs my zipper down, I let out a small gasp when she pulls my cock out and wraps her lips around the head. With her eyes on me, she slicks up the length, running her tongue from the base to the top. Then, when she swallows me down, I lose my head, a groan escaping as I melt into the sofa.

He's watching, and I don't even care. I can feel his eyes on me, and I remember he wants to see me let go, so I do. Digging my hand into her hair, I make eye contact with her as I force her down a little farther, watching the way she gags when I do.

I see him smile across the patio.

So, I do it again, thrusting my hips up until I feel the back of her throat, and this time she gags even louder, pulling her head away to gasp for air so I let her go. When she pulls her mouth off, there's a hint of shock in her eyes, then an arousal-laced smile. She goes back to stroking my cock with her lips and I have to concentrate hard to keep from coming already.

"Britta," Ellis barks, and I look up to see him nod his head at her. It's an obvious cue for her to go to him. And I watch as she crawls toward him on her hands and knees. Stroking myself, I can't tear my eyes away. She pulls him out, letting him fuck her mouth the same way I did.

The look of determination on his face. The cool awareness in his expression. The way he strokes her back gently while also jerking her head down. His controlling grip on her hair. It's so fucking hot to watch, so hot I have to stop moving my hand.

"I think she's ready for you, Nash," he mumbles, and she hums with delight as soon as he says it.

I've done this before. A few times actually. Sharing a woman isn't anything new for me, but right now, it feels brand new. Because there's something different happening this time. Something I didn't see coming. So, when I make my way toward her, pulling her dress up to find her moist and waiting for me, I do exactly what Ellis says, and it's fucking amazing, but it's still different.

And I can't seem to put my finger on why.

8

I NEVER SHOULD HAVE COME HERE. I'M BORED OUT OF MY mind, and as it turns out, trying to relax just means all you're left with are your thoughts. And after that strange encounter with Nash last night, it's clear I need to get back to the mainland. I don't want to be around my mother, but somehow being alone with myself is worse.

So, after spending the morning lying around on the beach without a soul to talk to, I decide I can't take another moment. Before texting Zara, I'll just ask Thalia if I can catch a ride back when everyone returns tonight.

I can't risk running into Nash again, so I wait until I see him crossing the yard to the office building next to the hangar before I rush to the house. It's empty at first, but I hear movement down the hall. Assuming it's Thalia, I head in that direction. It sounds as if someone is tidying up the bedroom, and the door is open, so I walk in without hesitation. Since Nash is in the office building, I don't have to worry about sneaking up on him and having another violent bathroom incident. I don't think my poor scalp could take it.

I nearly yelp when I come face to face with a shirtless man pulling on a long-sleeve button up.

"Well, hello there."

"Oh my God, I'm so sorry. I thought you were Thalia."

In a rush, I spin around and hurry down the hall and out into the living room. I am an idiot. At least he was mostly dressed. Unlike when Nash bombarded me in the guest house, and I was completely naked.

Which was embarrassing enough. Then I had to go throw myself at him last night basically inviting him to fuck me because *I was bored.* Get me the fuck off this island.

"Now wait a minute," the man calls, following me out into the main area of the house. His shirt is buttoned now, and this time my eyes actually make it up to his face. God damn...he's handsome. He looks a bit older than me... maybe late thirties, with warm honey-brunette hair, tan skin, a sharp jawline, and rich brown eyes.

"I'm really sorry. I didn't mean to just walk in on you."

"Well, the door *was* open." He puts a hand out, palm up, inviting me to put mine in his. "Ellis Prior. I'm here on business. And you are?"

I swallow, getting lost in those eyes. "Hanna Thurber," I reply, putting my hand in his. He lifts my knuckles to his lips, and suddenly it feels like I'm on stage again, roses being tossed at my feet with the crowd beyond the bright lights applauding for me.

"It's nice to meet you, Ms. Thurber."

Who the fuck is this guy?

Then, I remember my conversation with Nash last night. Before going full slut mode and trying to get him to sleep with me, Nash told me he had a business consultant coming to the island to stay.

"And what brings you out here, Hanna?" he asks as he buttons his tight-fitting shirt at the wrists. My fingers itch to reach out and button them for him, but I don't—because that would be crazy.

"Oh, just a short retreat. Get away from the hustle and bustle of the city."

"Alone?"

My eyes meet his. "Yes, alone."

"And what is it you do for a living?"

"I'm a dancer. Ballet."

His eyebrows lift and the spotlight burn of his gaze literally warms my skin. A flush rises to my cheeks as I send him an easy smile.

"That is very impressive."

"It's really not," I stammer with a blush.

"Of course, it is," he answers matter-of-factly.

It's silent a moment as I bask in the warmth of his attention.

"Listen, Hanna. I have to run. I have a meeting with Mr. Wilde in five minutes, but I hope I see you this evening. Perhaps for drinks when the workday is done?"

"Of course. I'll be here," I answer sweetly.

Then his hand lands gently on my arm, and he gives it a subtle squeeze before passing by to the door and heading out toward the office.

"Ms. Thurber, can I help you with anything?" Thalia enters the room, pulling me from my silent reverie.

"No, thank you, Thalia. I'm fine."

I spend the rest of the day looking forward to the evening in hopes of seeing this new mystery man again. There's a studio in the basement Zara has kept for years even though she has her own dance studio on the mainland now. I find myself down there sometime after lunch. I don't put on my shoes, but I feel a little closer to being able to actually dance.

I run through some basic warmups, letting my phone play a random playlist while I move. Staring at the girl in the mirror, I try to find the same woman who danced on stages and wowed audiences. I was a shell of a person then. I can remember how fast everything happened, how I never had a moment to breathe, reflect, enjoy it, before it was too late, and I suddenly had all the time in the world.

Now, I see a girl I don't recognize. I have no idea who I am anymore. What defines me now that the role is no longer filled?

My form is terrible, but in my defense I'm not really trying. It's no longer as effortless as it once was. And after about an hour, I stop trying altogether. Turning the music as high as it will go, something by Sia comes on and I practically deafen myself with the volume.

Losing myself in the poetry of the lyrics and the music, I let go. There is no form, no technique, just pure movement letting the rhythm pull my body along with it. By the time the song ends, I'm breathless, lying on the floor, gasping for air.

Then, the tears come. Draining me dry, I sob, glad to at least be feeling something. I don't even know why I'm crying, only that sometimes it comes, and I can't stop it. If I hold it in or keep myself from letting go, it festers and becomes explosive until I end up like I did last year. Mostly I think I cry because I'm alone, like always. Like maybe if I had someone to share in my sadness at least I wouldn't be so fucking lonely. But if I wasn't alone, maybe I wouldn't be so goddamn sad.

After my dance, I head back to the house to get showered up and ready for dinner. And yeah, I take a little more time on my makeup knowing I'll see Ellis again. And yeah, I hope he's the kind of guy who might be willing to bring me back to the guest house to fuck me straight into next week. I need it so bad, this is what I've resorted to. It's been too long.

Putting on a slick black shirt and a narrow black skirt, I slip on some heels and make my way to the house. It's just past six, and I figure I'll use the excuse of wanting a drink by the pool to explain my presence. The staff has just headed for the mainland, and the office looks quiet as I pass by.

There are men's voices when I enter the house through the kitchen.

"Because she's Zara's friend."

"That makes her off-limits?"

"It does for me," Nash snaps, and I freeze by the door.

They are silent for a moment before Ellis replies, a darker change in his tone. "You're harboring a grudge against me, Nash. If you'd like to talk about it, let's talk about it."

"I'm not harboring a grudge. I told you, water under the bridge, but this isn't like Britta, Ellis. Hanna is family to me."

And suddenly I realize Nash is trying to cock block me, and the blood drains from my face. That *asshole*.

"I understand," Ellis responds as their voices grow nearer.

"I'm being protective," Nash says while I consider slipping back outside through the patio, but it's too late.

"Protecting her from me?" Ellis says as they enter the

living room. I'm standing by the door, clearly having heard everything they said.

"Hanna," Nash blurts out.

Ellis doesn't even bother looking embarrassed. He wears a smug grin as he greets me. "Hello there."

"Did Thalia not deliver your dinner?" Nash asks.

"She did. I just...I wanted a drink..."

"Well, come on in. That's exactly where we were headed," Ellis says, waving me toward the bar. I can feel Nash's eyes on me, specifically on my outfit and heels. But I ignore him, holding my head up as I follow Ellis to the bar in the living room.

"Ellis told me you two met already," Nash says. There's some tension in his voice, and I peer back at him to notice his shoulders by his ears again. The urge to go over and run my hands down his back to ease some of his stress is intense.

"Just for a moment," Ellis replies as he pours me a glass of red wine after I pointed to the bottle. "Hanna found me getting dressed," he adds with a laugh.

"I apologized," I reply with a smirk.

"What would you like to drink, Nash?"

"I'll fix my own drink," he barks, and I glance up at him. I came over here to find Ellis, hoping for a connection I couldn't make with Nash, and now that he's watching, I feel unsettled. He won't stop looking at me.

Ellis puts his hands up and moves away from the drinks to come stand by me. "So, are you getting the break you needed?" he asks me.

"It's not so bad out here. It's so quiet though. Don't you ever get bored, Nash?"

"No," he answers abruptly.

"Because you work too much," I reply.

"I work a lot, but it's not too much."

"So, what do you do if you need a break? You already live on an island," I say playfully.

"I go to the mainland and find plenty of company there," he replies calmly. I know what he's trying to say, so my gaze lingers on his face for a moment. He's implying he finds women there. That women are his stress relief.

The three of us take our drinks and sit on the patio under the large cabana by the pool. There are two sofas shaped in an L, and when I sit, Ellis takes the spot next to me. I notice the way Nash watches him, sitting across from us.

"This place has changed a lot," Ellis says, looking around at the island. His arm rests on the back of the sofa.

"You've been here before?" I ask.

"He used to work with my dad," Nash interjects. "When I was a kid."

Ellis laughs, a deep, low rumble of a chuckle. "What he's saying is I'm old."

"How old?" I ask, leaning back so my cheek almost brushes his arm. It feels almost intimate.

He smirks at me, and I know I'm being bold by asking, but I'm nothing if not a good flirt. Plus, Ellis doesn't seem like the kind of man to feel ashamed of his age or keep secrets. He looks too proud.

"I'm thirty-eight."

"That's not old," I reply softly, and I feel his fingers touch my hair.

Nash shifts in his seat to get our attention. After taking a drink of my wine, I look back at Ellis. "So, what was Nash like as a kid?"

"Much like Nash as an adult actually."

"Fuck you," Nash growls, but Ellis and I laugh. When I glance over to see his expression, I'm disappointed he's not even smiling. It may have felt like a joke to us, but he's still so tense, and something is bothering him.

How did Zara put up with him for so long?

And why do I always feel the urge to heal him? To heal any man, for that matter? To fix them, comfort them, help them in any way I can when I'm the one who is usually drowning? Why do I do this to myself?

Then, I look at Ellis. If I had a man like him, I bet he would take care of me. I bet I could finally get the attention I want, the nurturing comfort of someone who doesn't need me, but has the time and interest to give me what I need. Would I get bored? Would a part of me be unfulfilled by not being needed by him?

"You have exquisite eyes," he says softly, staring so close I feel almost insecure about it.

"Thank you," I mumble, biting back a smile. "I usually wear contacts to hide it."

"You shouldn't," he replies.

"That's what I told her," Nash interjects, and I tip back my wine glass to hide the awkwardness I'm starting to feel between them.

We only have two rounds of drinks before it starts to get dark. Nash and Ellis talk mostly about business and a little about Ellis's time with the Wildes over a decade ago. And that's it. But I get the feeling there is more they're not telling me. Nash carries so much resentment in his shoulders, I can see it. And there is a mix of admiration and skepticism on his face when he looks at the man sitting next to me.

He's watching Ellis with intensity, and I'm not the only one who notices. A moment later, Ellis stands unexpectedly. "Well, we have a lot of work to do tomorrow. I think I'll call it a night." He turns toward me. "It was really nice meeting you, Hanna."

And with that, much to my disappointment, he walks into the house, shutting the door and leaving me and Nash alone outside.

He's still watching me coldly.

"What?" I ask casually.

"You know what," he growls.

"No, I don't think I do." My tone levels as I glare back at him, heat pulsing under my skin.

"The way you're dressed, the way you flirted with him. What is your deal?"

I scoff. "What the fuck is your deal? I can dress however I want and flirt with whoever the fuck I want."

"Yeah, well last night you were begging to ride my dick, but I said no, so you moved on quickly. Is that it?"

"Fuck you," I mutter, standing up and stomping away toward the guest house.

He doesn't follow me, at least not at first. But when I get to my room, my door is only shut a moment before he's opening it again, closing himself in with me.

"What do you—," I say through the darkness, but before I can get out another word, he stalks across the room and presses me against the wall. Then his mouth is on mine, and I'm struck silent. Nash is kissing me. It's rough, passionate, and so intimate I can hardly focus. His breath on my face rips every thought from my head.

"Do I still scare you, Hanna?" he whispers into my mouth, and I realize my hands are shaking.

I can feel his fingers against my thighs, slowly crawling the length of my skirt, gathering it up to my waist.

"Nash," I whisper, putting my hands against his chest. If I want him to stop, I can push him away, but I don't.

"I said, do I scare you?" he repeats himself so harshly in my face.

"Yes," I yelp.

"Good."

He lifts me abruptly off the ground, winding my legs around his waist as he presses me hard against the wall, his mouth on mine again. This time I do push him away, but he doesn't retreat. I can only feel his fingers moving toward my underwear until they get a hold of the hemline, tearing them down my leg, and he has to drop my legs back down to the floor to pull them off.

"You still want this? You wanted it last night," he mutters, and my blood begins to run cold. I do want this, fuck I want this! What is wrong with me?

I can still hear Ellis's voice in my head, but I can no longer feel the warmth of his presence. And then I see Nash, the pain, the frustration, the anger in his expression and I want to heal him from all of it.

Thinking too long, I don't answer until I feel his fingers at my core, running along the moisture gathering there. I let out a cry as he touches me, and I can't think straight anymore. I'm aroused, but also not. I'm too scared, too nervous, too in my head to be fully aroused, but the way his fingers are moving along my sensitive skin is enough to warm up the blood running through my body.

"Nash," I whisper, grabbing onto his shoulders. Then, he's on his knees, and I don't get a moment to collect my thoughts before his mouth is there. I scream. Not because it hurts but because it feels so wrong and so right at the same time. This is Nash. Nash Wilde. Zara's Nash.

Fuck.

Fuck, fuck, fuck.

She can't know about this. She'll never talk to me again. She'll hate me.

I keep repeating an apology to her in my head as he sucks, nibbles and licks at my pussy. God it's been so long, and I can finally feel that familiar heat building up, the feeling I haven't felt in so long. I should stop him, but I can't.

Then, his kisses are rough. Too rough. His stubble against my legs burns as he devours me, grinding his mouth against me so hard, I have to press myself against the wall while pushing him back with my knee against his shoulder.

"Nash, that hurts!" I cry out.

Then, I'm off the floor again. This time my legs are on his shoulders, wrapped around his head as he sucks every ounce of arousal out of me. Finally, his pressure lets up a little, and the sensitivity it left behind only makes my body react quicker. I have nothing to grasp onto except the wall and his head.

My climax hits hard without any buildup, and it leaves as fast as it came. Still, I let out a moan as my body freezes in his hands. I know I can do better. I know my body is capable of more. That wasn't enough.

But as soon as he feels it fade, he pulls back, letting my body melt to the floor. When I reach for his face, he moves away.

"Don't fuck with Ellis," he whispers, and it shocks me so much I glare at him in confusion.

"What?"

"Stay away from him, okay? I know he's good looking and charming, but he's just..."

"Just what?" I ask, still a little breathless and very confused.

"I don't trust him with you, Hanna."

My eyes squint as I stare skeptically at him. "You mean, you don't want him to have me."

"Will you just fucking listen to me?" His voice is growing heated, and I can feel my own blood starting to boil. The idea of Nash Wilde trying to tell me what to do, to corner me, keep me for himself, control my actions makes me want to spit fire.

"I don't have to listen to you," I snap, pushing him away. "You're so fucking jealous. Yesterday you didn't want me, but now that another man shows interest..."

My voice trails.

And he stares at me silently like he's trying to guess what I'm thinking.

"This is what you get off on, isn't it? You can't handle a woman alone, but you want there to be competition."

"Oh, fuck off, Hanna. I'm protecting you, okay? And this…" he says gesturing to the space between us, signifying what we just did—or rather what he did to me. "You looked like you could use the stress relief, and I did you a favor."

"No, you came in here because you think I'm weak. You think you could beat him to me, and I would fall down on my knees for you, Nash, but I won't."

"Fuck you, Hanna."

"No, fuck you, Nash!" Then I give him a good shove, and before I know it, I'm pressed up against the wall again, and when he rears back his hand, I flinch waiting for the impact. Instead, he slams his fist against the wall next to my head, and I hear the crack of his knuckles, letting out a scream.

"Get the fuck off me," I howl, fighting and kicking against him.

He hoists me up, carrying me, and at first I think we're going to the bedroom, and my blood goes cold. Not that. Not Nash. I can't handle that.

But then we're outside. My bare ass is in the air as I'm slung over his shoulder, and I know exactly where we're going. Still, I fight, clawing at his back and yelling.

"Will you shut the fuck up, you crazy bitch?"

"I hate you, Nash," I mutter, but the words taste sour in my mouth. I instantly regret them. But before I can say anything, I'm airborne, flying toward the ground but instead of hitting the cold pool deck, I'm submerged in water. It's not cold but it shocks me all the same. I sink toward the bottom before I pop back out, letting out a scream.

"You need to cool the fuck down," he growls at me before turning and walking away.

As I climb out of the water, I sit on the edge of the pool, shivering and replaying every second of that in my head. What the fuck was he talking about?

"You okay?" A new deep, cool voice travels across the silent patio and shocks me before I can start crying.

"I'm fine." I'm not in the mood to be charmed by Ellis right now, so I stand up and head back toward the guest house.

"Hanna, wait a moment."

"I said I'm fine."

"I heard you two fighting." He grabs a towel off the back of the chair and brings it over, draping it across my shoulders. I'm sure my makeup is melting down my face, but I stare up at him, looking for any sign Nash was right, and Ellis can't be trusted.

All I see is a confident man with a hint of something behind his eyes. Maybe it's loneliness too.

"Maybe someday you'll tell me what really happened between you two," I mumble. "For now, I'm going to bed."

With that, I turn away from him and walk silently back to my room. When I get there, I make sure to lock the door.

9

Nash is tense as hell. Poring over this business plan for the hundredth time, I don't have the heart to tell him he doesn't need me. He has crossed every T and dotted every I there is, but I'm still here. What he needs is to relax. Let go. Try to focus on something else for a moment, but he certainly won't hear anything like that from me.

Watching him across the table, hammering on about the budget, I can't help but notice he hasn't changed a bit in the past three years. He's matured physically, grown out his hair, started dressing like a business owner and not a punk kid. But he's still wound just as tightly.

It makes me wonder how Nash and I connected so

quickly in Amsterdam. When he stood before me that first night at the party, a fully grown man with fire and fear in his eyes, I wanted to know him more. I wanted to draw out the man inside, the one who could be whoever he wanted to be without fear.

I moved too quickly. The first night we shared the girl in my apartment was too soon for Nash. Not too soon for sex, too soon to have sex in front of me—*with* me. In the room, I mean. But there was a spark, and I knew it could be a blazing fire if handled correctly.

Well, I saw that fire eventually. I pushed too hard, and I got burned for it. I could handle the fight, the anger, the backlash. What I couldn't handle was the silence and then the absence, but that's what I got.

I'm still curious about last night with Hanna, and I want to ask him, but I keep my mouth shut. I heard them in her guest house. I'm pretty sure he wanted me to hear her screaming his name. I haven't gotten a good feel on their relationship yet, but I'm willing to bet they weren't much of a thing before I started flirting with her. Nash still has a jealous side.

"It's past seven, Nash. The budget isn't going to be solved tonight. Take a break."

He looks at his watch. "Fuck, I didn't even realize. I'm sorry. Have a good evening, and we'll resume this tomorrow."

When I stand to leave, he doesn't move, still running numbers on his desk. "Nash," I say in a stern, deep tone reserved exclusively for commands and not requests. I watch him pause, a subtle tic in his hand. Slowly, he looks up at me.

"It's late, Nash."

"You still think that shit is going to work on me?"

Holding back my shoulders, I stare down at him. "Yes, I do."

Which is true. Nash may love to wield his stubborn temper, but he can't ignore the part of him that likes to listen. I see it, even if he doesn't.

"Fuck you, Ellis," he snaps. It's the first time he's really used my name and it sends a chill down my spine. The sound of it coming out of his mouth, past those lips and through the air that drives me forward to place my hands on his desk and look him square in the eye.

"I'm here as your business consultant, and as your business consultant, I'm telling you you're strung too tight. You don't need to go over this budget again, and I don't know what kind of misdirected anxiety or grief this is, but if you don't learn to chill the fuck out, you're going to have a nervous breakdown and ruin your company."

He's clenching his jaw, staring up at me with acrimony, and I don't know why I'm tempting fate or poking the bear, but I lean in until our faces are only inches apart. So close I can feel his breath, smell his cologne—which he hasn't changed I notice. "But on a personal level, Nash, I'm telling you to cut your bullshit with me. I'm not going back down that road again with you, do you understand? You said it was water under the bridge, so believe me when I say..." I lean a little closer. "I have no desire to control you or own you, not anymore. So, get the fuck over yourself, you fucking brat."

He explodes out of his chair and throws his hands against my chest, the heat and anger in his eyes radiating from him like rays of sun. I don't throw my hands back at him, and I have no interest in brawling right here in his office like college kids, but I want to wrap my hands around his throat. Getting Nash angry is like blowing on the embers of a fire. So easily fired up, but I can tell he wants it. Nash loves to be angry.

It only took me three months with him in Amsterdam to figure that out.

"If you think I want to go back to the way things were, you're fucking crazy. Everything that happened between us was just another form of your manipulation."

"Okay, Nash," I respond, humor lacing my tone. This is what he does. He deflects responsibility, blame, guilt. He still blames me for what happened, for wanting what we did. For *liking it.*

"You had me right where you wanted me, didn't you? I told you I wasn't into that, but you found a way to manipulate me into it."

"So, that's how you remember it? Because that's not exactly how it happened, Nash. You know that, right?"

"I remember it very clearly."

"And what do you remember? Do you remember me forcing you to your knees? Making you believe you wanted to suck my dick? Does any of that ring a bell or was that all my fault?"

"Shut the fuck up, Ellis." He looks like he's about to burst. There are veins popping along his forearms as he squeezes his hands into fists.

"You have your own warped memory of how things went down because you don't want to admit something about yourself—"

"I told you, I'm not fucking gay, Ellis. You think I'd have a problem admitting it if I was?"

I can't help the sardonic laugh that slips through my lips. "You think that's all this is about. All it was ever about. You really have no idea, Nash."

He's staring at me, his brows pinched together as I turn

and walk away, leaving him with those words. And I hope they keep him up all fucking night.

It's late but not late enough to sleep, so I decide to go for a walk instead. I can't be around Nash right now. I came here to work but also to hopefully settle this thing between us, to see what it was we left behind, and I meant what I said—I'm not going back down that road again.

I don't like to admit Nash had an effect on me in Amsterdam, and the way things ended left me stunned for...well, years. Did I push him? Sure. At first it was fun, and I was intrigued by him and his fiery presence, but it wasn't long before it became something more serious. Something I couldn't walk away from. I found myself testing the waters, hoping for more, wanting things I had never wanted. And once I got a taste, it only got worse.

The sun still hangs heavy over the horizon, painting the sky a beautiful watercolor pink and orange. After a few moments of walking, I spot a figure sitting on a large rock jettying out toward the water. She's silhouetted in the sunset, her knees pulled up to her chest and her face pressed against the last light of the dying sun.

I like Hanna. She puts on a beautiful facade, a fearless prima ballerina who holds the world in her hands, but there's something more beneath that mask. She says she's out here to get away, get away from what? Work? Pressure? A man?

In a quiet moment last night, I did my research on Ms. Thurber and found out she did eight years with a prominent ballet company, working her way to being the principal dancer during her last two years. Out of nowhere last summer she missed a performance due to, what was later claimed as a medical episode before the show. She hasn't performed since.

She's single, never been married, and has been seen

around town with a chorus line of underwhelming boyfriends who all looked too self-absorbed to know what to do with a creature like her.

And that little dark voice in my head reminds me I know exactly what to do with her.

I know Hanna's type, and I'm willing to bet she's very much like the cocky prick I left fuming in his office. She's too caught up in her head, so sure she knows what she needs, but doesn't settle easily. I'm dying to crack her open to see what's inside.

As I approach Hanna sitting peacefully on the rock, I stand a few feet away, putting my hands in my pockets and clearing my throat to make my presence known. She's so peaceful and such a contrast to the tension-filled discussion I just left with Nash.

"Oh hey," she says with a smile, instantly straightening her spine and painting a soft expression on her face. If I had any desire to preserve this moment of beauty, I'd take a picture of her right now. In this light, the warmth of her skin absorbing the sun's glow, she looks stunning, but it's not exactly the outer beauty I'm interested in.

"I hope I'm not bothering you."

"Not at all," she replies, throwing her wind-swept black waves out of her face.

"Care to walk with me?" I ask. There is a spark of interest in her eyes as she hops off the rock.

"Absolutely."

I don't head back toward the house yet. There are approximately six miles of beach on this island and while I'm not interested in walking them all now, I want to prolong this quiet moment with this girl.

"So, I have a confession," I say, watching for the way she tenses and looks almost guilty already.

"Ich kanne eine bischen Deutsch."

Freezing on the sand, she lets out a clipped laugh and swats at my arm. She seems almost disarmed, a little looser than she was yesterday, and I wonder if it's my presence or the lack of Nash's.

"You can speak German? Wait," she says, looking up at me with a dimple in her cheek. "How did you know I was half-German? Did you look me up? Have your spies done their research?"

An easy smile spreads across my face. "I might have done a little stalking online last night."

She laughs for a moment until the humor drops off of her face like water running down the panes of a window. She's realizing at this exact moment that by looking her up I've discovered the moment she's ashamed of.

"You have nothing to be embarrassed about," I tell her flatly as we walk.

"The media loves to tell their own story sometimes."

"I'd like to hear yours. Someday." When I do look at her, there is so much sincerity in her eyes I worry, not for the first time, that this woman could work her way under my skin. She is easy to be around, so genuine, like a jewel that requires nothing from you except to admire how beautiful it is. And that's all I want from Hanna, to admire her.

And maybe to push her, just a little. Find her limits. I bet she'd surprise even herself.

"Want to go back to my room?" she blurts out, and my head practically snaps as I look at her.

"Why do you want to go back to your room?" I stroke the side of my chin as I notice her swallowing. I know exactly why she wants to go back to her room, but it was a little sudden. And to be clear, I'd like nothing more than to go back to her room and do exactly what she has in mind. But there's something not quite right about the way she came out with it.

"I think you know, Ellis…" She's staring down at her feet in the sand, and I reach out, lifting her chin to bring her eyes to mine.

"And what about Nash?"

She scoffs. "I belong to no one. I'm just looking for a good time. Aren't you? Can't we skip all the formalities. I know what you want. You know what I want. So, why wait?"

I step forward, put a hand on her waist, and she tilts her head up toward me, as if she's waiting for me to kiss her. I underestimated this girl from the start. I knew there was something beneath her beautiful mask, but I have a feeling it's far more complex than I originally thought. She's not just broken. She's shattered into a million little pieces.

"Let's go back to your room," I whisper. Her eyes brighten for a moment as she takes my hand and pulls me toward the guest house.

10

Thank God. I need this, and I have faith Ellis Prior has what it takes to get me out of this dry slump I've been stuck in for the past eleven months. Living so long without arousal does things to a person. Sure, Nash got me off last night, but it wasn't quite the release I was looking for.

Something about his forcefulness turned me on, but more than anything, the fear was like ice cold water on my body. It was a desperate, fumbling orgasm full of resentment and regret. Not exactly how I wanted my first time with Nash to be.

So, I need Ellis to wash it all away. Like a palate

cleanser. A thirty-eight-year old, hot as fuck, confident, rich palate cleanser.

When we get to the room, I pull him in and offer him some wine from the bottle I have sitting on the small kitchenette.

"No thank you," he replies as he puts his hands in his pockets and walks toward me. The eye contact is disarming.

"Okay then." I keep waiting for him to take the lead, tear off my clothes or something, but he doesn't. So, I walk up to him instead and reach for the buttons of his shirt. His hands snatch mine before I can get one undone.

"Sit with me."

"We really don't have to—"

"Sit down, Hanna." A chill runs down my spine as I silently obey him, moving toward the couch. As I take a seat, I look up to him, waiting for him to sit too.

When he finally takes the spot next to me, he still doesn't move to kiss me. What is his deal? Instead, he leans his arm along the back of the sofa and looks at me.

I reach for his pants, thinking maybe he wants me to take the lead.

"Stop."

I pull my hands away.

"Ellis, I don't need you to be polite about this. We don't have to pretend we didn't both come here to fuck."

"That's not why I came here, Hanna."

I let out a sigh and a sarcastic laugh. "Why are you fucking with me right now?"

"Because I like you, and I want to know what has you acting like this."

My eyes widen, and I pull away, ready to snap at him, but his hand reaches out, grasping the back of my neck as he pulls me forward. Our lips hover an inch apart as he stares into my eyes.

"So, what is it? Why are you so eager to get me into bed?"

"Is the fact I'm attracted to you not enough?" I ask. A small smile lifts the corner of his mouth.

"I'm attracted to you too, but you don't see me trying to fuck you like it means nothing," he replies.

"Oh, it definitely wouldn't mean nothing to me," I whisper. "Don't tell me you never have meaningless sex. I don't believe that for a second."

"Not with people I like."

Finally, he pulls my face toward him, closing the distance and pressing his soft lips to mine. First, it's a gentle kiss, our lips locking in warmth and velvet until his tongue slips through, stroking mine in a soft friction that lights a small spark behind my ribcage.

He kisses me for a long time, holding my head like I'm some small fragile thing. I melt into his embrace, crawling onto his lap while he takes his time with his mouth exploring mine. I can't remember the last time I just kissed someone, making out like we're teenagers, but suddenly I'm in no hurry to do anything else.

When his lips move from mine to trail kisses along my jaw and down to my neck, I forget my own name. Letting out a soft hum, I suddenly get hungry to have him touch me. For the first time in almost a year, my body is warm, but the arousal hasn't quite reached my panties yet. It's like my heart and body is warmed up but nothing is going on down there.

"Let's go to the bedroom," I pant.

And just like that he stops kissing me.

"I'm not going to fuck you." His words are like ice. I pull away in a rush.

"What? Why?"

He touches my cheek softly. "Patience, Hanna."

"Fuck patience."

"Why the hurry?"

"I can feel your cock against my leg and it's rock hard. Why on earth would we wait?"

He laughs, actually fucking laughs, and I want to scream. Then, he puts his hands on my hips and presses me against his erection, grinding me on him with a groan. "Trust me, I want it too, but you are worth the wait."

I freeze, looking into his eyes. After last night with Nash, this feels like a cruel joke. One man has no patience. The other has too much.

"Tell me what happened between you and Nash," he whispers, tucking a strand of curls behind my ear as I shift off of his lap to put a little distance between us. If he's not going to fuck me, being so close to him feels like a tease... and too intimate.

"You first," I reply, and this time it's his turn to flinch.

"What makes you think there's anything between us?" he asks.

"I'm not blind. He hates you, and Nash only bothers to hate people he cares about."

There's a deep rumble of short laughter from his chest. "That's a good way to put it."

"So, tell me."

"Just old friends, that's all."

"And why does he hate you?"

He strokes my fingers in his hand. "Nash is jealous and hot-tempered. You can figure out the rest." Then he kisses my knuckles, and I melt. Looking up at me, he adds, "So Nash told me you were off limits, but what I heard last night says something else."

Oh great. I was worried he heard everything that

happened before he found me crawling out of the pool without underwear on. "You heard that? It was a mistake. It won't happen again." My voice trails. What do I say? There is no word for what happened between us. It wasn't quite consensual enough to be sex, but it wasn't anything worse than that. I just wish it had been on better terms.

And now talking about it with the guy I'm currently trying to have very consensual sex with feels wrong, and well, it's not making me feel very good about myself.

"Have you two slept together?" he asks.

"No," I answer, assuming him assaulting me with his mouth doesn't count. "Zara is my best friend…and we really shouldn't have…"

He lets out a sigh, as my gaze drifts across the room, focusing on nothing at all. The moonlight streaming through the window, soft sound of the air conditioner, the feel of Ellis's soft hands on my fingers.

"What are you thinking about?" he asks, and my gaze jolts back to his face.

"Oh, nothing. I was just…zoning out, I guess."

Gently reclining on the couch, I pull my feet up to the couch, and he takes them into his lap, looking down at me as if there is a sudden intimacy between us. It's easy comfort, and I'm almost glad we didn't immediately have sex. It'd probably be over by now and he'd be wanting to leave, or I'd be wishing I hadn't rushed things.

But him looking at me, actually looking at me, it's better than sex.

"So, about Zara…" he says, and my attention perks again.

"You both seem to be protecting her feelings so much. I can understand she's your best friend, but Nash…why does he care so much?"

"How much of that story do you know?" I ask, squinting at him before I continue.

"All of it."

"Okay, good. Then, you know for a while, he was a part of that relationship. And then...he wasn't anymore. So, I almost wonder if it's Zara he's still stuck on, but the bond between them. All of them."

"A little strange, don't you think?"

Feeling suddenly sleepy, I rest my head against the arm of the couch, and focus on the feel of his hands along my ankles and then my calves. "Who's to say what's normal and strange? Nash is probably too much for one person anyway."

He laughs again, but then the room grows quiet as he strokes my legs, and his gentle touch is the last thing I remember before sleep takes me.

11

It's well after midnight when I hear Ellis coming back in from Hanna's guest house. Watching him cross the yard toward the house, I'm seething, anger building from thinking about them together. I'm sitting in the living room when he sneaks in, the lights still on so he knows I'm there. After stepping in, he takes one look at me, showing no emotion as he passes through.

"I told you she was off limits," I snarl. He freezes in the doorway, glaring at me with a cold, cynical expression.

"Since when do I take orders from you?"

"This isn't a joke, Ellis," I snap, standing up and crossing the room to get in his face. He's so fucking smug, like he knows everything. I used to admire that about him. Now I hate it. I hate his confidence, and I especially hate how he has me so pegged, like he thinks he knows me.

"Does it look like I'm fucking joking, Nash?"

"You are a joke," I mutter. Okay maybe that was the vodka talking, and I completely deserve the harsh, hateful glare he sends me. He should punch me. Knock me out. I would, but he doesn't because this is Ellis, the calm, collected man who never loses control. Well, almost never.

"Fuck off, Nash." It's all he gives me before he tries to leave, but I'm not ready yet. I still have so much I need to say, things I need to get off my chest.

"Stay the fuck away from her," I shout at him, crowding him toward the corner of the room.

"You're the same reckless kid you were three years ago, Nash. You don't deserve a woman like her, and after what I heard last night, she's better off in my hands."

The next moment is a blur as I drive my forearm against his throat and shove him against the wall.

"This isn't Amsterdam. I used to think you were a fucking god, now all I see is a lonely man with no one because he never got over the one person he couldn't have. You're pathetic."

He snarls at me, and I think for a moment he's not going to fight back. His eyes are glued on mine, and I get lost in those dark brown orbs. Memories come flooding back. This was my friend. I trusted him, and he blinded me. He manipulated me at a time when I was vulnerable, and I gave in. And now, my stupid, naive heart thuds a little harder in my chest as he has the fucking nerve to look hurt. No, he doesn't get to be hurt. Not after what he did to me.

My grip against his throat loosens, and before I know it, he gains control, grabbing my arm and in a struggle, he manages to get it behind my back, flipping me around and shoving me against the couch. He's pressed behind me as he folds me over the back. I let out a snarl as I fight him, but every time I move, he shoves my arm up farther, sending a jolt of electric pain through my shoulder.

"Calm the fuck down," he says, using that deep authoritative voice I remember so clearly.

"You want to call me pathetic?" he says, seething as I feel his lips against my ear. "I'm not the one in denial here, Nash. You can blame me all you want for what happened, but you know as well as I do you fucking *liked* it. I'm not going to make you feel better about how much you loved my cock, Nash, and I'm sure as fuck not going to put up with your little tantrums about it. You walked out of my life, and I didn't follow you, just like you asked. So why did you hire me, huh?"

"Did you tell her about us?" I ask.

He winds his arm around my throat, pulling me up so I'm flush against his body. I hate the way my heart nearly drops to the floor with that familiar old feel of his rippled chest and thick biceps. I hate the way I love it.

Then he whispers harshly into my ear. "No, I didn't fucking tell her. Because when I'm with her, we don't talk about you."

I jerk against his hold again, but then I feel something warm and wet run a long line from my shoulder to my ear, and I realize it's his tongue. My body freezes in his hold.

"Hundred bucks says you're harder than cement right now," he whispers, his warm breath against my ear. "Can I check?"

I grunt against him, but he's got a vice grip on my neck, cutting off my ability to speak. I can barely breathe as it is, but I'm not sure that's from the chokehold.

Then, he releases my arm, and slides his hand down

my chest. I shudder as he reaches the front of my pants, and no matter how much I fight, I can't get away. Before I know it, he's cupping my dick, and as he predicted, it's hard as stone.

A low groan hums against my back as he squeezes me tighter, both around my neck and cock. Suddenly I lose the will to fight, and I find myself shoving into his hand, grinding it against the back of the couch.

"Is this my fault too? How much you love my hand on your cock?"

"Fuck you," I mutter. This is totally his fucking fault. He gets in my head, making me think some shit that was never there before. I'm not attracted to dudes, and I've never wanted dick before, but all of a sudden Ellis gets a hold of me, and my body can't fight how fucking good it feels.

"No, Nash. More like fuck you." He thrusts his hips against me, his thick erection shoved into the crevice of my ass.

"Get the fuck off of me, Ellis."

"If I let you go, can you agree to stop being such an asshole to me? Can you just fucking listen to me?"

"All I do is listen to you."

He thrusts me against the couch again. "Say it," he seethes in my ear. "Or I swear I'll jack you off right here. You'll love every second of it and hate yourself for it."

I growl against him, trying to shift out of his hold, but the more I do, the more friction there is against my cock, and I'm weak to it. A part of me wishes he would unbutton my pants and wrap that big hand around me, squeezing it so tight I could barely manage to come, but he's right. I'd hate myself for it.

"Fine," I mutter.

"What was that?" he replies in a dark, teasing tone.

"Yes." Fuck, please don't make me say it.

"Yes, what?"

I struggle again. "Just fucking let me go."

With a laugh, he says, "Fine." And with that, he releases me. I feel the absence immediately, mostly the pressure against my dick. He pulls away slowly, and I turn around to see the tent he's pitched in his pants. I remember the way it felt in my hands, among other places. The memory of it hits me so hard, I have to force myself to swallow and look away.

"You can touch it if you want," he says with a smirk, and I glance up at him.

No, I don't want to touch it.

"Fuck you."

"You really hate me, don't you?"

When I look at him again, I see that pain again, and it makes me seethe with hatred. He doesn't get to hurt. Not when he's gotten the best of me. Not when I've spent the last three years of my life in constant torture, unable to wrap my head around how he made me bend so easily. How he had me right where he wanted me.

"Just stay away from Hanna."

"Do you have feelings for her?" he asks coolly.

"That's none of your fucking business," I snap back at him.

"Be careful with her, Nash. Whatever she's been through, it's broken her, but I see a strong woman trying to build herself back up. Whatever you do, don't push her back down. She'll make it easy for you."

I can feel my nostrils flare as I remember what I did to her last night. I hate that he's right. She will make it easy. Hanna will follow the path of least resistance, even if it sends her down into a spiral. How the fuck does he think he knows what she needs more than me? He's known her for two days.

"You don't think I know that? The last thing she needs is two assholes fighting over her. So, you leave her alone, and I will too."

"I'm not going to fuck her, but I'm not going to leave her alone," he says, and I feel my spine straighten.

"You didn't…?"

"No, I didn't fuck her. She wanted me to, but I did her one better."

"Yeah, what's that?" I ask, expecting him to tell me how he gave her a better orgasm than I did or some shit.

But as he turns away and moves toward the hallway where his room is, he calls back over his shoulder, "I listened."

12

THE SOUND OF THE HELICOPTER APPROACHING PULLS MY attention from my laptop. Nash is going over the budget, again, when he looks up too, and I hear him mutter a curse.

"Who is it?" I ask.

"My dad," he mumbles, his voice taking on a thickness I haven't heard yet.

The last few days he's been acting almost civil toward me. I know he still blames me for what happened in Amsterdam, as if being someone he was attracted to was somehow my fault. I bore the brunt of that blame for three years. It's nothing new to me now.

But I could also feel him peeling back a little bit of that pain and showing the real Nash underneath.

"Did you know he was coming?" I ask.

"No."

He looks back down at his computer, ignoring the presence of his father and his new wife standing outside. I watch as Hanna approaches them, going first to Alistair to give him a quick embrace. Then, she goes to Zara, tucking herself at her side as they walk toward the main house.

Alistair turns the opposite way and comes to the office. When he pulls open the door, we both look up.

"Working on a Saturday?" he asks, eyebrows raised and gaze leveled on Nash. I toss him an easy smile as I lean back in my chair.

"I've tried talking him into a break, but he won't listen to me. So good luck."

"Well, he's certainly not going to listen to me." Alistair walks over to see what he is working on, and I watch as Nash stiffens in his seat, his jaw clenched as his father looks over the budget on the screen.

"Thalia prepared lunch for us. Let's go eat and we can talk."

"Again, don't you guys have a new baby? Do you ever spend any time with her?"

Alistair rolls his eyes. "I have a son too, and sometimes I like to spend time with him, so put the work away and come eat with us."

"Let's go, Nash," I say, standing up from the desk. He finally shuts his laptop, and stands along with me. There's a curious flinch in Alistair's brow as he notices the way his son listens to me, and not him, and I notice it. We all notice it.

And fuck me, I like it.

The patio is set with lunch as we approach. Hanna and

Zara are already sitting across from each other with cocktails in their hands. Hanna looks up at me with a spark in her eye. For reasons I don't understand, I wink at her, sending her a warm smile. It became clear after the talk we had the other night there is an instant chemistry between us, an easy comfort, and I find myself looking forward to the few moments each night we have to talk. Hanna is genuine, smart, and I want to know the depths of her. What I see on the surface is a woman who is at war with herself while hiding the confidence I know she has. I'd like to change that.

I met Alistair's new wife on the day he flew me out to Del Rey, but she sends me a smile and greeting anyway. Zara is a beautiful girl, and I see how well she complements him, but I also have to bite back my judgement. I don't blame her for what happened with Nash, but I was the one who picked up the pieces after it all went down, so it's hard not to reserve at least a little judgement.

"I hope Nash isn't giving you too much trouble," she says with a bright smile as she takes a sip of her drink.

"Nothing I can't handle," I reply, but when I glance back at Nash, I notice a softness in his expression as he looks at her. I had a suspicion he still harbored feelings for the girl who was once his, the one who slipped out of his grasp, and I remember how he told me in Amsterdam he would have never made a good boyfriend for her then, but I can't help but wonder what it is that exists between them now. It's like a strange combination of family, friends, and ex-lovers.

We all take our seats and immediately I regret the way it happens. Alistair is next to his wife. Hanna is sitting next to me, and Nash sits alone at the head of the table. There's a clench to his jaw, and his fists are so tight around his drink they're blanched white at the knuckles.

Zara puts her hand through Alistair's fingers as the girls go on about Zara's dance studio.

"How is the acquisition going?" Alistair asks me, talking aside from the women. Nash takes a drink, looking away from his father, as if he's actively avoiding that question. As if it doesn't bother him his father didn't direct the question to him.

"You said no work talk," Zara complains. She runs her hands through his hair, and I glare at her. Does she know what she's doing? Sure, Nash is okay with them being together, but he's still struggling with the physical touch between them. How do they not see that?

Because he puts up a wall, hides it all…just like Hanna does.

"You're talking about work," Alistair argues softly.

"That's different." Her eyes dance over to Nash, and I want to scream. The messages are all wrong. She'll touch Alistair in front of him, but pretend she's protecting him from the stress of talking work with his overbearing father. The boundaries are all wrong here, and it's making me crazy.

Just then, I feel Hanna's hand run along my back, and I stiffen, my eyes immediately bolting over to Nash to see his reaction. He seems to be too busy sipping down his vodka soda with lime to care.

"So, Ellis told me he used to work here years ago when Nash was just a kid," Hanna says.

Zara laughs. "So, what was Nash like as a child?"

"That's what I asked," Hanna replies. They're all looking at me, and I try to keep a casual expression on my face, remembering how I answered this question three days ago. I had said he's the same spoiled brat now he was then.

But when I glance at him, I see a man in the margins. Shoved out of the only relationship he's ever been in. No significant other, no friend, no brother. It's enough to remind me he's not as tough as he lets the world believe. And I feel instant regret over the way I answered the question before.

"He was a good kid," I say with a shrug.

His eyes snap up to me, and instead of looking pleased with me, he stares daggers at me, his brow furrowed with anger.

"He was the good one," Alistair adds, taking the attention of the table, well everyone except from Nash who is still seething with his eyes on me. It's not so obvious everyone else will notice it, but I do.

"It was Preston who was the troublemaker." Bringing up Nash's late brother seems to be the only thing that draws his glare away from me. He nods his head at his father as they both share a subtle, silent moment.

Then, Zara winds her fingers in Alistair's and when he looks at her, she leans up to plant a kiss on his lips.

"He may not have been a troublemaker when he was a kid, but he certainly is now," Zara says as she looks over at him with a soft smile.

I know she thinks she's being friendly with him, and with the way he smiles back at her, it's obvious she's buying his front. But I see what they don't.

Nash is holding onto something. And it grates on my nerves.

"Well, being a troublemaker makes him a great CEO. I don't think I've ever seen business in such good shape when I get to a job."

Again, he glares at me because speaking kindly of him when he so clearly wants me to hate him as much as he hates me is enough to set him off. He thinks I'm fucking with him.

"He cares about his company and not in dollar signs.

He loves his job because this company means everything to him," I add.

"What Nash needs is to learn to let go of some responsibility. He has control issues. He knows that," Alistair adds, taking a bite from his sandwich.

There's a short moment of silence as I look around at the table, trying to bite my tongue. Trying, but failing.

"Yeah. He does. But it's pretty clear he has trust issues." The words slip out of my mouth, and I feel the tension land like a brick against the table. His eyes squint as he levels his glare at me. Meanwhile, Zara is staring down at her lunch, pushing around her food while chewing on her inner lip.

No one will dare to argue Nash doesn't have trust issues. They can't argue because they were the ones who instilled them. He can feed me all the bullshit about it being consensual and how he was the one to let her go, but I see it for what it is. He gave her up because she fell in love with his father more than she fell in love with him.

It's quiet for a moment, and I already know Alistair will have words for me, but I don't give a shit. It's like I'm the only one who sees things clearly here, and it's infuriating.

"We need more drinks," Hanna says, breaking the tension.

"I'll get them," I snap, standing quickly and grabbing their glasses. When I get inside, I slam them against the bar top a little too hard. They don't break, but I almost wish they had.

What the fuck is happening to me? It's like the feelings I've been ignoring for the past three years are bubbling up as if they never really went away. I pushed away everything that happened with Nash. I thought I could get past it, but when I see him at that table, struggling with his pain alone, the pain of accepting what we did in Amsterdam on top of it, I feel so fucking unsettled, I want to break something.

I rinse out the glasses and refill them with ice when I see Nash come inside, shutting the patio door behind him. He's fuming, nostrils flaring and brow angsty and folded in.

"What the fuck is wrong with you?"

"What are you talking about?" I ask, trying my best to look unbothered.

"This is none of your fucking business. So, stay out of it!"

I drop the ice bucket on the counter with a bang. "You're right. It is none of my business. I'm just an outsider, Nash, and I wasn't there when all of this happened, but I was there after it happened. I remember how terrified you were that I'd leave you too. Do you remember begging me to stay?"

"Shut the fuck up," he mutters through clenched teeth.

"I picked up the pieces in Amsterdam. I tried to give you what they couldn't, something I knew you wanted, and do you know what you did to me in return, Nash? You broke my fucking heart!"

He flinches, his eyes going wide, and it takes a moment before he reacts, stomping toward me and shoving me back until we're in the hallway behind the kitchen. Out of view of the party, he holds me against the wall, his hand pressed firmly against my chest.

"I swear to God if you don't drop that shit, I'm going to send your ass packing off this fucking island, do you hear me?"

I brush him away easily. "I'm already gone. I can't stay here, not with you." When I try to move out of his grasp, his hand lands against my chest again and this time when he shoves me against the wall, his eyes are trained on my face, wild and…terrified.

"I never should have come here. You're even more fucked up than—" He stops my words with his mouth, crashing against mine. Grabbing onto his neck, I devour his touch, his mouth, the warm velvet sensation of his tongue as it sweeps past my lips. A low groan shudders through me as I latch onto him, feeling him fist my shirt in his hand.

"Quiet," he whispers, his hand reaching for my pants, gripping my cock through these thin, linen trousers. "I fucking hate you," he mutters as he quickly pulls down the zipper and reaches inside, wrapping his hand around me and sending my mind far away where it can't think, only feel.

The harder I squeeze his neck, the tighter his fist strangles my dick. Pulling away from our kiss, he looks down at what he's doing, and I watch as he spits on the head, using it as lube as he strokes me, fast.

"You don't hate me," I whisper, grabbing his dick through his shorts, but he swats my hand away.

"Don't touch me."

Keeping up his assault on my cock, my breathing starts to stutter. Just when I feel myself start to build up, I grab him by the throat and look him in the eye.

Realization dawns like a cruel monster, intent on destroying everything good that comes our way. Nash wants me to lose control. He wants to have me vulnerable, to feel the way he did, helpless to this desire. It's why he won't let me touch him. Why he fights me, denies everything, blames me for it all. He wants me to foot the bill for everything he wants.

I don't lose control. And I don't do vulnerable.

My build-up recedes, and with my hand on his throat, I shove Nash down. He fights me at first until he can no longer deny what he wants, dropping to his knees and staring straight ahead at the red, engorged cock in front of him.

"Open up," I mutter, and he looks up at me, the boiling hatred still obvious in his eyes.

Then he does. Slowly he lets his tongue roll out of his open mouth, letting me drop the head of my dick against the warmth of it.

"Still hate me?" I ask as I slide the small beads of pre-cum against the surface. Then, I slide myself in, and he closes his lips around me like he's been dying to do it again. A tingle slides its way up my spine remembering the first time he did this. How fucking hot he was, taking my dick in his mouth. So nervous and unsure. So turned on he had to stroke himself at the same time.

"Do you, Nash? Do you still hate me?"

I nearly hit the back of his throat as he practically swallows my cock, but he doesn't let up. He starts bobbing up and down almost angrily, but he won't look up at me anymore, practically suffocating himself. When his eyes start to water, I run my hands through his long hair, pulling his head back so he can look up at me.

"Those tears tell me all I need to know."

With my hands buried in his hair, I fuck his mouth, five or six hard strokes until I shoot down the back of his throat.

When he pulls away, he wipes his mouth, staring blankly ahead as I stuff myself back into my pants.

Neither of us says a word for a moment until he stands, glaring at me with something new. Not anger, but resignation.

Surrender.

Defeat.

"I'm sorry shit is complicated, Nash. I'm sorry the last time you were in love, you had your heart broken, but I'm not sorry you are the way you are. And I'm not sorry about anything that's happened between us, so if you want me to apologize, then you can fuck off."

Leaving him there, I turn away and head back down the hallway that leads to the kitchen, but the moment I reach the room, I stop, frozen in place as I stare at Hanna, who is watching me with wide eyes, heartbreak written all over her face.

13

OH MY GOD. I JUST HAPPENED TO CATCH NASH PUSHING Ellis down the hall, and I only came in hoping to defuse the situation, but what I ended up overhearing was definitely not a fight. It was most definitely the sound of Nash choking on Ellis's…

Fuck, I'm such an idiot. How did I not see this? I threw myself at Ellis, and I wondered why he didn't want me back. Now, I know it's just because he's…

And Nash? Is he?

Thoughts are firing off in my mind, the sounds of him and Nash replaying in my head, the words he said to him.

"Hanna," Ellis states so clearly I don't know if he's announcing my presence or making a plea.

Out of everything going on in my head right now, not one thing is what I *should* say. Instead, I turn on my heels and rush out of the room toward the patio. I don't get far before his hand is latched onto my arm.

"I'm sorry," he whispers.

"Don't apologize to me," I snap, glaring up at him with fire in my eyes. "You could have told me. You didn't have to lead me on."

"Lead you on? You were the one throwing yourself at me."

With a scoff, I tear my arm away. I don't want to be mad at Ellis, but my anger boils, threatening to spill over. Why am I so mad at him all of a sudden? Because he let me make a fool of myself. He let me kiss him, try to fuck him, and he could have spoken up at any moment.

Before going to the patio, I snatch the two drinks off the bar and rush out the door. As I reach the patio, Zara and Alistair are still sitting at the table, both engrossed in their phones.

"Everything okay?" she asks immediately, noticing the serious expression on my face.

"Yep," I lie.

I should leave. I know that now. I should leave with them right now, and I won't have to face my humiliation anymore. I can run from this easily too. I found myself wanting Ellis so desperately after such a short time, and not in the same way I've wanted other men. I wanted him because with him I feel safe and wanted, but apparently that was one-sided because not only is he interested in someone else, but that person is Nash.

Nash.

I really don't need to be around him anymore either.

That strange encounter the other day is branded into my brain, and it's not exactly a memory of him I'd like to keep. The moment Zara stepped foot on the island, guilt stained my mind. How could I look at her, laugh with her, pretend everything was fine when just a few days ago, *her* Nash had his head buried between my thighs.

"Sure you're okay? You look like you've got a lot on your mind?"

"I'm really fine," I say. "I just—"

At that moment, Nash steps outside, slamming the door with a little too much force. His eyes meet mine instantly, and the eye contact feels like an attack. I know what he did. He knows I know, and instead of looking embarrassed or ashamed, he looks furious.

"I have to get back to work." Without so much as a goodbye, he marches over to the office, leaving us all sitting there in confusion.

"Nash," Alistair calls.

"I'll go talk to him," Zara says, and I don't know why, but for the first time in our friendship, I feel the hot sting of jealousy.

"Let me," I bark, standing up too quickly.

The look she gives me is a mix of shock and hurt. To her, Nash and I have always been barely friends, only really related through her, and now I'm taking her place, pushing her aside to have him to myself.

I have never felt a sense of protectiveness simmer to the surface the way it is right now.

"I'll be right back," I say carefully, trying to force on a fake smile.

"We should probably get going," Alistair replies. "If he's in a mood, there's nothing she can say to get him to come back out. In fact, I think he's been in a shitty mood all day."

Zara won't take her eyes off me, but when her husband puts his hand on her leg, she relaxes. "He's still working too hard," she whispers.

"None of us are going to be able to talk him out of that," Alistair replies. "I was the same way when I was his age."

I can still see Zara's urge to go to him, so I quickly distract the conversation. "I'm so glad you came out. It was nice to see someone else for once. All these boys do is work, so I've gotten a lot of alone time."

"That's good. I hope they're not bothering you too much," Alistair adds.

"Not at all."

As they stand up, Zara comes to me first, wrapping me up in a hug. A moment later, Ellis emerges from the house. "Sorry about that. I got caught up on a call. Are you leaving?"

"Yeah, we have to get back to the baby."

The men shake hands with a clap on the shoulder, and I sense the tension between them. I know it's because of the awkward conversation at lunch, but I can't help but wonder if Alistair has any idea about Ellis or what Ellis has been up to with Nash? Did everyone know about this but me?

"Thank you again for everything," I tell the couple as they walk out to the helicopter. The men walk ahead as Zara pulls me back.

"Do you know what's gotten into him?" she asks, and I know she's referring to Nash. I don't want to lie, but it's not exactly my secret to tell. So, I swallow everything down and try to answer as honestly as I can without giving too much away.

"I think he's having a hard time collaborating with

Ellis," I say, doing my best to sell it. Her mouth twists in concern, but then she levels her gaze on me.

"Speaking of…" she whispers. "What's going on there?" Her eyes dance over to where the men are talking, and I'm sure this question was inspired by the intimacy between us at lunch, a reminder I am an idiot and clearly put myself in a stupid situation, making a complete fool of myself.

"Nothing," I answer, glancing at him. "We're just friends."

"Just be careful," she replies, touching a strand of curls that hangs on the side of my head. "I don't feel right leaving you here with these two. This island does things to you."

"I can handle them," I answer with a laugh. This time the guys look over at us, and we both grin back at them.

Ellis and I stand together as Zara and Alistair take off, and at the exact moment I feel him turning toward me ready to say something, I give him my shoulder and head toward the office. I need time to cool off, a moment to come down from the initial resentment so I can have a real conversation with him. Like I said, Ellis is the one person here I don't want to hate.

He doesn't follow me to the office. I half-expect him to, but he goes back to the house instead. When I enter the office, I find Nash bent over his laptop again. When his eyes flash up to see me, they soften when he realizes it's me and not someone else.

"I really don't want to talk right now, Hanna."

"Okay," I reply, walking over to the empty table and leaning against it, crossing my ankles and looking down at him.

"Then why are you still here?" he says in a low growl.

"Because I don't believe you."

"Believe me. I don't want to talk about it."

"About what happened in the house?"

His fists slam against the table. "Jesus Christ, Hanna. I'm serious. Get out."

It takes everything in me to keep from flinching. There's not a part of me that's not still scared of Nash in some way, his volatile nature, but in my first week here, I've learned what Zara never told me about him. He's just as scared as I am. And that gives me a sense of comfort and power.

I have never felt this intense draw toward someone, the sudden need to shelter him, fix him, nurture him. It's the only thing keeping me in here right now. The old Hanna would have bolted the moment he told me to get out.

"How long has this been going on, Nash?"

With his elbows on the table, he runs his hands through this hair. "There's nothing going on."

"Then, what was that in the house? Because two days ago, you assaulted my clit with your mouth in my room, and now you're hooking up with Ellis, so tell me, Nash. What exactly is going on?"

He bolts out of his chair, looking at me with wild eyes. I knew that would get his attention.

"I didn't hook up with Ellis. He just…he gets in my head. He makes me think I want this shit, but I don't. I just…you don't understand him, Hanna. He has a way of controlling people."

"There was something before this week, wasn't there? Between you two."

His shoulders soften, and I sense the resignation in his stance. More than anything, Nash looks tired, so I do what comes natural, pushing off the table and crossing the room, I place myself between him and his desk. Then I wind my arms around his neck, pulling his face down to rest against my shoulder. He folds easily, taking a deep inhale as his arms wrap me up tightly.

Something splinters around my heart as he relaxes into my body as if he's trusting me with his heart.

"Please talk to me," I whisper.

"We ran into each other in Amsterdam. We were friends. It was great, and then it got intense, banging girls at the same time, then fooling around with each other, and it all happened so fast, I freaked out and left. I think he's fucking with me as payback. He's still mad that I took off."

I stroke the back of his neck as he folds into me. He's so much taller and wider than me, but he seems to fit so easily into my arms.

There are a hundred questions floating around in my head at the moment, questions like… How far did things go between them? Were feelings involved? Is Nash really gay…or I guess, bisexual? And if he didn't want this to happen again, why did he hire Ellis to come here?

I'm not going to ask Nash any of these questions now because I know better. I have him in a moment of sweet vulnerability, and it feels so good to hold him like this. The more I poke and prod at him, the more backlash I'll receive, and I don't want any of that.

Instead, I stroke his back.

"I haven't told anyone that," he admits. "I don't know why I told you."

"Because I asked."

"Because you won't judge me."

I pull away, putting his face into view. "I would never judge you."

Our faces are so close our noses are practically touching, and the moment our eyes meet we become locked there. This is the closest I've ever been to Nash, and the sliver of emotion he etched into my heart a moment ago opens like a stab wound, and I find myself feeling an intense attachment to the one man I deemed off-limits. And this is somehow far worse than inviting him to fuck me a few days ago and having him making me come the next night. No, sex is one thing. Zara probably even expects us to fuck at some point. But feelings? Strong feelings, no. That's where I know it will break her heart and shatter our friendship into a million pieces.

But when he presses his lips softly to mine, I can't pull away. It's a soft, dry kiss, at first. But after a moment, his tongue slips far enough into my mouth to scrape against my teeth, and I drip like melting wax onto the floor.

"We shouldn't," I mumble, pushing him away.

"I don't care."

I lose the fight as he forces me against him, kissing me deeper, but somehow still as soft. Soon our kiss becomes heated, panting into each other's mouths.

"Nash, I'm serious."

He doesn't argue, because I know he sees it the same way I do. This kiss is about more than sex.

With our mouths still only a couple inches apart, he whispers, "I don't care about him, Hanna. I want you."

Pushing his shoulder until there is more space between us, I stare at him. "But do you? Want him?"

"I don't know." And that's the most I can expect out of him on this issue now.

There is sincerity in his eyes, and for a moment it's the real Nash. No tough exterior, no walls or aggression. Just Nash.

But with a blink of an eye and completely out of nowhere it changes. "Do you?"

"Do I what?" I ask, pulling away, but his grip on my back won't let me.

"I know he was in your room until midnight. I heard

what he said to you today. You threw yourself at him, and I mean, I can't say I'm surprised, but here you are kissing me. So…do you want Ellis or not?"

Everything warm and comfortable is immediately sucked out of the room, and the nurturing emotion I felt a moment ago is gone. This time I shove against him violently, and he finally releases me. I want to slap him. I want to claw at his face for the way he makes me feel, so easily he breaks me down, making me a speck of dust.

"I can't fucking believe you. Is that what this is all about? You're jealous of him. Jealous I went to him and not you. That I want him and not you!"

He grabs me by the arms, squeezing me so tight I know it'll bruise as he shoves me toward the door. "Get out, you fucking slut. You're all the goddamn same."

I let out a loud, "Ha!" as I spin around toward him. "You think I'm her. You're still so stuck on Zara you think this is *that* situation all over again. Is that why you sucked his dick, Nash? To keep him from wanting me so you wouldn't end up broken hearted again?"

The sudden change of tone nearly makes my head spin, and I know I'm being too fucking harsh, but I'm too fired up to care. Nash plays with emotions, and he had me for a second. Or rather I had him, for a short moment before he covered it all back up and pushed me away. Well, as much as I want to help him, I'm not going to let him call me names and treat me like shit and take it. Fuck that.

"Or is it the other way around?" I snap. "Are you trying to distract me so you have him all to yourself? You and your fucking daddy issues, you can have him!"

"Fuck off, Hanna!" This time when he comes to grab me again, I come out swinging. He blocks the first hit, but my second swing ends with my closed fist against his face, and that's the last blow I can get before I'm shoved against the glass wall of the office.

As he sneers into my face, pressing my arms painfully against the glass, I realize this is worse than us catching feelings for each other. Hating each other to this point is far worse, and I already know Zara can never know about this.

Suddenly the office door flies open, and Ellis charges in like a storm, grabbing Nash by the collar first as he tosses him away from me. Nash comes back at him like he wants to fight, but there's a stern, harsh glare on Ellis's face that suddenly stops Nash's movement, freezing him in place.

"That's enough," Ellis barks.

They stare at each other for a long moment before Ellis turns to me, touching me lightly on the elbow and ushering me out the door.

It's a blur, him taking me to the house, inspecting my hand he notices me cradling, and then watching me as I break down in sobs on the kitchen island.

How did this happen? How did we get here? And it all becomes painfully clear.

Nash said he wanted me. Just like he wanted Zara, but she chose his father over him. I had a short glimpse of Nash without the armor, but he could only keep it off for so long, and the moment he admitted his feelings for me, he had to put it back on. It's no different than the armor I wear, my defenses against feeling anything real, knowing we never get what we truly want in this life. All three of us know this truth too well. Love is only there to destroy us, especially when we're at our weakest.

"I FUCKING HATE HIM," I sob into the dark, charcoal gray sheets on Ellis's bed. After forcing me to drink some water and making me breathe, he ushered me to his bedroom and ordered me to lie down. Now, I can't seem to stop shaking. There is no poetry in my head right now. I can't focus on words or images or feelings.

At first, I panicked when the tremors took over, thinking the attack was back and I was spiraling again, but Ellis just stroked a hand down my back and told me it was just adrenaline.

"You are both very intense," he says, putting a glass of water on the table next to the bed. I can't stop the tears. I hate when this happens, as soon as they start, it's endless. Ellis is quick with a tissue, leaning over to wipe them for me as I turn to my back, draping my arm over my head.

Then, when he seems to notice I'm not getting any better, he does something unexpected. He slips off his shoes next to the bed and crawls in next to me. Without a word, he pulls me under his arm and rests my face against his chest. Then with his large, strong hands, he runs a steady line down my spine like a steady current, and it actually starts to ward away the crying.

It's quiet between us for a moment before he finally says, "Feeling better?"

"We kissed," I blurt out with a small hiccup. It feels like I'm confessing something, but he doesn't react. Tilting his head to the side, he looks down at me with those wise eyes and strong brow, and I suddenly feel so guilty like I've disappointed him even though I know I didn't do a damn thing wrong.

"Did you want to kiss him?" His voice is balanced, calm.

"I did at the time. He was being honest and real. That was before he shut down and started being a sociopath."

He nods solemnly and I glance up at him again. "He's confused and his reaction is to lash out."

"You think?" I reply with a laugh. When he looks down at me, wiping my tears, I feel them start to well up. He seems to have this effect on me, my safe space. And I'm still mad at him, but I'm far less mad at him than Nash so he's literally the lesser of two evils right now.

"I'm sorry you had to hear what happened between us at the house," he says quietly.

"Why couldn't you just tell me? You let me throw myself at you, and all the while you and Nash…"

"Hanna, stop. There is no me and Nash. And it has nothing to do with you throwing yourself at me. I only turned down your invitation for sex because I didn't trust your reasoning." His hand runs tenderly down my arm. "It wasn't because I didn't want to."

"So, you sleep with women?" I ask out of curiosity.

"And men," he replies. "Is that a problem?"

"Not at all." Feeling suddenly a little closer to him, I squeeze him tighter around the chest and feel his head rest at the top of mine.

We lie there for a moment, him still holding me tight against his body and my tears have finally dried. It's comfortable and quiet, and yet, Nash is still here in this space. I wish he wasn't. I wish he could let go of me and Ellis could let go of him, but we've somehow turned into a vicious little triangle.

"What happened between you two?" I ask, the curiosity overwhelming me.

He clears his throat. "Amsterdam happened."

I don't know what that means, but I wait patiently for him to expand on it, and it takes him a moment before he continues. "At first it was fun until it was serious, and when things got serious, Nash panicked. For a short moment in Amsterdam, I actually thought I had found what I needed, but then he broke everything we had built, but it was my fault. I should have known he was still fragile from what happened with his dad."

"What was it?" I ask.

"What do you mean?"

"You said you found what you needed. What did you need?"

"Someone who made me want to stop…everything I was doing. Someone who needed me."

I want to tell him I need him. After only a few days, I do need him, or rather someone like him. But I have a feeling he wants someone else to need him more.

14

Amsterdam

It's become a bit of a habit, this little thing Ellis and I started with Britta. And now it's other girls too, tonight a kinky little thing that goes by Lilac. She was here when I came over, sitting on the couch in black leather pants and a bra. That's it.

I don't leave Ellis's apartment often. I'm here after work, on the weekends, and most nights I crash in the guest room or on especially wild nights, in Ellis's bed with someone between us. It's quickly starting to feel like work is just this thing that keeps me from my time here. Of course, there are days when there isn't a fucked up three-way going on. We also have nights when we work, him at his desk, and me on the couch, pouring over manuals and test booklets. I know this shit like the back of my hand, and sometimes I ask myself why I'm even here, but Ellis keeps me grounded.

"Nash, this is Lilac," he says from the kitchen as he pours a bottle of seltzer water into two glasses, handing one to his guest. I notice he's not drinking tonight, and I pause.

"Hi," I mutter, taking in the girl on the sofa. She puts up a hand to greet me, and instantly I have a weird feeling. Like something is different tonight, not a bad feeling…just a feeling.

It's not like Ellis doesn't have a line of women waiting for a ride every weekend, but something about this girl is different.

When I get to the kitchen, I give him a sideways glance, and he answers with a smirk, full of fucking secrets and mischief. Yeah, the asshole is up to something. Whatever it is, I'm game. I'm always game. Mostly when it comes to him. If Ellis suggests it, I'll do it.

Ever since running into him again I feel like everything in my life plan has changed. I can hardly remember the pain I felt six months ago when I got here. Now, I see a new future, and mostly it involves freedom, money, and a lot of fucking sex. If I'm half as confident and happy as Ellis in ten years when I'm his age, I'll be happy.

"So, Lilac and I have known each other a while," he says, and I glance over at her. She smiles at him, like they're in on some kind of joke. A sudden rush of dread and angst passes over me. I hate feeling like the odd man out. I fucking hate it, and Ellis knows this. "When she called me today, I wanted to have her over, but I wanted to include you. She said that was okay."

"Okay…" I reply. There is never so much formal introduction and it's starting to make me uncomfortable. It's usually a scenario of drinking then fucking.

"I wouldn't have invited her if I didn't think you'd be okay with it."

"Okay with what?" I ask, sick of the cryptic bullshit.

He turns toward me, his back to the counter as he takes a sip of his drink, looking too fucking cool, and yeah, I can admit it, hot. Ellis is hot. He's tall, with a perfect sweep of amber brown hair, a warm short cut beard and broad shoulders. It doesn't hurt that he's always dressed well and when he looks at you, it's with so much intensity you feel like the only person alive.

"A little bondage, some pain. She likes when I tie her up, turn her back bright red, make her beg me to come."

My drink tries to come up through my nose, but I swallow it down. Holy shit, that came out of nowhere.

"It's nothing serious," he says. "Just a little fun she and I like to have from time to time."

I try to keep my emotions from showing this shit has an effect on me. Like I'm really fucking excited, curious, and…nervous.

"Of course, you're welcome to just watch. She likes it when people watch," he adds with a wink toward her.

"Fuck watching. I'm in."

The smile that spreads across his cheeks makes my heart pound a little harder in my chest. Damn, Ellis has me wishing I swung both ways. He has me thinking some crazy shit lately. Like I don't care he's a man and has a dick. Like I don't care that I love pussy. This man is in my head, and I don't hate it.

After sitting around and getting to know each other for a few minutes, Ellis looks at Lilac with a lazy smirk and hooded eyes.

"Come here."

I watch from the couch as she slides down to the floor, lust in her gaze as she crawls toward him. He's sitting in the upholstered chair as she kneels at his feet. Something in Ellis changes as he looks down at her, stroking her chin and pulling her face up to softly kiss her lips. She keeps her hands at her side as he deepens the kiss, eliciting a low moan from her tiny body.

So far, this isn't really any different than what we normally do. At some point, he'll tell her to suck his dick or mine and then things will progress from there.

But then, he holds her by the chin, pulling away from the kiss. "Bedroom."

Again, she crawls toward the room with him following close behind. When he glances back at me, I swallow. Here we fucking go.

The first thing I notice in the room are the things lying on Ellis's bed. The first is a bundle of black rope tied together with a piece of black silk. Next to that is a paddle, nothing too big or intimidating. It's narrow with diamond shaped cut-outs. The last thing is black leather fringe with a corded handle.

Suddenly, I wish Ellis had mixed actual drinks because right now there's a tremor of excitement deep in my bones, and I could use something to relax me. Although I guess it makes sense why he didn't. This isn't shit you mess with drunk.

I know I said I wasn't going to be an observer, but I find myself standing to the side, because watching him, the way he controls her and the way she submits to him is way more intoxicating than I expected. With a few simple commands, he has her naked on the bed, facing the headboard, kneeling as he grabs the rope. Unbinding it, he hands one strand to me.

"You said you didn't want to watch."

I nod, taking the nylon and moving to the opposite headboard.

"Lilac, you'll be a good girl for Nash, won't you?"

"Yes, sir," she purrs, and my dick twitches.

He walks me through binding her wrist to the bedpost, and I do my best to hide the shake in my hands. What the fuck is wrong with me? Of course, Ellis catches it. He catches everything, and as he glances up from my hands, he gives me a coy smirk, and I shoot him a grimace Lilac doesn't see.

Soon, she doesn't see anything because he uses the black silk to blindfold her. Just the sight of her, naked and bound at our mercy is so fucking dirty and somehow goddamn beautiful. I can't take my eyes away.

Ellis looks at the other items still on the bed, browsing through them like he's shopping for a new suit. Finally, his hand lands on the paddle, and he picks it up, swinging it side to side like he's warming up. His hand reaches out and strokes Lilac down her spine gently.

"We're going to start with twelve. If you need a break, you know what to say."

"Yes, sir," she whispers, a quiver to her voice.

"What does she say?" I ask, and I almost feel bad breaking the scene a little, but Ellis only looks up at me with a delicate smile on his face.

"Lilac's safe word is trust."

Safe word. Of course, there's a safe word, but something about him saying that sends a lightning bolt of excitement up my spine. This is really fucking happening.

"Count for me, Lilac."

"Yes, sir," she says, and I watch as she lets out a big exhale, her shoulders relaxing almost as if she doesn't want to tense up as he takes his first swing. The immediate smack of the paddle against the bare skin of her ass makes me flinch, and my eyes dash over to him. Lilac lets out on a small gasp, and I watch her pale skin turn pink almost immediately.

"One," she says with more composure and calmness than I'd expect. I mean, yeah, I get she signed up for this and literally asked for it, but fuck, that sounded like it hurt.

When he swings a second time, it's lighter, but the smack still echoes through the room.

"Two," she says with no real change to her voice.

By five, her counting sounds strangled, and her cries are louder, almost like she can't take it anymore. There's a part of me that wants her to use the safe word, tell him to stop. She's clearly in pain and I can hear that it hurts like a bitch, but she doesn't. Instead, she hangs from the bed posts and counts like he told her to.

It's around nine when I realize my eyes are no longer on Lilac. They're on him. With each swing, some soft and some hard, his determination captures me. Every single movement is intentional, controlled, and complicit. We both pulled off our shirts when we first came in the room, and my eyes get caught for a moment on the veins of his forearm with every swing and smack of the paddle. There's a heaving to his chest, and an evil-looking delight in his eyes as he inflicts the pain.

I'm so caught up in what I'm seeing I hardly notice my dick is trying to bust out of these pants like it's fucking Shawshank Redemption down there.

It's not like I'm naive to this shit. I used a belt on Zara for fuck's sake, but this is different. It's so intentional, and watching him has my body reacting in ways I did not see coming.

When I hear her say "twelve" in a strangled sob, I realize Ellis is looking at me, or rather, he catches me looking at him. Then his gaze travels down to my crotch to see the very obvious erection in my pants. When our eyes meet again, it's charged, a special glint in his eye.

"It's your turn," he announces as he strokes Lilac's hair, his hand traveling all the way down to her bare ass which is now painted red. She's breathing heavy, her posture sagging, but she doesn't protest or say her safe word. "Lilac wants another round, don't you, my little flower?"

"Yes, sir," she whispers. He climbs up next to her, kissing her on the mouth, and I see her reaction in every little movement of her body. The way it tilts toward him like a magnet, so eager and desperate for his attention, and I get a twinge of something like jealousy in my stomach.

He climbs down and hands the paddle to me. "She's ready for you."

I don't even know this girl. Sure, I've fucked plenty of girls I didn't know, maybe even spanked a few, but this is different. Still, I take the paddle and look at Lilac. Mostly, I feel his eyes on me, his arms crossed over his bare chest, and I want to do this right.

Squeezing the leather wrapped handle, I take my first swing, back-handed and holding back, but not too much. Lilac lets out a beautiful cry as my spine erupts with some sensation I've never felt before. It skitters across the skin of my arms as I paddle her again. I'm only aware of two things while I take her from panting to all-out gasping for breath. One, Ellis is watching me. His eyes haven't left me since he gave me the paddle, and I feel it. I feel his gaze on me, the way he's watching, and how bad I want to please him. And how something about his posture and expression changes as I land the paddle on her upper thighs and bright red ass.

The other thing I'm aware of is I fucking love this.

All too soon, the twelve smacks are up. When it was

Ellis's turn at bat, I almost wanted him to stop, afraid he would really hurt her, but when it was my turn, I didn't want it to end. The more she cried, the more excited I got. I mean, I don't really want to hurt the girl; it's not about that. It's about giving her the punishment she wants.

I'm almost disappointed when he begins to untie her wrists, but he's not done with her yet. As Lilac relaxes from the binding against the bedposts, there are tears streaming down her face, but she still doesn't fight or argue. Not even when he fists her hair and practically drags her over to me.

She's on the bed in front of me on all fours when he says, "He's already so hard and ready for you, Lilac. Take out his dick and suck on it."

"Yes, sir," she says with a residual shake in her voice.

My lips part and I watch as she does what he tells her, and when her soft lips wrap around my cock, I let out a groan.

Then, I make a big mistake. I look up. With her on my cock, pleasure painted across my face and in my eyes, I stare at *him*. And he stares back.

We look at each other too long. Too fucking long. The only time he breaks the eye contact is when he goes to the drawer to get two condoms, removing his pants and slipping one on. Even when he slips into her from behind, he's looking at me.

And yeah, it's with my eyes on his face, those sharp cheekbones and abyss-like dark brown eyes, when I feel my balls tightening, ready to come.

"Lilac, stop," he barks, and just like that she pulls her mouth off of me, leaving my body on edge, not quite over the precipice, but dangling there. "You're such a good girl, but we don't want him coming yet." She bites her lip, no longer crying but now wearing a mischievous smile. Then her hands reach out and wrap around my balls, pulling down and forcing a moan from my lips.

I'm still panting when she releases me and he yanks her up, flush to his body. With his mouth next to her ear, he whispers in a husky voice, "How did his cock taste?"

And I swear if he didn't want me to come, that was not the thing to say because my now my body is confused as fuck.

"It tasted good, sir," she replies. "Do you want me to bring him over here so you can try it?"

I get tunnel vision, but I try to hide how fucked out of my brain I am right now, and it's not because I'm scared of him sucking my dick. It's how scared I am by how much *I want him to*. The thought of his lips—

"I don't think Nash is ready for that," he replies, smiling at me as he kisses her cheek. Suddenly, I'm the odd man out again, and it makes me irritable and defensive. I don't like when people speak for me or dismiss what I do or do not want. That's the only reason I blurt out, "I'm ready for whatever you got. You want a taste, then come get a fucking taste."

His fire-hot stare blazes into me as he taps her hips and barks, "On the floor, Lilac." She crawls away from him, climbing down to the floor to kneel at my feet. Then, I watch him as he walks around the bed, meeting me toe-to-toe. Did I say too much? Maybe Ellis isn't into sucking dick and I just fucking insulted him? Although that's not what my gut is telling me here. My gut is telling me I just invited Ellis Prior to suck my cock and that is exactly what he's about to do.

Without a word, he kneels on the floor next to Lilac, both of them staring up as he takes her by the hair again and presses her toward me. She swallows my length without hesitation.

After a few strokes, he pulls her off and puts his own mouth in her place with his soft lips and bright red tongue waiting at the edge of his mouth. It's all I can focus on as it engulfs my body in warmth. A low, growling hum vibrates out of my chest as he takes me deep, deeper than she did, all the while keeping his eyes on me. Nothing about my body or brain wants to reject this, and I can chalk that up to us being freaky as fuck.

How can I refuse the fact that Ellis gives some legendary fucking head? I'm too busy focusing on that and not on the fact that a guy has my dick down his throat.

"I'm going to—" I say in a warning, my voice strangled and tight as I pull away, Ellis popping off, and I immediately wish I could have finished in his mouth.

"You were right, Lilac. It does taste good. Now get back on that bed."

"Yes, sir," she replies and does what he tells her to do. I'm too busy trying to get my head on right as Ellis stands and gives me a quick *are you okay* glance with his eyes at which I nod. Yes, of course I'm fine, too fucking fine. So, fucking fine, it's scary.

A GOOD HOUR LATER, the three of us collapse onto the bed with nothing left, completely spent. Lilac is lying on her stomach next to me, and finally, it feels like she's out of character, free to just be herself. No more sir and submission shit.

"I like you," she says sweetly. "He's good," she says to Ellis as he stands up and strokes her backside tenderly.

"I know he is," he says, and it catches my attention. He knows I'm good? I'll assume he means at sex, but it feels like there's more there.

Just as he moves toward the bedroom door, she calls out for him. "Where are you going?"

"To get you some water and something to eat. You know the drill."

She rolls her eyes and looks at me. "He likes to do things right. This is the part where he's supposed to coddle me and pamper me, but I don't need that. I mean, don't get me wrong, sometimes I do, but tonight, you pampered me plenty. I don't think I've ever come that many times in a row. Not in a long time at least."

She's so talkative now, almost like she's a different person than the tense girl who I met on the couch.

"How often do you guys do this?" I ask.

"Me and Ellis? I don't know…every couple of months or so. It's just an outlet, no big commitment to it, know what I mean?"

"Sure," I reply even though I don't.

"Did you like it?" she asks, a bright smile on her face for a girl who probably won't be able to sit without wincing for a week.

"Fuck yeah."

"Did you like him sucking your cock?" she asks quietly. "I could tell that was your first time."

My eyes go wide. "Uh…I mean, yeah. Of course, I liked it."

"Ellis is amazing, and he likes you. I can tell."

There's a quickening in my chest, and I try to shove it down. Of course, Ellis likes me. We're friends. Practically best friends at this point. We almost live together. We share girls regularly. I've told him everything. So yeah, of course he likes me.

When he comes back in, he tries to force feed Lilac some cheese, fruit, and bread which she obliges and does it to please him. The water takes less coaxing.

"Are you staying tonight?" he asks.

"Nah, I have to work tomorrow. Thanks for a good evening though. I needed that." Suddenly, she's jumping off the bed, dressing casually like she came over for pizza and a movie, and we didn't just fuck her brains out.

"You boys have fun though," she adds with a wink, and my cheeks flush hot.

"Let me walk you out," he says, moving for his pants.

"No," she barks at him before running up to kiss him on the cheek. "You two are too gorgeous lying together naked and I want to take this vision with me. I'll be thinking about it later." Then with a wink, she waves goodbye and rushes out the door.

For a long quiet moment, it's just me and Ellis…naked together. There's no girl here, and with everything we've done, I really shouldn't be self-conscious about it, but I am.

"You should sleep in here tonight," he says finally, getting out of bed to pick up the discarded clothes on the floor and tossing them into the hamper. "You earned it," he adds with a chuckle.

"Okay." It seems like the most natural thing to say. It's not weird to sleep next to your best friend. It's not weird that I *want* to sleep in here.

"I'm going to go shower real quick. You can go after me. Eat something."

"Okay," I reply again because I apparently can't think a thought on my own anymore.

When he leaves the bedroom, I lie naked on his bed, my mind spinning. After a few minutes of running through the options, I settle on a couple of excuses as to why my brain can only seem to think about Ellis and his cock.

It's just curiosity. I've never had sex with a man before, and after experiencing what his mouth felt like around my dick, it's not wrong to want more.

After everything we've done together this year, it's normal that my mind has connected Ellis to sex. So naturally the thought of his naked body turns me on now. What did I expect to happen?

As I get off the bed and move toward the bathroom to pee, I walk into the foggy haze and see his naked form on the other side of the frosted glass and realize this is about more than sex, isn't it? I want to be Ellis's first thought, his number one, his go-to. That's what I've wanted this entire time, but being his best friend doesn't seem to define what this is anymore.

"You okay?" he asks, probably noticing me standing there, staring at the mirror.

"Yeah. Just tired."

The shower door opens. "Come on. It's a big shower. I'm almost done. Wash up and then you can get some sleep."

Shower with him. Am I going to pass that up? No. Just like I didn't pass up the invitation to sleep with him. I'm out of my mind.

He was right. It is a big shower, but only by European standards, and our bodies aren't all that far apart. I can't take my eyes off of him as he tilts his head back, letting the water run the soap out of his hair and down his back.

"That was your first time having a man give you a blow job, wasn't it?"

I glare up at him. "Yeah, of course."

"I could tell by the look on your face."

"I'm not gay."

"Neither am I," he replies, switching places with me so I'm directly under the spray.

"But…"

"I'm bisexual, Nash. I've been with men. Does that bother you?"

"No," I answer quickly. I'm almost offended he has to ask me that, but I guess I can understand with how wigged out I am tonight. It was a lot to take in at once. The bondage, the blow job. I need a drink and a minute to process this.

"Good," he replies, pouring shampoo into his hands, and I don't quite know what's happening until his hands are in my hair. He's washing my hair, and I'm letting him, like I'm a fucking child. But it feels good. His nearness, his attention. I'm soaking it in.

That's the last we talk about the blow job, and I do climb into his bed after the shower. It doesn't feel weird. Luckily, it's a king with plenty of room for both of us, and once we both sink into the mattress, I hear his breathing slow to a sleeping cadence after only a few minutes.

Through the darkness, I can see his chest move and the silhouette of his face in the moonlight. I could never see a future without a woman in it, but these past six months have changed something in my head. Like I'm drowning in him, and I never want to come up for air.

15

As the helicopter touches down on the landing pad just outside Wilde headquarters, I let out a heavy exhale. It feels good to be off the island. Just to clear my head, ground myself in reality for a moment. Unfortunately, I couldn't escape my company on this little trip. Ellis is sitting next to me, and Hanna is stewing silently in the back.

She asked to hitch a ride so she could handle some things, and Ellis offered to help her. He wanted to come to the meeting I have with the design team, but I assured him it's just boring engineering stuff. Nothing to do with the acquisition, and he accepted that, deciding to accompany her instead.

The car takes them away while I head into the building to hopefully handle the issues we're having with the dash design on the new model. I was content to leave it the way it was, but once Alistair Wilde made his little comment about the layout, I knew I would have to change it.

So that's what we spend the next three hours doing. I end up skipping lunch trying to figure out how we can make room for the redesigned altimeter without rewiring the entire electrical panel. I hate the way it turns out, but at least he can't say anything about it now.

After signing off on the blueprints, I grab another company car and head toward the city center.

I don't really know what it is Hanna had to do in the city, and it's not my business to ask. Neither of them are really talking to me after our little fight on Saturday, and it's been two days. It's not exactly the cold shoulder. More like they're fine talking to each other, so they don't need to talk to me.

It hurts.

But I brush it off. Neither of them are really supposed to be here anyway and in a few weeks they'll be gone, and I can go back to my solitary existence with nothing distracting me from work.

I shoot a quick text to Ellis asking for their location, and he drops me a pin. Once I find a parking spot down-town, I take it and text him back.

He responds a moment later letting me know they are on their way.

Nothing about being on the mainland today has cleared my head. Somehow, I feel fucking worse. Like how if I wasn't so obsessed with things I could easily delegate to others, I could have joined them for lunch in the city and helped Hanna out with whatever he's helping her out with.

No, I'd rather work. I know that.

Then they round the corner, side-by-side, and it's like salt in the wound. He has his arm around her, hanging over her shoulders and she's leaning into him. They both look so damn happy and relaxed it has me instantly putting up my defenses. Fuck them. Fuck this feeling I get every time I'm stuck being the odd one out.

The sickening feeling of jealousy hits me hard as I watch them both looking so happy. He's looking down at her with a smile in his eyes and she's practically glowing under the spotlight. I hate how he's touching her. I hate how she's letting him when she won't let me. And I hate how she gets his attention when he won't give it to me.

Why?

Because I'm a fucking asshole, and I've dug this very grave I'm lying in.

We make dry small talk in the car on the way back to headquarters, and my eyes keep checking on Hanna in the backseat. She's purposefully avoiding me.

"Did you get everything done you needed to?" I ask.

"Mostly," she replies without looking at me.

"Everything okay?" I ask, digging for information.

"Yep."

Things between us remain this cold during the ride back to Del Rey. When we touch down, she immediately climbs out and says goodbye to Ellis without acknowledging me.

She passes by me on her way to the guest house, and I suddenly can't go another second with her giving me this cold shoulder. Hanna and I have known each other for too long. We were friends before this for fuck's sake and after she leaves here, there will be more times we'll be around each other with Zara and my dad. I can't leave shit like this.

Before she can disappear into the guest house, I jog after her and make the dumb ass mistake to reach out and grab her by the forearm. Her head snaps in my direction as she snatches her hand out of my grasp.

"What are you doing?" she gasps.

"Sorry, fuck. I just…" Fuck this. Why can't I just apologize? "Never mind."

"What is wrong with you?"

"I don't know," I mutter, turning back to the helicopter. Her heels click against the pavement, but after a few steps, they stop. When I hear her coming back my way, I turn toward her.

She stops directly in front of me, and for a moment neither one of us speaks, she keeps her eyes unfocused on my suit as thoughts clearly turn through her mind.

"I don't understand why you're so insecure, Nash. I don't know why you don't see what I see."

"What does that mean?" I ask, feeling my defenses rising again, readying myself to hear her call me what the rest do—a spoiled brat, a possessive jerk, a wild card. But she only lays her hand soft against my chest.

"Nash Wilde, you're punishing me for not wanting you, but you're the one pushing me away."

Her hand stays on my chest a moment before she turns away and walks off toward the guest house, leaving me with words that shake me to my core.

THE WARM BUZZ of vodka running down my throat settles my nerves instantly. I'm sitting at the bar in the kitchen watching the sun set over the water and trying not to think about what Hanna said to me today or how it felt to see the two of them so happy together.

She's wrong. I'm not pushing anyone away. I didn't push Zara away. I poured my heart out for her. I told her I fucking loved her, those words to be exact too. And she still chose him. Fuck, even Preston's girlfriend chose him, like he's a goddamn pussy magnet or something. And he acts so innocent about it, like he had nothing to do with it. But he gave her his heart, willingly, and she took it. Meanwhile I'm over here torn between two people who would rather fuck each other.

There are footsteps down the hall. When he enters the kitchen, dressed in casual shorts and a T-shirt, my eyes refuse to drift away from the way his biceps fill the sleeves and the V-cut reveals a small patch of light hair. I hate the way he still has this effect on me.

We don't speak as he walks to the kitchen, pulling out a bottle of whiskey he bought in the city and holds it up to me, as if he's offering me a glass, noticing the vodka in mine is gone. I should refuse. I should walk away because I know what happens when Ellis and I start drinking together. I've had myself convinced for three years the only reason he liquored me up all those times in Amsterdam was to get me to do what we did, but I know goddamn well I was sober for the first time. The first time he touched my cock I was sober as a nun and I liked it. I wanted it again. The only time I drank after that was to give myself the courage to let him do more.

"Sure," I reply.

"Did you get done what you needed to with the design team?" he asks calmly.

"Yeah. It was a pain in the ass, but we managed it."

"Good."

He hands me my drink, and we don't talk for a

moment. But he doesn't leave either. Standing on the other side of the island, he keeps his eyes on me as he takes a sip, and I warm under his gaze and from the drink. I should apologize for what happened the other day. I should make it very clear right now it won't happen again. But my mouth won't form the words.

"This is delicious," I say instead because it is. I'm not much of a whiskey guy, but it's a lot more fucking smooth than vodka, and the flavor doesn't assault my senses as it slides down my throat. I'm getting drunk tonight. Fuck, I'm already halfway there.

"It is," he replies. "It's the best stuff I can get stateside. Nothing like what we could score in Europe."

Bringing up Amsterdam instantly raises the hairs on my arm, and we make sudden eye contact, but I glance away as fast as it came.

"I think I'll go drink this on the patio. It's nice out." He takes his drink, letting his gaze linger on me for a long moment before he leaves through the patio door and sits at the table next to the pool.

That was definitely an invitation. I'm not a fucking idiot, but the question is whether or not I should take it. We're not going back to the way things were in Amsterdam. I can't.

I want Hanna, not him. Or at least, I *should* want Hanna more than him.

But I brought him out here for a reason, to mend the friendship we shared before things went overboard. And with that, I grab my glass and the bottle he left behind, following him to the patio.

The two of us sit in silence for a while, making small talk about work when I notice movement in the guest house. Part of me wonders if he wanted to sit out here because out here, we could be seen by her. If she sees us together, sharing a drink, being civil, maybe she'll come too. Maybe I can mend two broken friendships. Two birds, one stone and all that.

A moment later, just as I suspected, she emerges from the guest house in nothing but her white bikini with a towel draped over her arm. It catches both of our eyes, and neither of us can look away as she saunters toward us. Those long legs of hers carry her with so much grace it's intoxicating. And that white suit in contrast to her golden skin shining in the setting sun makes her look like a goddess in our presence.

Fuck, I want to make this work with Hanna. And I don't really care anymore if she's off-limits or what Zara would say. It's my turn to be happy.

And what if I stop pushing her away? What if I let her in and give her everything, will she take it? Or will she choose him and fucking crush me? Knowing my luck, she'll somehow end up choosing my dad too. Fucker.

But as she reaches our table, giving us both a warm smile, creating beautiful dimples in her cheeks, I know it's worth it. I'll risk it. I'll tear my heart out of my chest right now and hand it to her if that's what she wants. If she'd just choose me.

"Is this dinner?" she asks, pointing to the whiskey.

"It would seem so," Ellis replies.

"Are you hungry? Let me make you something?" I ask, starting to stand.

Her eyes widen at me, but she puts up a hand before I can dash off to the kitchen. I may not be as good of a cook as my dad, but damn, I can try.

"I'm fine," she says softly toward me. We're not screaming at each other, so that's a start. We just have to keep this up.

"Would you like something to drink?" Ellis asks as his

fingers gently run up her arms in an intimate loving gesture, like they're already committed or some shit. The minute my jealousy wants to rear its ugly head, I take a drink and push it down.

"I think some white wine would be nice," she says, and Ellis is up before me, jogging off to the house to fetch it for her. If this is going to be some pissing contest for her affection, I'm going to win. I've known her longer. When he's gone, I'll still be around.

"Going for a swim?"

"Yeah," she replies with a smile. "It's beautiful out tonight. I figured I should soak it up while I can."

My eyes flash up to meet hers. What was that supposed to mean?

"I'm going to head back tomorrow."

Suddenly it feels like I'm swallowing glass. She's leaving already. I mean, I guess she's been here a week, and no one can avoid their life forever, but I'm not ready for this. I don't like the idea of this island without her already.

"You don't have to." It feels pathetic to say, but I'm afraid it's because of me. I did this. Scared her away.

"I have some things to take care of. Ellis helped me get it started, but I need to do this." She looks like she's putting on a brave face, and I think back to that night I picked her up outside the bars, drunk and clearly in some bar fight. I don't want her going back to that life.

"Anything I can help with?"

"No, Nash. Letting me come here to get away was help enough."

"I want to help," I reply, giving her a pleading expression. I want to help. Fuck I want to do everything for her.

"I know you do, but I need to do this part on my own."

"Okay," I answer, not knowing what we're talking about at all, but whatever it is, I'll do it.

Ellis comes out a moment later with a stemless glass full of white wine, handing it to her with a warm smile. She bathes in his attention as my grip on the glass I'm holding tightens.

"You guys want to swim with me?" she asks playfully, looking at both of us.

"Maybe in a bit," he replies, taking her towel and draping it across her lounge chair like she can't do it herself.

Suddenly, I jump up. "I will."

My reaction was a little bit too fast because the ground starts to tilt a little as soon as I'm on my feet, but I don't let them see the way the alcohol has affected me so far. Then, I tear my shirt off and her eyebrows shoot to her forehead.

"In your underwear?"

"Yeah, you got a problem with that?" My shorts come off next, and I'm standing in my tight black boxers which were not made for swimming, but I don't care. Yeah, I've had too many drinks already today, but it doesn't stop me from grabbing my drink and beating Hanna to the pool. Setting it down on the deck, I make a quick dive into the water. It's warm without being hot, perfect for tepid nights like tonight. It's not too hot out here this time of year, but just right for an evening swim. Just as I come up, I spot her sitting on the edge, her legs dangling into the water.

"That's not swimming," I say, gliding over to her, placing my hands on her legs.

Is it too obvious I'm trying to play nice? Can they tell I'm trying way too fucking hard to not be an asshole? Probably, but the whiskey helps convince me I'm doing the right thing.

Thanks, whiskey.

"Nash!" She yelps as I pull her under, my hands gliding

up from her legs to her soft waist, my fingers dancing over her ribs, feeling each bone under her skin.

I should have made her dinner. Now I feel like an asshole, but as we both pop back up, the water running in rivulets out of her thick black curls and over her skin, I fight the urge to kiss her.

"You're too skinny," I say as soon as we come out of the water, and her smile fades in a blink.

"You know that's just as rude as telling someone they're too fat."

"Well, you are." She pushes against my chest, but I wind my hands around her waist, holding her to me. "I'm sorry if that's rude, but I want you to eat more." I'm not trying to start a fight, but the harsh expression on her face tells me she thinks I am and she's readying herself for battle.

"I'm just worried about you, that's all."

With her one blue and one brown eye laser focused on my face, her struggle dissipates.

"I'm fine, Nash."

"Are you?"

It's a quiet, intimate moment as we stare at each other and I guess I'm probably bringing up the elephant in the room, but I was the one who picked her up that night. She never wants to tell me what's going on with her, and maybe she thinks I don't care. But I do care. I care she had a very public breakdown last year. I care that she's living in such misery now that she ran off to my island to escape. I care this was supposed to be a safe place for her and instead, I yelled at her and called her a slut.

I care that she should hate me, but I hope to fucking God she doesn't.

From the corner of my eye, I see Ellis approach. In his hands is a round wooden tray, and he sets it down on the pool deck next to our drinks. Hanna and I both look over and notice that while we weren't looking, he must have put together this cheese tray assembled with two different kinds of cheese, sausage, crackers and some grapes.

"Thank you," she says sweetly to him.

Why couldn't I do that? Why do I have to push her buttons? Basically insult her when all I wanted to do was what he just did?

He gives me a momentary glance before he goes back to his chair around the patio table.

Hanna dives into the food Ellis brought out, and we both watch with satisfaction as she practically demolishes it. When she takes her last sip of wine, he's quick to replenish it for her.

"Thanks guys," she says. "I could get used to this. You two could really take good care of me, couldn't you?"

Our eyes meet immediately. The innuendo was obvious, wasn't it? That wasn't just in my head, and suddenly as I glare at him over her head I'm back in Amsterdam, sitting around with some girl, waiting to take things to the next level.

But this isn't Amsterdam. And Hanna is not just another girl. That is not happening with her.

What is happening is at the end of this night, she will be in my bed. I'm going to make things up to her the right way, without fighting, without letting my insecurities win, without hurting her in the process.

Just thinking about it has my dick twitching in my soaking boxers.

The sun has gone down, and the outdoor lights have kicked on, bathing us in a warm glow under the night sky. I can first tell Hanna is tipsy when she swims over to me and laces her long legs around my waist from behind, latching onto my body like a floatation device. My hands glide against the softness of her shins when she whispers next to my ear.

"Think he's ever going to join us?"

"I bet if you ask him, he will."

Wait. What am I doing? I don't want him in here. I want Hanna to myself. If he comes then it'll be his waist she latches onto. It'll be her he gives his attention to.

"Ellis, Nash wants you to come swimming," she sings to him, and he responds with a subtle lift to the corner of his lips. I know what she's doing—we both do. Trying to pretend I want him here to make us make up.

"I'm happy just watching you two."

I swallow down the lump in my throat. When my eyes meet his, I try to decipher the look he's giving me, but I can't. He's leaning back in the chair, a few feet away from the water, drink in hand as he watches us, and a shot of excitement dances up my spine. We're on the brink of something. I can feel it.

"Watching us swim? That doesn't sound very exciting?" she replies with a laugh. I hear the soft slur to her voice, and I assume at her weight, it doesn't take much, but her second glass is already gone, and this is starting to feel dangerous.

"Then do something more exciting," he says flatly.

An eerie calm blankets the island as I suddenly realize where things are headed.

"Like what?" she asks with a little less playfulness in her tone and a good deal more severity. Meanwhile I'm standing here, her on my back, his eyes on her as he says, "Why don't you kiss him?"

Her hands roam the landscape of my chest. The air stops, dropping like lead in my lungs as she climbs down from my back and comes to stand in front of me.

"Ellis told me to kiss you," she whispers.

What are we, sixteen?

Well, fuck it. If we're going to play, then I'm going to be in charge this time.

"Yeah, well he likes to be in control," I reply, pushing her to the edge of the pool.

"Is that so?"

Once her backside hits the edge, I lean down, pressing my lips to his ear as I say, "Yeah, and I like to let him think he has it." Then with my hands under ass, I lift her back up so her legs wind around me again, and I attack her lips with mine.

She hums into the kiss, and I instantly remember what it felt like to kiss her the other day when everything went to shit. This time I'm not going to let her go. If he wants her back, he's going to have to fight me for her.

Our mouths move in perfect harmony as her teeth pinch my bottom lip, and my fingers dig into her backside. I almost forget he's watching us until we pull away, gasping for air and we both look his way at the same time. He hasn't moved. But the look in his eyes has grown in intensity, staring down at us through hooded lids.

I want to kiss her again, and since I'm sure she can feel how hard my dick is between us, it's clear that I want to do a lot more than kiss her. But it's like we're both waiting for him to say something else, like we're waiting for instructions.

"That had to be more fun than watching us swim," she says to him, touching her bottom lip softly with her fingers.

"It was."

"Are you sure you don't want to join us?" she asks, her legs tightening around my waist.

Instantly I glare up at him, but he's quick to reply. "I'm sure."

I don't wait for his direction before I lay kisses against

her neck, tasting the pool water as I move down to her chest. Her bikini top is a strapless band that covers her breasts, so when my fingers work to unclasp the back, I expect her to hesitate, but she doesn't.

Her eyes meet mine as the tension releases, and the water takes her top, leaving her bare from the top up in my arms.

There's a low hum from the chair on the pool deck just as my lips take a gentle bite of the soft flesh of her chest. Moving my hungry mouth down, I pull the soft hazel peak between my teeth and she lets out a delicious moan, arching her back.

"Is he hard, Hanna?" Ellis asks.

"Yes," she pants, high pitched and needy. She rubs her body against the stiffness in my underwear and the ache to be inside her grows so intense I can hardly breathe.

"Reach into his boxers, Hanna. Touch him."

With my mouth still on her tits, she does as he says, snaking her hand under the waistband of my briefs and grasping my cock in her hand. I can't help the low growl that comes out of me as she squeezes.

Contrary to popular belief, water is not a lubricant, and it becomes instantly clear, mostly based on the harsh tug of my cock, that we need to move this out of the pool. But I'm impatient, so with her legs still wrapped around me, I carry her to the steps, and once I have the water at my waist level, I set her on the top step, so she's sitting in shallow water.

This also gives me a perfect view of Ellis who is calmly watching this with his whiskey still in his hands like we're performing for him. I guess we are.

I also take notice of the fact he's not joining in. Usually he does, and part of me is anxious for him to, but I'm also processing the fact that he's letting me have this. Maybe in some way he's letting me have her.

She leans back on her elbows so her body is sprawled out before me as I continue to devour her, my lips traveling from her stomach to her breasts and up to her neck. When I kiss her mouth, she hums, touching my cheek with her hand. I don't know why, but the intimate gesture sends my heart beating a little faster than it already is.

Sitting up, she begins to kiss down my neck and chest, and I suddenly know where this is going, but I can't bring myself to stop it.

"Do you want to taste him, Hanna?"

"Mmhm…" she responds with her lips near the waistband of my boxers and so fucking close to the head of my dick. I nearly stumble as chills run over my skin.

"Do it."

My eyes dance up to meet his gaze when I hear that familiar authoritative voice. And it's with our gazes locked that she pulls down the fabric and places her warm lips against the head, making my eyes nearly roll back in my head. When she swallows me down against her tongue and I feel the back of her throat, my fingers dig into her hair, and I fight the urge to lose it already. He's not here with us, but with him watching us like this it's like he is.

Hanna's mouth is working up and down on my length, and I hold back the urge to fuck her without mercy. Maybe an old Nash would have, but for now, I stare at the man in the chair as she drives me closer and closer to my climax.

"Hanna, stop." Ellis's voice pulls me out of my pleasure-laced daze, and I look down at the brown and blue eyes staring up at me. It takes me softly pulling on her hair for her to tear herself away. Her wet lips look so delicious I can't help but lean down and capture them with my own. She hums into my mouth as our tongues tangle in warmth.

"I think she's ready for you," a cool, gravelly voice says from the chair outside the pool, and when I pull my lips from hers, I stare down with a question on my face.

"I'm ready," she whispers against my mouth.

My body takes over, or maybe it's an old version of Nash that flips Hanna over, putting her knees on the steps as she lets out a raw, guttural yelp. I kiss a line down her spine, hitting each vertebra before peeling down her bikini bottoms.

A tremor ripples through her body as I plant a kiss right at the bottom of her spine. My hand slides between her legs, feeling how ready she is for me, and I can't wait another second. Covering her bent body with my own, I put my lips to her ear as I grunt, "He's watching you. Does that turn you on?"

"Yes," she cries, high-pitched and desperate, and I look up at him too, both of us staring at Ellis who seemingly hasn't moved since the first kiss.

In a swift movement, I thrust into her, pressing my hips hard against her backside. She grips the pool deck as she cries out. With my hands tight on her body, I pound in again.

"Yes!" she screams, and I notice the way she shoves her body back against me. And soon it feels like we're fighting again, her struggling for control.

With every thrust, I'm losing my mind, being taken over by this pleasure. Her body feels so perfect in my hands, as if she was made for me, and I can't stop moving. I can't take my eyes off her delicate nails scratching at the cool bricks of the pool deck. Then, I notice her eyes are still glued to Ellis in the chair. They are staring at each other, an intense connection between them.

But he's not moving. Fuck, I wouldn't have made it this long in the chair. He should be over here by now, guiding her mouth to his cock or at the very least stroking himself as he watches, but he's not. Why?

"Harder, Nash," he commands, and the guttural moan that comes out of me at his words is completely involuntary, and my body can do nothing but obey him as I slam into her again, this time making her scream.

Fuck, am I hurting her? I almost stop when he says, "Don't stop. She's almost there."

Almost as if she can feel me hesitating, Hanna shoves her hips back again, impaling herself on my dick. Something instinctual takes over as I take her body fast and hard, losing all control.

We're all lost in this torrent, stuck in the whirlwind, until Hanna finally lets out a cry and her body tenses then quivers and shakes so violently, I almost don't pull out in time.

My orgasm rocks me to my core, and I spill myself all over her back. Fuck, I don't know the last time I've come that hard, and my heart is pounding so loudly, I feel it everywhere, in my head, in my limbs, in my chest. As she collapses against the steps of the pool, she lets out a tired and sweet sounding, "Finally."

I don't quite know what that's all about as I quickly wash away the cum covering her back.

Hanna and I are busy catching our breaths when I look up and see Ellis standing there with a white towel open for her. Giving her a hand, I help her out of the pool into his arms where he dries her tenderly without touching her or even looking at her naked body. A moment later, I pull my boxers up and climb out behind her, fishing a towel out of the storage bin.

She's standing in his arms, his hands sliding up and down her arms to warm her.

"Ellis," she whispers, looking up at him and touching

his chin. My heart stops as I watch them. His lips press against her forehead.

"You should get to bed, beautiful."

"But—"

"That's enough for tonight."

Almost on cue, she lets out a large yawn and even I can see how sex-swept she is. When she turns around to look at me, I give her a nod. A moment later, she's walking my way.

"You okay?" I ask as she stands toe to toe with me, a post-orgasm glow on her face.

"I'm more than okay." Then she leans forward and presses her forehead against my chest, and I squeeze my arms around her wishing I could take her to bed with me. I want to feel her warm body against mine while I sleep.

Reluctantly, I let her go, and Ellis and I watch her walk to the guest house alone.

"Night, boys," she calls back with a pout on her face. She almost looks like she wants to come to my bed as much as I want her to, but I'm not fighting for this one. I'm still reeling from how hot that was.

Hanna and I just fucked. It was raw and dirty and hot as hell.

Ellis only sends me one cold, blank look before he turns toward the patio to head inside.

"Why did you do that?" I blurt out.

He turns and looks at me with skepticism. "Do what?"

"You didn't… It was like you were letting me have her. You could have…"

"I know what I could have done, but I didn't. You said she was off-limits."

"But I mean, if that was the case, I shouldn't have fucked her either," I argue.

With a tilt of his head and a hint of a smirk on his lips, he adds, "Nash, you almost sound disappointed."

It hits me like a heat wave. I'm not disappointed. If he wanted to join that was on him, no skin off my back. But that's not what I say because something else is bothering me. "Did it ever occur to you that she wants you? She would have let you do whatever you wanted to her?"

"Did it ever occur to you she's not the only one I want to please?"

With that, he turns and walks into the house, and I watch through the window as he takes his bottle of whiskey to the kitchen. I swallow what's left of mine and stare down at the empty glass.

And I realize something major. I expected him to be a part of what just happened, almost like I wanted him to.

16

We're not talking about what happened last night. And I guess I should feel bad that I finally had sex with Nash, but I don't. Because for the first time in eleven months, I felt something. And not just a mind-blowing orgasm, but something deeper than that. Something that made me feel alive. So, when I finally laid my head on the pillow last night, I fell into an easy sleep, dreaming of Nash's hands and Ellis's eyes.

There's a soft knock on the door after I get out of the shower. When I open it, Nash is standing there but instead of his regular business suit and shoes, he's wearing shorts and a snug-fitting T-shirt. As our eyes meet, I expect there to be awkwardness between us, but he only smiles at me, and a grin stretches comfortably across my face.

"Good morning," I greet him.

"Morning. I know you said you were leaving today, but I realized you haven't even been out on the boat yet, so Ellis and I decided you need to have a little fun before you go."

With a twist of my lips, I gaze at him with a skeptical glare. "Out on the boat? Don't you have work to do?"

"I can take a day off."

"Nash Wilde take a day off?"

When he winks at me, I feel my knees weaken. I could blame him for trying to coax me into another scandalous situation like last night, which definitely will not happen again, but I don't bother telling him that. Instead, I tighten my grip on the towel wrapped around me and say, "Let me get dressed. I'll be out in fifteen."

THE BOAT DOCK is on the other side of the island, so when I come out of my room in my swimsuit and cover-up, Ellis and Nash are packing up the UTV with supplies, mainly a cooler and towels. When he sees me approaching, Ellis's face lights up with a warm smile and he walks over to greet me with a hug.

"Sleep well?" he asks.

"Yes, thank you." Already we're dancing around what happened last night. I can feel it, but it's not awkward. It's almost...exciting. I've never done anything like that before. I loved it, I mean, clearly. Being ordered around and watched like I was some kind of sex slave...it was the dirtiest thing I've ever done, and that's saying something.

"So, I thought we could head to the cay south of here. There's a beautiful place to swim and a local bar and restaurant on the island," Nash says, coming up to stand next to us.

"Sounds perfect," I reply with a smile.

"We packed drinks, but if you want something specific—"

"I'm fine, Nash."

He's being weird. In fact, he's been weird since yesterday when we came back from the city. More attentive, more generous, and it's nice, don't get me wrong, but he's trying too hard. Or I guess he's trying, period. And I'm not used to the new Nash.

Once the supplies are all packed, we take off on the lightly paved path around the island to the opposite side where there is an old hangar and the boat dock. We load up the speed boat, the smallest and yet most expensive looking boat they have parked out here, and as I climb aboard, I admire the two men working to get everything ready to go.

I've always appreciated the fact that Alistair was the kind of man who could have all the money in the world and was still willing to get his hands dirty and break a sweat. It seems he instilled that in Nash too, because watching these two men working is doing something to me.

The spirit between us is light as we take off from Del Rey, heading south. If living on the island is like another world, then being on the open ocean, the breeze through my hair and the sun on my skin, is like reaching another plane of existence. I'm sitting up front while the two of them are standing near the wheel. We're not going super fast, but with the gentle motion of the water beneath us as we glide across the endless blue, I start to feel the weight of everything melt off my shoulders.

Pulling out my phone and for the first time in a long

time, I type out a couple lines to a messy nonsensical poem.

Endless blue
  World of infinite waves.
  A cage and freedom in one.

It feels good to write something, anything. I'll never share these words, but they belong to me. When it felt like nothing truly did, I had this.

Yesterday, I went into the city with the plan to put a down payment on my own apartment. Ellis helped me look at a few that would work, and something my savings could cover until I figure out what I want to do. It's a start. I didn't tell my mother, and aside from ignoring a few of her messages, I haven't heard from her at all. Being out here, so removed from everything and being rightly distracted by these two men who are pulling me in two different directions, I haven't even given much thought to how she's going to react to the news I'm moving out and I'm giving up ballet, forever.

I decided it not long after getting here.

And it feels good to finally accept the decision, but I'm still unsettled. Something is still not right. Almost as if I know once I get back home, she'll be there, ready to undo all of the confidence I've built here. She will tear every ounce of it out of me before I've even had a chance to live with it.

When I open my eyes, pulling myself out of these doom-like thoughts, I'm caught by the way Nash is staring at me. Those bright blue eyes are boring into me, and I'm struck by the emotion I feel in his gaze. Or maybe I'm feeling what's happening in my heart. How since I've gotten here and that first night in the guest house, I've had to face my feelings for him and how badly I want to bury him in my arms even though all the good sense in my head is telling me how bad of an idea that is.

Nash is toxic, broken, and cruel. He will pull me down with him if I let him, but somewhere in my dumb head I have myself convinced I could love every single one of those things out of him.

And maybe he's thinking the same thing as we stare at each other.

Next to him, Ellis is looking down at his phone, but I catch the way his eyes lift, and maybe he doesn't see me staring, but I watch as his gaze locks on Nash. I see the way he absorbs him with his eyes, living in some kind of one-sided love affair and I see what it is he won't say. I know whatever happened between them was intense, maybe more intense than what happened with Alistair and Zara because Nash isn't just over Ellis, he's actively avoiding him.

Ellis never really told me what happened between them, but I think I have a feeling whatever it was, feelings got involved. And if there was sex, Nash must have felt something pretty intense for Ellis because he seems to be struggling with it right now. Whatever it is, they are both terrible at hiding it.

When we pull up to the swimming lagoon about forty-five minutes later, I'm left speechless by the beautiful blue and white alcove of rock and water. Nash drops the anchor as close to the jetty as he can, and I don't hesitate before diving headfirst into the water. There's another splash after mine, and I pop out of the water to see Ellis smiling at me, brushing his wet hair out of his face.

We both look up to see Nash still on the boat, looking

down at us with a signature Nash scowl, and my face falls for a moment, afraid he's going to find something to fight with us about, but he doesn't. Instead, he peels his shirt over his head and dives in after us.

Ellis is the first to climb onto the low rock. "Don't hurt yourself," Nash calls in a mocking tone.

"Fuck you," Ellis replies, and I let out an easy laugh. It feels so good to be alone with them. I wish it could be like this all the time. This is what I've been missing for so long, and I want to call it friendship, but I know it's more than that. It's almost like a sense of family with them, or is it belonging? Whatever it is, I don't know if I'm ready to leave it yet.

Ellis stands on the lowest ledge of rock, his hands on his wet trunks, which are already short and tight, revealing the thick muscles of his tan thighs. I can hardly tear my eyes away, and I honestly wonder if he's not doing this on purpose, standing up there like he's on display, all of the sun's rays highlighting every sharp edge of muscle on his chest and stomach.

And I'm not the only one looking. As I turn in the water to look for Nash, I catch him staring at Ellis too. After clearly being caught gawking, he swims away toward the rock so he can begin his climb too.

Nash takes a different route up the rock face, obviously aiming for a higher ledge.

"Be careful!" I call, seeing him so high up. The water is deep here, and I trust him, but my anxiety kicks up at the thought of him falling.

"Show off," Ellis barks at him with a playful scowl.

Hanging onto the rock, I watch as Nash takes the dive first, and my stomach literally leaps into my throat at the sight of him falling headfirst toward the water. Ellis and I both let out a sigh of relief when his head pops out of the water. Next, Ellis dives in, and they both look at me.

"Your turn," Nash says.

"Me?" Immediately, I think about my mother. She would have my head if she knew I did something so reckless, something that could ruin my career. An injury wouldn't just ruin my life, it would strip me of my value.

Fuck that.

When I swim toward the rock Nash climbed, I hear Ellis call my name, but I ignore him. With each foot of rock I climb my heart beats faster. When my bare foot slips, they both yell my name, but I don't stop. There's a scrape on my knee, and I can feel a trickle of blood seeping down my leg. It only motivates me.

"Come on, Hanna," Nash yells. "You can really hurt yourself, for fuck's sake."

"Please be careful," Ellis echoes.

When I reach the small flat area where I can stand, I turn around and stare down at the huge cliff beneath me. Oh fuck, this is high up.

"You should see your faces right now," I yell with a laugh. They are both staring up at me with expressions of terror, and only Ellis cracks a smile. "I'm fine!"

"Please just jump far away from the rocks," Nash adds.

I don't know why, but standing up here with the sun on my face, I feel exhilarated, and the reminder my mother would never let me do this only excites me more. With my hands in the air, I let out an exhilarated whoop.

"Just jump, Hanna!"

"Oh, relax. Let her have a moment," Ellis scolds him.

"I've never, *never* done anything like this."

When I look back down at the two guys in the water, both of them treading water, gazing up at me and waiting for me to jump, I feel a bolt of something in my chest. It's something profound, bordering on pain and all I know is I want more. My feelings are getting caught up in this and I don't want to go back to the life I left behind. But I can't have both of them, and my heart refuses to lean in one direction more than the other.

Pushing away the reminder that this feeling has an expiration date, I finally gather the courage to jump. The moment my feet leave the rock, I try to make time stop. Floating feet first toward the water, I leave everything behind.

AFTER ABOUT AN HOUR of swimming in the lagoon, we head to the opposite side of the island where there is a large island bar with a huge patio that reaches out to the water. The three of us sit around a plastic patio table with margaritas and tacos. No one is fighting or talking about what happened last night. No one has tried anything with me, and it feels so comfortable and fun, I hate my heart for loving every second.

I'm still leaving as soon as we get back to Del Rey.

During our second round of drinks, Ellis's phone buzzes on the table, and he excuses himself to take the call. Almost as if he was waiting for him to leave, Nash takes the opportunity with us alone to lean in and reach for my hand.

"Don't leave," he says, and I see the restraint in his expression. He's trying to be civil when he wants to be abrasive.

"Nash, I have to. I didn't come out here to stay forever. I have a life to get back to."

"A life you were miserable in. You're happy out here." I give him a pointed glare with a head tilt, and he adds, "When I'm not being a complete asshole."

"I still need to get back," I argue.

"Then come back next weekend."

"For what?" I ask, running my thumb over his knuckles before trying to pull my hand away.

"For me, Hanna." He snatches my hand before I can hide it in my lap. With every touch, I feel myself crumbling. I'm helpless to him, but I have to keep my head about me. There is no future for the two of us.

"Nash…"

He cuts me off, so eager, and almost desperate. "I'm sorry I brushed these feelings aside for the past three years, but I love having you here, Hanna. I love having you with me."

"No, this cannot happen. We would be terrible together."

Please don't beg me, Nash. I'm so afraid one little plea and I'll be useless against my own defenses.

"No, we wouldn't. Last night was amazing."

I let out a sigh, resting my face in my hands. "Yes, it was, but Nash, we are both too volatile to make it work. Yes, when it's good, it's very good. But when it's bad…"

"I'll be better," he begs. "I'm trying to work on that."

My eyes dance around the patio looking for Ellis. He can't hear this. I don't know why, but I hate the idea of him hearing us talk about a relationship.

"Are you looking for him? Is it him? You're choosing him, aren't you?"

I can see the erratic way he's working himself up, and I put up a hand to stop him. Lowering my voice, I glare at him. "I'm not choosing him, Nash."

"Then, why can't you give me a chance?"

"Because there's something going on between the two of you, and I can't be with either of you until you work it out."

His face pales, his eyes widening as he leans back. "Hanna, there's nothing. I'm not…" He lowers his head, whispering to keep our conversation private even though I'm sure the tables around us can hear every word. "I'm not gay."

I scoff. I hate that I do that, but I can't help it. Nash lives in denial, about himself, about us, about the future. For once, I wish he'd let go of everything he's holding so tightly, wearing everything like armor. There are brief, beautiful moments when he looks at me and it's the real Nash, and he's gorgeous, open, vulnerable and real. But then just like that, he throws up the armor and he's gone.

"What exactly did I walk in on the other day then? What happened in Amsterdam?"

"He told you about that?"

"No," I reply, trying to hold back the harshness in my tone. "But I'm not stupid or blind, Nash. And you're not either because all day long while you were looking at me, he was looking at you."

The table falls silent, and I watch the Adam's apple in his throat bob as he swallows. The cold look of shock on his face is frozen in place as Ellis returns. He can sense the tension immediately, and when Nash turns his eyes toward him, I'm afraid he's going to make a scene now, but he doesn't.

Instead, his gaze shifts to the horizon, and I turn to see what he's squinting at. Just off in the distance, there is a cluster of dark clouds spreading like ink over the bright blue sky.

"Looks like a storm rolling in. We better head back now before we get stuck in it."

It feels appropriate to how I feel right now, except I'm afraid the storm is here, and we're already stuck in it.

WE ARE NOT BEATING THE STORM. JUST AS DEL REY appears on the horizon, the rain starts. Nash picks up the speed and I sit next to Hanna at the back, holding her tight against my chest trying to cover her as much as possible because strangely enough, the hard torrent of rain hurts against bare skin.

No one said much after I came back from my call, and I could tell there was an argument or at the very least a heated discussion between the two of them. I'm just grateful I didn't return to find them full-on brawling on the patio.

I have a feeling I know what was being said though. If

I had to guess, it was Nash trying to convince her to pick him even though I'm not putting myself in this race. I won't take Hanna from him. As much as I hate to admit it, it's best if she just leaves. They are both too hot-headed to make it work, and I don't think I'd feel comfortable leaving them alone.

But when I'm there to balance it out, they're fine.

With her pressed tight against my chest, I try to enjoy these last few moments of having her close. It's only been a week, but this girl got under my skin fast. I've even found myself imagining her in my life, and not just for short moments or quick fucks. Hanna is easy to be around. Flawless in her beauty, inside and out. She swallows her flaws, keeping them inside, and I want to know each and every one of them.

But I could never do that to him. So, when she leaves, I won't contact her. As much as it pains me to do that.

Somehow, I don't think he would believe me. He's been giving me harsh glares ever since we paid the tab at lunch, as if I have a target on my back.

The rain somehow gets worse as we reach the dock. The wind picks up, and I hear Hanna screaming as we both try to stand to run up the dock.

"Take her to the hangar!" Nash yells through the tempest. "It's unlocked."

"What about you?" I reply.

"I have to tie it up. I'll be fine, just go!"

Hanna's scream spurs me into action, scooping her up into my arms as I run up the paved way to the hangar, which is unlocked like he said. Tearing the door open, I carry her through. Setting her down, I check to make sure she's okay, and we're both breathing heavy. The heavy clouds keep it pretty dark in here, but she seems fine. A little shaken up from the sudden hit of the storm. These things can come in so fast, it's unsettling.

We both move to the door, looking for Nash. He should be coming up shortly after us, and the wind has only gotten worse. But he's used to this. I know for a fact, he's been driving and docking boats since he was a little kid. I shouldn't be worried, but with every moment that passes without him running up the drive, I feel the panic settle into my bones.

"Where is he?" she cries.

"I'm going to check on him." I feel her grab my arm, but I don't stop. Leaving her in the hangar, I run down the path toward the dock. The rain slaps even harder against my skin as I run, and the feeling of panic suddenly turns into ice cold dread when I reach the dock and he's nowhere to be found. The boat is tied, but it's rocking violently from the wind and waves.

"Nash!" I shout in pure panic.

My eyes dash to the water, checking for any sign he might have fallen in, but if that were the case, I'd have no way of knowing. The water is dark and moving too fast.

I yell his name again, terror seizing my chest. *Where the fuck is he?* He better be okay. I keep repeating it to myself over and over again, scanning the area, but there are only a couple of other boats and jet-skis tied to the dock, and literally nowhere for him to be hiding.

After two minutes, I feel sick. *No, no, no, no.*

Finally, I catch movement out of the corner of my eye and see him climbing out of one of the larger boats with a bundle of rope in his hands. He slips as he reaches the dock, barely making it out of the rocking boat without falling in. Rushing over, I grab him by the arm and drag him to shore.

"What the fuck? You had me scared to death!"

He's staring at me as if I punched him in the face.

"I had to get extra rope," he yells, the heavy winds drowning out his voice.

I want to squeeze him, shake him, hit him, anything to make him feel something. Say something, give me literally anything. Burying my fists in his shirt, I yank his body toward mine, sneering in his face with all of the pent up anger and frustration over the last three years.

"I said I was worried about you," I seethe.

"Why do you care, Ellis?" Shoving away, he tries to get out of my grasp, but I don't let him go.

"What do you mean, why do I care? I never stopped caring, Nash."

"Well, stop! I can't be what you want."

"What do you mean?" I yell, still holding his shirt. It's not the best place to have this argument, but the words are spilling out of me, and a minute ago I literally thought he could be dead, so I can't stop them now. "You are exactly what I want, Nash. I never asked you to be anything more than you are."

This time he pushes harder, tearing his shirt from my fists. Dropping the rope on the ground, he lays two palms directly into my chest causing me to stumble.

"I couldn't live up to him, Ellis. How could I possibly live up to you?"

"What the fuck are you talking about?"

"I'm not Alistair. I'm not my father. I will never be my father, never be good enough. And you…Mr. Fucking Perfect. I can't be your…what? Your boyfriend? Fuck that, Ellis. Fuck that and fuck you. I'd rather be alone."

"Rather be alone than be with someone who thinks you are perfect? I don't understand you."

He's raging, the wild fury in his eyes as he shoves me in

the chest again. "Yeah, well I don't need you to understand me. Just leave me alone."

"I can't. You're the one who brought me out here! You're depriving yourself of something good, of real happiness because you can't bear the thought someone will find your flaws?"

"Fuck off, Ellis!" I see the clench of his fist, and I'm waiting for him to let it fly. I almost crave it. Hit me. Hurt me. Something.

"Stop it!" a small voice screams, barely heard over the downpour. Hanna clings to Nash's arm, tearing him away. "Both of you, stop it! Get inside before you get yourselves killed out here!"

"Come on, Nash, hit me. Punch me! You know you want to."

"Ellis, stop it!" she shrieks.

It's not that I'm ignoring her. It's that her words are not registering past the rage. "Will it make you feel better? Just fucking hit me! Then we can be done with this!"

"I'm already done," he grits out through clenched teeth.

"You guys, please!" She's clawing at both of us now, but were both too locked in this battle.

"Bullshit," I reply with a dark laugh. "Come on, hit me!"

He's pulling back his elbow, and I'm ready for it. I'm waiting for the impact. I clench my jaw, and tilt my face, hoping he gets a hit on my cheek and not my jaw. But just as he's about to swing, Hanna moves in a desperate reflex to stop us. She bolts to his arms, pulling down his face and latching onto his mouth with her own.

I watch in shock as the hot poker of jealousy stabs me right in the heart, and somewhere in my head, I register the fact that she's choosing him. Even after I mentally pulled myself out of the race, I must have been holding onto hope, but this pretty clearly stakes a claim. His shoulder relaxes as he melts into her kiss, even in this harsh storm.

Watching them touch each other, my fight fades. Before I can do anything, she pushes away from his arms and turns to mine. I don't even know what's happening until she's kissing me. It's a harsh, rough kiss, her nails hard against the back of my neck. It immediately registers that she's doing this to defuse the situation and stop us from beating the shit out of each other, but when she's ripped from my arms and back in Nash's, I'm hit with a wave of possessiveness, and I clutch her to my body even as he's kissing her again.

She lets him kiss her for a moment, but when I string my hand around her throat, she pulls away from him panting and turns toward me.

What are we doing? We're going to tear this girl in two, but I can't stop kissing her.

Just then, we hear the unmistakable sound of thunder cracking heavy overhead, rattling the island and shocking us out of whatever this is we're doing. Hanna stares at me with terror, and I feel a sudden flush of shame for keeping her outside in this for so long. She is literally soaked to the bone. We all are.

"Inside, now." In a deep command, they both immediately start running up to the hangar like I told them to. Following close behind, even I can admit my head is spinning right now. This big question of *what now* hangs in the air between us.

I am the one they listen to. I'm the one who calls the shots and holds the answer to that question.

As we rush into the hangar, still dim without light through the windows, I let the door slam behind me as my hand finds the back of Hanna's neck, pulling her to me as I land a hard kiss on her mouth. I keep the kiss short because I can feel his presence, so I pull her away, pushing her toward him. They don't hesitate, fusing like they were made to kiss each other. He gathers her in his arms, melding her body to his as he curves himself around her.

Stepping into the fray and setting the pace, I reach for the hem of her long cover up and pull it over her head. Suddenly, all of the energy we built up outside is poured into this moment. With Hanna's back against my chest, I kiss her neck, tasting the rain on her skin as she pulls off Nash's shirt. When she spins and reaches for me, mine comes off next.

Nash unties her bikini top, and at the first sight of her breasts, cold and covered in goosebumps, I pull one into my mouth, covering her with warm kisses. She lets out a hum that echoes through the silent space. Moving to the other one, I devour every inch of her delicate skin I can. She tastes so good, like ocean and perfume and *her*.

"Wait," she cries in a hoarse gasp. Immediately, I pull back, looking at her face for any sign she wants this to stop. With one hand on my chest and one on his, she moves her hands to our necks at the same time, and I know where this is going. And I admit, thrill skates up my spine.

This could either go very right or very wrong.

With a gentle push, her request is clear.

When our eyes meet, I still see a hint of that seething hatred toward me in his eyes, but it doesn't make me want to kiss him any less. Fuck, I want a lot more than a kiss.

But I'm going to wait for his reaction first. Nothing happens for a moment while she waits until he suddenly reaches, grabs my neck and pulls my lips to his mouth.

At first, it's an impersonal, rough kiss. Nothing to ease the tension between us, but as I pull him closer, my fingers running along the ridges of his ribcage, remembering the way his body feels, he softens, and I feel him run his tongue along the inside of my mouth.

My cock flinches in my heavy soaking wet shorts I'm suddenly fucking desperate to get off. Giving him a squeeze against my body, I purposefully press my hard length against him. I want him to feel it, remember it. And not like he did the other day, like some sort of hate fuck. I want him to feel it and want it.

When he groans into my mouth, I celebrate inwardly. That was enough of an answer to me.

Nash and I break the kiss, and both turn to see Hanna biting her lip and staring at us with lust in her eyes. "Fuck, that was hot," she gasps before latching onto my body.

When Nash disappears, I almost panic until he returns a moment later with a large rolled blanket in his hands. Hanna is pulling down my shorts when he throws the blanket out onto the floor in the broad space between two helicopters. That's when her bottoms come off and the three of us are completely naked, our wet clothes in a puddle of water on the floor.

Her warm hand wraps around my cock, and I let out a growl, squeezing her tighter to my body. Then, he's there, stealing her kisses, and we are a flurry of hands and mouths and skin until Hanna is flat on the blanket, laid out like a buffet for Nash and I to devour. With every taste of her skin from the gentle slope of her waist to the soft flesh of her thighs, I become more and more intoxicated by her. Desperate for more, hopelessly addicted until my mouth finds her center, burying my tongue deep inside her just to see the way it makes her hips buck and squirm.

Gazing up over her body while I'm still deep in her warm folds, I watch as she takes Nash into her mouth, much like last night, but this time, he's letting me in. My eyes find his face every moment or so gauging whether or not he's going to push me out, putting the emotional barrier up like he always does, afraid to set himself up for pain again, but he doesn't, and when I sit upright, her juices still on my face, he snatches my chin and licks them straight off my lips.

Hanna moans, something guttural from her belly as her legs wrap around my hips and pull me forward.

"Fuck me, Ellis," she cries.

It would seem I am no longer calling the shots. In fact, Hanna has had control of this whole thing, hasn't she? From the very first kiss in the rain, she's had the reins, and as I align my cock at her entrance, I let go of my need to control, and I give in to her. It's not something I do often, but even I'm having a hard time holding back.

So, with one powerful thrust, I'm deep inside her warmth, and the empty hangar sings with the echoes of our lust. It is the pounding flesh against flesh with moans and heavy breathing, and it's far more than anything we ever did in Amsterdam. It's more because of her.

"Hanna," I moan while I move inside her, lost in her eyes.

Covering her body with mine, I watch as she takes Nash into her mouth again, but I see the struggle in her angle. "Come here," I beckon, pulling her up. Then with a quick flip, I lie on my back and help her settle her hips back down.

She bounces hard on my cock, all the while working him to the point where his mouth hangs open, pure ecstasy written on his face.

"Fuck, you're perfect," I moan, helping her to keep a steady rhythm.

"So perfect," he repeats, stroking her still wet hair out of her face.

I'm on the edge, so fucking close, but she hasn't finished yet, so I press a thumb to her clit and pick up the speed, slamming roughly. She lets out a muffled cry, pulling Nash out of her mouth as she falls swiftly toward her climax.

"I'm so close," she moans, still stroking him at the same fast tempo I'm thrusting into her, and it's like the growing electricity in the room strikes us all at once. She goes tense and breathless at the same exact moment Nash releases, the warm jets landing against her chest.

God I want to come in her so fucking bad, but I wait for her to ride out her climax before I let myself go, pulling her off in a rush as it slams into me. Tremors quake through my body, my fingers digging into her hips as I come.

We're all left panting. Nash is still on his knees next to me as he leans down to press his lips to Hanna's neck, cheek, and lips, like he's worshipping, and I watch the way he devotes himself to her. And it hits me that I can't take this away from him. And it hurts. Leaving her, leaving him.

As she collapses onto my chest, not caring we're both sticky and covered, I gather her into my arms, feeling the erratic beat of her heart against my chest. Nash gets up and jogs away, disappearing between the parked aircrafts. When he returns a moment later with a warm, wet washcloth, he takes care in wiping us both clean, placing a kiss on her cheek before his eyes freeze on my face.

This isn't like Amsterdam, I want to tell him, but I don't. And maybe he knows. This is different. She's different. She's…more.

18

It takes another hour for the storm to subside. Our clothes are still soaked and too cold to put back on, so the three of us are left riding back to the house wrapped in towels. As I drop off Hanna in front of the guest house, she climbs off and stares back at us. It's only a little after three in the afternoon, and with the sky clearing up, I see the question brewing on Hanna's face as she turns toward me, clutching her towel to her chest.

"Is it still safe to fly?" she asks, looking at the helicopter parked behind me on the helipad.

I could say no. I could tell her some shit about the weather or about how I don't fly after storms because of what happened to my brother, but that would be bullshit, and Hanna deserves better than that.

"It's safe."

Next to me, I see Ellis clench his jaw, but I keep my eyes on her, hoping she remembers our conversation at the restaurant. How much I'll change to make this work. How hard I'll try, yeah even after what just happened. Even after I watched another man fuck her. I still want her to stay.

She's contemplative, chewing on her lip and thinking it over.

"Your apartment won't be ready until the first of the month." His deep voice cuts right through the tension between Hanna and me, making us both look his way. "Stay with us for a few more days."

I wish I could understand what he wants. I can see his attraction to Hanna, but not that long ago he was talking about how he never let go of things between us.

But as I watched them together, I noticed how different he was with her than the other girls I've seen him with. There's a connection between them, something I almost feel guilty about wanting to break.

Hanna looks at him, her expression relaxing as she nods. "Okay, maybe a couple more days."

"The launch party is next weekend," I add, remembering after the acquisition there's a big event in the city at the Wilde Aviation headquarters. "Stay until then. I'll take you back that night."

"Next weekend?" she asks, looking first at me then at Ellis. Technically it's almost two weeks away, but I don't add that part in.

"You can go back whenever you want, Hanna," he adds. "But it would be very empty out here without you."

At that she smiles, a warm, pleasant expression, and I hate how fucking smooth he is. No one talks about what just happened or about the fact that if she stays, we're all hoping and expecting it to happen again, and I'm still waiting for time to stop for a moment so I can really figure out if this is what I fucking want. Do I want him in on this? No, I want her to myself.

But then I remember how hot she was riding him, her tits bouncing as she chased her orgasm, him taking over at the exact moment she needed him to. And yeah, I did get off on that, like I did in Amsterdam, but fuck, this is Hanna.

This is Zara's Hanna. What am I doing?

"No pressure, Hanna. Whatever you want to do, baby."

"I know," she answers with that signature Hanna sass. "I'm going to shower up and I'll meet you guys at the house for dinner, okay?"

"Okay," we both reply in unison.

Ellis and I don't talk as we pull away, taking the UTV to the house where I park it and we start unloading the cooler and gear. It's when we finally end up inside and we nearly collide in the laundry room where he tosses the dirty towels and clothes that he finally says something.

"This isn't Amsterdam," he mutters.

I stop in my tracks, turning on him and giving him a scowl.

Fucking relax, Nash.

"You don't think I know that?"

"Well, maybe I'm telling you, so you know that I know that."

He folds his arms over his bare chest, the white towel still cinched around his waist, and it takes serious concentration on my part to keep my eyes from falling down there.

"After the launch party, she will go home, and you will

fly back to your office, and all of this will be over. You'll stay away from her."

He grinds his teeth together, his brown eyes boring into me, and I feel my heart race. "That's the deal," he adds before turning away and heading down the hallway that leads to his room.

But my dumb ass wants to know something that's been on my mind since the storm. "Did you mean any of that shit out there? In the rain?"

He stops, slowly turning and holding his chin high, glaring down at me impatiently. "Remind me, Nash. A lot has happened since then."

I swallow my nerves. "You said." I clear my throat. "You said I was all you wanted. You said you cared. Is that true?"

He scoffs, shaking his head, and relaxing his shoulders, but then a look of anger crosses over his features. As he glares at me, I feel myself shrink in his gaze. It's not the Ellis attention I want. And as he steps toward me, I know whatever he's about to say I'm not going to like.

"No."

It's such a simple response I'm not sure I understand, furrowing my brow at him. But I wait for him to continue.

"As far as you're concerned, Nash, I didn't mean a fucking word of it. I'm not going back again, not with you." He steps toe to toe with me, pushing me back as a show of dominance, and I stumble back because I don't have it in me to fight with him anymore. "You will never understand what it's like for anyone to love you, Nash. How perfect you fill this space," he says pointing to his chest. "You are this untamable animal except you fuck with hearts and heads, and I fell for it once, Nash Wilde. I won't fall for it again, so no, I didn't mean shit I said out there. And if you choose to pursue Hanna, I beg you to do her right. If you fill that space in her heart, don't run from it. Don't leave her like you left me."

With that, he spins away, leaving me with my confusion. "So, what if I told you I don't want you touching her again? Would you listen to me?"

"If I thought that's what you really wanted, I would."

I'm about to shout that it is what I really want, but I'm too busy running his words through my head, replaying every single one of them. Walking to my room, I drop my towel on the tile floor as I lean against the cool countertop, my mind spinning with his words.

That first night three years ago replays in my mind again and again. Asking myself if it was a mistake. Doing what we did. It didn't feel like a mistake at the time, but damn, I was so deep into his mind fuck I wasn't thinking clearly.

But it was just fun…until it was more than fun. At least for me. He never felt anything for me like I felt for him. This is Ellis fucking Prior. He could have literally anyone, so why the fuck would he want me? Why is he acting like I broke his heart or some shit? I mean, yeah I get I was a dickhead that night, and sure what I did was fucked up, but he can't still be stuck on me like that.

I'm moving on with Hanna. Everything with her will be so much easier, and I will be happy. I can watch my temper, be better for her. He'll step back and when he leaves here at the end of the month I'll finally be at peace, knowing I mended our friendship. I made things right. Buried the hatchet. Said my piece. And he's fine.

But fuck…he said love. The motherfucker said love. How I don't know what it's like for anyone to love me. I don't make it that fucking hard. He didn't love me. He's trying to get in my head again, and I have to ignore it. Keep my eyes forward, be better for Hanna.

No, fuck this.

Shoving away from the counter, not even caring that I'm stark-ass-naked, I march out of my room, down the hall and across the house toward Ellis's wing, once my dad's. The shower is running, and I don't give a fuck as I burst into the bathroom.

The sight of him, standing under the dual shower heads, clouded in steam, his golden tan skin and dark chest hair through the hazy shower glass making me pause. Why does he still have such an effect on me? He's not in my head anymore. I'm not the same guy I was in Amsterdam.

I stand there silent and stupid for a moment before the shower door opens slowly and he lifts his chin at me. It's a dare, and not an inviting one. Every tiny feature on his face is telling me not to fuck with him, but I don't understand how he is still fucking with me so much. Why do I want to climb into the shower, rub his wet body against mine, feel the length of his hardness against me…*inside me.*

"Fuck!" I bark at him before bolting out of the room. I'm not doing this again. I'm not.

As I reach my hallway again, I try not to think about the urge billowing inside me, the sudden fucking need to go back into that bathroom and shut off every thought in my head with his body.

Instead, I clench my fist and drive it hard against the drywall of my bedroom. The plaster cracks as the pain travels like lightning up my arm and I swallow down the urge to scream.

Why did I bring him here and why the fuck can't I just move on?

19

I can't focus. Truth be told, I haven't been able to focus
on much at all lately, not when every free moment of my
day is spent thinking about that night last week and everything that happened. The feel of that paddle in my hands,
the way it felt making contact with her backside, the pain
that came out in cries from her mouth, and then of course,
the sight of him, tongue out and tasting me.

Tasting me.

"Fuck," I mutter, tossing my laptop aside on the couch.
There's no denying the thoughts in my head, and they are
fucked up. He's my friend. No, actually, he's *my dad's friend*.

Not to mention, a man, and if I was into dick, surely, I'd know by now. Wouldn't I?

Picking up my phone, I shoot him a quick text.

WHAT'S THE PLAN TONIGHT?

HIS RESPONSE COMES BACK IMMEDIATELY.

THERE IS NO PLAN. Come over.

I'M STARING at my phone for a long time. I could call it an early night, say I'm not feeling well, pass on any plans like drinking or inviting some girls over.

I won't, but I could.

Instead, I go to the bathroom, fix my hair, throw on some cologne, and march out the door. On the ride over, I rehearse the plan in my head. We are going to drink. Maybe call someone. Maybe go out to the bar. At the end of the night, I will ride home. No more staying over, especially not in his bed. No more blurring these lines.

It's not my fault Zara fucked me up so bad, but I can't spiral like this. That's all this is. Maybe I'll call my therapist tomorrow, talk a little more about those phases of grief. Is wanting to fuck your best friend one of them? Probably not.

Ugh, the thought turns sour in my head. *Get your shit together, Nash.* It's fucking embarrassing.

Regardless of the silent pep talk in the tram on the way over, I'm a ball of nerves when I get to Ellis's apartment. Using the extra key he gave me, I slip inside, hoping to wipe every thought from my head. But he's not in the living room or kitchen when I enter.

"I'm in the office," he calls, and I give him a nonchalant response that sounds way too forced in my head. Why is my voice coming out all deep like this? *What the fuck is wrong with me?*

Slipping off my shoes, I go to the kitchen first. I need a drink. The fridge is stocked with beers, Heineken of course, so I grab one and pop the top, downing almost all of it at once. Hopefully this will help calm my damn nerves. The nerves I'm feeling for no fucking reason at all.

Now that I think about it...drinking probably isn't the best idea. *Oh well*, I think as I finish the bottle.

"Come take a look at this for me," he calls from the office. Even his voice has the hairs on my arm standing.

After tossing my bottle in the recycling bin under the sink, I head toward the office with every fucking intention of sticking to my plan. What I don't expect is Ellis standing there in front of the floor-to-ceiling windows in nothing but a pair of loose jeans, no shirt, and still-wet hair from the shower.

I pause in the doorway. He's facing his desk, holding a few papers in his hands.

"Read this and tell me if you can find a clause about confidential provisions. I'm not signing shit until I know it's clean and my lawyer won't be up until tomorrow morning. She's in the states."

He's rambling, and I barely hear a word, my eyes glued to the way those jeans hug his ass. After a moment of me not answering, he finally turns toward me with an arch in his brow.

"Here, take a look." He holds a paper out to me, and I silently step forward taking it from his hands and trying to read the words on the page, but like the work manual I was supposed to be studying today, the words don't register. My brain is literally not working.

Instead, I smell the fresh soap on his skin. The product in his hair. The aftershave on his face. And I remember last week when he uttered the words, "I've been with men." That electric shock of arousal hits my nervous system like a storm.

I let the paper settle on the desk and tell myself I need to leave.

I need to leave now.

But I don't. Instead, I turn toward him, letting my gaze settle on his face when he finally looks up from his paper and stares back. At first his expression is shrouded in curiosity, until his eyes meet mine, and maybe my internal struggle is written all over my face. Maybe I'm not fucking discrete at all, but his face slacks and he gazes back at me like he knows.

Like he fucking knows.

I move first, leaving every thought behind, not giving a shit what could happen or what will happen next as I grab him by the back of the neck and pull his mouth to mine, desperate to taste his lips.

He's only thrown off for a second. Pure shock I'm sure. Well, I'm fucking shocked too.

But then he's kissing me back, tasting my lips, my mouth, sucking on my tongue as I force it between his teeth so I can claim his mouth for myself. And he doesn't stop me. His papers drop to the floor as his hands grip my hips and shove me against the desk, pinning my body with his. A low growl echoes through my chest, and I don't know if it came from him or me—because he is an extension of me. Or am I an extension of him?

The kiss intensifies until all that exists is the taste of his lips, his breath, his scent, just Ellis. Every tiny movement of his body registering in mine like I'm on his frequency.

"Nash," he gasps, pulling away to look at my face. "Are you okay?" he asks with a hand on my chest.

Fuck that. I swat his hand away and go in for his mouth again like it's the only thing I need, the only thing I want. His kiss is oxygen.

With my hands against the soft planes of his chest, I slide them down along the ridges of his ribcage, feeling his skin against my fingers like it's the first time I've touched anyone. And when I reach the waist of his jeans, he doesn't bother stopping me again. He doesn't need to fucking check up on me; he needs to never stop kissing me.

As my fingers fumble with the button on his pants, he stumbles forward, like he's short circuiting, shoving my body even harder against the desk. That's when he starts tearing at my shirt, but he's taking too much care with the buttons. Forget that shit. I tear it off, hearing the buttons pop, too anxious to feel his bare chest against mine, and like I expected, it's fucking heaven. The soft patch of his chest hair against my bare skin doesn't feel wrong or strange. It feels right.

Somewhere in the deep recesses of my mind is a voice telling me to stop. This isn't who I am, but I don't care. Right now, I'm indulging. Just this once. Just for fun.

And since this is the only time I'm doing this, I want everything. Every single thing.

So, I make quick work of his pants, unbuttoning them and pulling them down, and of course, he's not wearing anything underneath. His hard dick is staring up at me, and there is nothing stopping me from wrapping my hands around it.

So, I do.

Maybe a little too tightly. He moans, deep and husky

before latching his teeth onto my jaw, kissing roughly. "Oh fuck, Nash."

He said my name. I'm holding his cock in my hand. And all of this is happening, and all I can think at the moment is I want to come, so fucking bad. But I want to make him come even more, so I stroke him slow and tight, learning the feel of him in my hand, so surreal. His dick is wider than mine, smooth and harder than a fucking rock.

"Come here," he groans, jerking my hips forward and tearing my pants open.

"Fuck, yes," I grit through my teeth as he makes contact. His hand is hot around my cock, stroking to my rhythm, and I'm going to come way too fucking fast. "Wait. Stop."

His touch leaves me immediately. We're frozen in place for a moment, and my hand is still wrapped around him while he waits for my next move. I realize he thinks I wanted to stop completely, as if I'm backing out, but that's so far from the truth.

My body is on fire, and I haven't felt this good in a long time. There is no stopping me now. So, while I have the chance, I do what I've been thinking about all fucking week.

My eyes still glued on his face, I drop slowly to my knees and look ahead at his beautiful tan and pink length, tight round head, veins bulging, and warmth radiating into my palm. It is a perfect fucking dick, and I really never considered myself admiring another cock before, but here I am.

Placing a warm, wet kiss directly on the head, we both shiver at the same time. Then I trail my lips along the bottom side, all the way to the base before licking my way back to the head. Every texture and sensation is so new to me, and I feel the shake of nervous excitement in my spine as I part my lips pulling him in. He glides easily along my tongue, and I'm almost afraid he won't make it very deep when my gag reflex kicks in, but fuck, this is the only time I'm going to do this, so I'm going to do it right. I'm going to please him. I have to.

Relaxing my throat, I try again. Adding more saliva to his staff, I let him slide even further, feeling him at the back of my throat. His hands go to my hair, gripping the locks at my scalp as he jolts forward.

"Fuck, Nash. Fuck."

I'm totally lost in the movement of my mouth around him, taking him a little deeper each time, saliva running down my chin and tears pooling in my eyes.

"Your mouth is perfect on my cock, Nash."

The praise spurs me on, sucking him down faster, tasting the beads of pre-cum on my tongue. And the question in my head, what will I do when he comes, steals my thoughts. Will I swallow it down?

This is the only time I'm doing this, so I guess I will. I want it. I want him.

I don't even realize I'm doing it, but I have one hand on my own cock, stroking shamelessly, and I feel myself building toward my orgasm at the same speed he is. And just when I think I'm there, he pulls out, and I stop my moving.

"Stand up," he orders me, breathless.

His cheeks are red, his eyes dark and dilated with lust. As I stand, my lips wet and swollen, he grabs my jaw and pulls me in for a deep kiss. Fuck, I love his mouth on mine. More than I thought I would. Something about kissing a man as opposed to a woman is hot as fuck. Like I can be as rough and hard on him as I want, and he can take it.

But as he pulls away, still holding me by the throat, he

glares into my eyes. And my heart won't stop hammering in my chest because I know what comes next.

This is the only time I'm doing this. The thought echoes.

"Turn around," he says.

My chest heaves as I pause.

Make up your mind, Nash. I can't let this moment pass.

One, two, three, four.

I turn toward the window. Facing his desk, my pants at my feet, I place my palms against the cool wood before feeling his body hot against my back as he hums low and inviting. With one arm around my waist, he takes my dick in his hand, stroking slowly as his other hand rifles through the top drawer. Glancing there, I see him drop a small bottle of lube on the desk, and bring a condom wrapper to his teeth to tear it open.

My heart is going to explode in my chest.

He lets go of my cock long enough to put the rubber on his own. Then, comes the lube. At first he drops some onto his fingers and I wait, trying to tell my chest to stop pounding so hard. It's his fingers, slick and warm against my back entrance I feel first, making me jolt and clench from the sudden touch of him there.

First, he's just rubbing, and I know I should do something. So, I press back into his hand. *Just do it, Ellis. Just fucking do it. I can take it.*

"Relax," he mutters against my shoulder. And I do, enough for his finger to breach the tight entrance, and I let out a ragged gasp.

At first, it's all wrong, and I almost panic. I can't do this. I can't fucking do this.

Then he pushes a little deeper, and everything changes. My spine turns into lava, pleasure sliding up until I'm choking on it. He's only one knuckle in and I'm rocking my hips back toward him.

More.

"Slow down, baby." He chuckles, twisting his finger a few times before adding a second and sliding a little deeper. Then he hits a spot inside of me that makes my cock jump and my eyes roll into the back of my head. *Fuck yes.*

I moan, my fingers clawing at the desktop.

"Just fuck me," I say in a ragged pant, the words foreign in my ears.

But he doesn't, not right away. He spends another few minutes prepping my hole, slicking me up, and I hear his voice grow hoarse as he does. This is turning him on, and that shit turns me on.

When he pulls his fingers out, I take my first full breath in what feels like hours, but I miss the sensation. I need it back. The top of the lube bottle clicks again, and I hear the unmistakable sound of him covering himself with it.

Then he's there. The broad, moist tip of his cock pressing in. It's too big, *way too fucking big*, but as he eases forward, he whispers, "Just bear down." With that, he pushes inside of me, sliding all the way to the hilt, and we both groan, guttural and animalistic. Neither of us move for a moment, and I'm breathing in this new sensation of being so fucking full. Full of him.

More.

With his hands on my hips, he slides out and back in, hitting that spot again that turns my body into fire. Oh, I am not going to last long. Fuck I might come without even touching my own dick.

More, I repeat in my mind

He laughs. Oh, shit. I guess I said that out loud, but I want more. I want him faster, harder, deeper. I just want him.

Wrapping his strong arm around my chest, he pulls my

body upright against his, still buried deep as he thrusts his hips hard, pinning me to the desk.

"God, you feel so good on my cock, Nash. Like you were fucking made for it."

I reach a hand back, holding onto his leg as he pounds into me. And the minute he grabs my cock, I'm done. He doesn't even need to stroke. He picks up his speed, fucking me harder, his masculine grunts in my ear, and I shoot right into his palm. I'm on another planet as my body shakes and explodes in pleasure. It's all too much and not enough at the same time.

A moment later, he thrusts and tremors, emptying his cock into the condom between us. And we're both left gasping for breath. I feel his warm breath on my neck, clutching my body, and I don't know how much longer I'll be able to stand. I sink against his hold as he slowly pulls out, leaving me empty and missing him immediately.

It's like coming back to earth. My head starts to clear as he disappears from the room, returning a moment later with a warm washcloth he uses against my ass and then to clean up his desk.

"This contract is fucked now," he says, throwing away the pages that ended up crumpled or covered in cum.

"Sorry," I mutter, pulling up my briefs and jeans. "About that."

Ellis throws the washcloth in the wastebasket, and looks at me with sincerity. He walks up to me, touching my chest and pulling my face close to his.

"Don't apologize. Not to me. I thought it was going to take you a lot longer to get here."

Then, he kisses me and for a moment I forget what this is. We're just friends. Friends who fucked.

But just once. I let my guard down once. I'm not doing it again.

20

"WHAT THE HELL HAPPENED TO YOUR HAND?" I ASK, THE moment I walk into the kitchen and notice the beet red, swollen knuckles on Nash's hand. He's opening the fridge, and I notice the way he's barely using that hand.

"It's fine," he mumbles.

Uh-oh. Something happened after we separated earlier. I knew this would happen and at this point, I'm over it. I grab him by the shirt and drag him to the counter so I can get a closer look. "Nash Wilde, tell me now what you did."

"He didn't hit me if that's what you're worried about." Ellis walks into the room, looking too handsome, freshly showered and dressed in a casual T-shirt and sweatpants.

Glaring at Nash, I try to be stern with him, but the moment he gives me those tortured eyes, I fall apart. Running my hands through his hair, I place a kiss on his temple. "Listen here, boys," I say as I grab a towel from the drawer, laying it on the counter and going to the freezer to get ice. "I'm not going to stay if you two are going to fight. And we are definitely not doing what we did today again if this happens every time." I wrap the ice in the towel, holding it on his fist. He gives me a pitiful, stubborn expression like he's too tough to be taken care of by a woman, but he knows as well as I do it's what we both want.

Let me take care of you, Nash Wilde. Let me love all of the hate right out of you.

"So, you're saying you want to do that again..." Nash says, teasing me with a pinch of my ass.

"No, it was terrible. Hated every moment." Giving him my best eye roll and sarcastic tone, I wait for him to crack a smile which he eventually does. It's not a big smile, but it's something.

"Just until next week," I add, going to the sink to wash my hands.

"Perhaps we should set some ground rules," Ellis says, leaning on the back of the couch and watching us.

"Do we need to?" I ask.

"Do we?" This time he's looking at Nash.

The room grows silent for a moment, and I wonder if these two are finally about to snap and have it out with each other.

"No," Nash says finally.

"So, what do you guys want for dinner?" I ask, looking through the fridge. Nash let the staff have the day off since we were gone most of the day anyway. Which means we are on our own unless we go to the mainland, but I'm much more into the idea of eating something here then possibly talking these guys into laying on the couch with me to relax and watch a movie.

My plan mostly goes down without any issues. There's chicken in the fridge, which I season, and Ellis puts on the grill. Nash helps me put together a kale salad, and the three of us eat on the patio with white wine, and for the most part they get along. That is to say they completely avoid looking at or talking to each other.

It's disappointing.

Today was so perfect, and I'm not just talking about the hangar. Everything before that, the boat ride, swimming, and being together was fun. Natural. Complete.

Nash lets me nurture him in the same way Ellis strengthens me. Strangely, it works. When everyone is happy, no one is jealous or territorial. I almost wish it could be like this forever, but that's crazy.

I'm not Zara. When all of this is over, I'm not choosing between Ellis and Nash. I could never do that. If I can't have both of them, then I can't choose one.

I just wish I could help them mend this bond and get over whatever issues they're holding onto. What did Nash do to Ellis that fucked him up so much?

After dinner, we head inside, and the guys indulge me with a movie. As we pile onto the couch, I sit between them, pulling a large throw blanket off the back to cuddle under. Nash has the remote and immediately pulls up his Netflix, and the first thing I see when the screen lights up is my face.

My heart stops.

There under *Continue Watching* is a thumbnail image of the ballet, Giselle, with my face in full makeup in a red dress on stage. I completely forgot our production was recorded and produced for streaming. I've never even watched it…but apparently, Nash has.

"What's that?" Ellis asks immediately.

"I forgot this even existed," I mumble.

Nash fidgets next to me as I glance at him. "You watched it?"

He shrugs, and I see him trying. Instinct has him wanting to put up walls, block us out, avoid being caught with emotions, but he doesn't. It's not easy for him, but he manages to reply with, "Yeah, I watched it. Why wouldn't I?"

My lips stretch into a thin smile I try to hide in the blanket. Nash watched me dance. Zara told me about the night she and Alistair came to see me in this production, how it was supposed to be her and Nash instead. But he said he hated ballet.

What if it had been him that night? Would things have been different? Would he have ever looked at me then how he's looking at me now?

"Let's watch it," Ellis says, putting an arm along the back of the couch.

"Noooo," I whine, hiding under the blanket.

"Oh yeah," Nash says casually before hitting play.

As the music starts, I'm battered by memories. This was the peak of my career, right before everything went to shit. Before it all became too much. Flashbacks of my mother forcing me to spend my weekends in the studio, working until I'd collapse, missing entire meals at a time, and only getting about three hours of restless sleep each night. It was like the moment she got a taste of my success she wanted more. She had my agent on the phone more often than not, talking about modeling, movie parts, endorsements. It never ended, and I started to see only one way out.

But Giselle…this memory is a good one. And as I watch with them, I don't see the mistakes she would point out. I see the look on my face, and I remember how it felt on that stage. I remember I loved it.

The boys next to me keep making oooh and aaaah comments with every leap and spin, like it was some superhuman feat. Shaking my head at them, I laugh. But then I glance at Ellis, and he's staring at the screen with adoration. Me. He's looking at *me* with adoration. Sure, it's a version of me from a few years ago, when I was at the top of my game, but still…there's something like love in his eyes, and damn it feels good.

Nash's hand clutches my leg gently under the blanket and not in a sexual way. He's looking at the TV with the same expression as Ellis, biting his lip with a smug grin. It's Nash's version of adoration.

And for the first time since I arrived on Del Rey, I start to consider maybe dance isn't done with me yet. I may never be in a Netflix production again, but that doesn't mean I can't feel that good on stage again. This is what I want, and a week ago, I was ready to give up the fight on the things I wanted, but these two have managed to renew this drive in me again.

Before my breakdown, dance was this thing I loved but it was used against me. And now I think I'm ready to take it back.

21

THE GUYS GET SWAMPED WITH WORK THE NEXT DAY, SO I'M alone with my thoughts and a renewed sense of excitement and purpose. Of course, the anxiety and dark thoughts are still there, waiting in the wings, ready to rear their ugly heads, but I manage to keep them at bay all morning. And it's enough to go back down to the studio and actually lace up my shoes this time.

Music plays from the speakers as I touch the barre, feeling the smooth surface against my fingertips. I slowly move through the routine of *demi-plies*, feeling more than a little rusty. The gentle stretching moves remind my soul of the life I used to live, and I'm happy to find the muscle memory is still there. The day slips away in a meditative trance as I completely lose myself in the basement, and before I realize it, it's early afternoon, and I haven't seen the boys all day.

After a quick shower and grabbing a bite to eat, I head over to the office once the staff has left. As long as they're around, I don't exactly feel comfortable being around the boys alone. I don't need them catching on to what's going on between the three of us.

I creep into the office in just my bikini, and they both look up from their laptops with coy smiles on their faces.

"What are you working on?" I ask, crawling onto Ellis's lap.

"It's boring," he replies, stroking my arm with his thumb.

"When will you be done? I'm bored."

He smells so delicious, and I'm anxious to get him undressed as fast as possible. I already miss his kiss. After the day I've had, I'm feeling good, uncommonly good. And nothing would top this day more than getting naked with these two.

"This has to be done by Friday. And we're not even a quarter of the way through."

Nash looks stressed again. Over the last couple of days, we managed to peel away some of this armor he hides behind, and I realize now it's his work. Nash buries himself in his work to keep from feeling or thinking things, and I guess I can relate to that.

"Do you think if I took my top off, he'd change his mind?" I ask, whispering to Ellis loud enough for Nash to hear.

"Worth a try," he replies.

"Don't even think about it," Nash barks as Ellis starts fooling with the clasp on the back of my bathing suit.

Just then my phone vibrates on the table, and I pick it up, assuming at first it'll be another spam call or at the very least, Zara. But when I see my mother's name on the screen, my blood runs cold.

"You okay?" Ellis asks, noticing my expression.

"I have to take this," I stammer, jumping up from his lap and rushing to the door. I can't talk to her in front of them. Once I'm outside, I hit the answer button.

"Hanna!" She bellows, and I freeze. "*Was ist falsch mit dir?*"

What is wrong with you?

And just like that, I'm a child. No, smaller. I'm reduced to a thing, a small, stupid thing.

"You disappear for two weeks and then I get a call from the bank telling me you put a deposit down on an apartment in the city? Are you stupid?"

"I'm not stupid," I mumble.

"You don't have money. You can't afford this apartment, Hanna. You missed your auditions. Who are you with? Some foolish man, I'm sure. Is he rich? Is he going to pay for your apartment? I'm sure he doesn't even love you. Why would he? You think because they will sleep with you, they must love you?"

"I have enough saved to pay for my own place."

"And then what, Hanna? How will you pay your rent? You lost your job dancing because you can't take care of yourself. You can't do anything right, Hanna."

"Mother," I snap. "I'm getting that fucking apartment and you can't stop me! I'm not a goddamn child. I'm a grown woman." It feels so good to stand up to her, something I should have done so long ago, and when I think I have her silenced, she manages to knock me right back down.

"A grown woman? This is how you talk to me after

everything I've done for you? I raised you by myself. I have given up everything for you. I'm the one who paid for all of those ballet lessons. They were very expensive, Hanna. I'm the one who made you a ballerina. You'd be nothing without me, and now you're running away from me. So ungrateful."

I can't speak. I have nothing to say. No defense. No words to fight her although I've rehearsed them in my head a thousand times, all the ways my mother has mistreated me, reduced me, broken me. But now they are all gone.

"I cancelled the deposit on your apartment, Hanna. It's gone. You need to save that money until you get hired again in another dance company, but until then, you need to be practicing and auditioning, but you're probably not doing anything. I made you a star, but I couldn't stop you from being so stupid."

The line goes dead.

My hands are shaking as I stare down at the blank screen. I want to throw it, but I don't. Instead, I carry myself on wobbling legs to the guest house. Once inside, I toss the phone against the couch.

I'm such an idiot. I've been out here living a fantasy while my life goes to shit. I'm not clearing my head. I'm just ruining my own fucking life.

The room is silent, a deafening silence filled only with the hateful thoughts in my head, the ones reminding me I am not worthy of the fame, the love, the happiness. None of it.

I hate the silence, so I let out a scream, bringing it up from somewhere deep inside, straight from the source. It doesn't make me feel any better, but it shuts up the voices.

Once the scream is out, I pick up my bag and start packing. I have to leave. I don't know where I'll go or what

I'll do, but I can't stay here. I can't keep pretending these men care about me or that I deserve any of this. I don't belong out here; I'm not even welcome. Nash never invited me, and now it's so fucking obvious how much I've imposed myself.

Fuck. What is wrong with me?

Does he care about me? He does. He does, he does, he does, I tell myself, but it hurts to even say it. It hurts to lie to myself. Nash doesn't care about me, and neither does Ellis. I let them fuck me like the slut I am, so of course they want me to stay now. God, I'm so stupid.

In a fit, I toss my bag against the wall, tears streaming down my face as my chest starts to burn, radiating out from the center and spreading like fire across my skin all the way down to my fingers and toes.

No, no, no. Not again. Please not again.

All of my energy drains out of my body, and all I want to do is lie down, and scream and break things and cry. So, I crawl into the bed and sob, trying to stop my chest from moving so fast. My lungs refuse to take full breaths, and I feel like I'm suffocating. Clenching the bedsheets in my fists, I wait for the episode to subside, but it won't fade away, and I know the more I panic, the more intense it becomes.

I can't breathe.

I'm going to die here on the guest bed on an island where I'm not welcome surrounded by people who don't care about me.

"Hanna!" The front door slams against the wall as heavy footfalls chase into the bedroom.

"Jesus Christ," Ellis mutters.

"Please go away!" I gasp, trying to speak through strangled breaths. It hurts to speak, my oxygen-deprived lungs burn as I try to force the words out. "Leave me alone."

There's a weight on the bed. "Fuck, she's pale."

"Let's fly her to the hospital," Nash says in alarm, and I feel his arms trying to pry me away from the bed, my face still buried in the pillows. On reflex from being touched, I panic and start swinging at him. The first thing I feel is his face against my palm, and I cry even harder.

"Don't touch me!"

"Okay, baby. It's okay." His hands are gone.

"What's happening?" Nash asks. I can't see him, but I hear the fear, no, disgust in his tone.

"Panic attack," Ellis answers, and I gasp loudly for breath again.

"What do we do? She can't breathe!"

"Nash, relax. Give her space. How about a cold washcloth?"

There's a hand on my back, and it's running smooth circles. It's like needles on my bare skin, but at the same time, it's warm and comforting.

"That's it, baby. Just keep breathing."

With my focus on his hand, I don't even realize the tightness in my chest has subsided. It still hurts to breathe, but I can take deeper breaths.

"Here," Nash stammers in a panic before I feel ice against my neck, and I jolt and shiver from the contact.

"That's my girl. It's passing."

With my face in the pillow, I try to pretend they're not here. I want the room to stop moving and my chest to stop aching, so I think about the motion of his hand on my back, the new scent of Nash's cologne in my nose, and before too long, I'm left with only my tears.

And they come on strong. The thrumming in my ears is gone, and the exhaustion in my body feels like I swam a thousand miles.

"Hanna," he whispers. As I peel my eyes open slowly,

I'm surprised to see Nash's face, lying on the pillow inches from mine. He's sprawled next to me, but it's not his hand on my back. I can tell by the weight and movement Ellis is behind me, but I don't turn toward him.

Instead, I bury my face again and sob. This is so fucking humiliating. I hate myself so much right now. Why am I like this?

Nash's hand touches mine, releasing it from the clench around the blankets to lace his fingers with mine.

"Please go away," I whisper against the wet pillow.

"We're not leaving you."

I don't know which one of them says it, but it doesn't matter because they don't leave. They both settle close against me, still rubbing my back and squeezing my hand until the exhaustion takes over and I'm lost to sleep.

WHEN I OPEN MY EYES, Nash is still there. He's lying next to me in the dark room with his eyes closed. Shifting back, I feel someone behind me too. Ellis's clothed body is pressed tight against mine, and I'm covered in a soft blanket in just my bikini.

Then I remember everything. From my mother's phone call to the breakdown, and Ellis and Nash calming me down. It feels like a bad dream. Or a hangover.

Very carefully, I climb out of the bed and tiptoe to the bathroom. When the light comes on, I stare at my reflection in the mirror. There are heavy dark circles under my eyes, makeup streaking down my cheeks, and cracks through the soft skin of my lips.

Before going back to bed, I wash my face and try to avoid looking at the ugly thing staring back at me in the mirror. I know it's my delusions, the evil voices in my head, telling me I'm too ugly to love.

When I get back to the bed, Nash's crystal blue eyes are watching me from the darkness. He doesn't say anything, not at first. He just curls my body against his, holding me tight in his arms.

"That used to happen to me after Preston died. I kept them away with vodka and pot, and I didn't even care I was only making it worse."

Looking up into his face, I try to remember the first time I met Nash, how young he seemed then. Pushing his shaggy brown hair out of his face, I still see the same pain I recognized then.

"Do you want to talk about it?" he asks.

Ellis shifts behind me, and I feel him bring the blanket back up around my waist, covering my body. Then his lips are on my shoulder. It's a gentle kiss, nothing like what happened in the hangar or the pool. It's like these two actually care about me, but how is that possible?

And what's the point? I can't choose one without hurting the other. So why am I doing this to myself, letting my heart get attached?

Because I'm stupid and I put myself in these situations.

"I don't know what's wrong with me," I mumble, swallowing down my humiliation.

"There's nothing wrong with you," Ellis replies, close to my ear. He's pressed against me, so I'm literally sandwiched between the two of them, and it's so comfortable and inviting I hate myself for how much I love it. I wish it could always be like this.

"Who was on the phone?" Nash asks.

Shutting my eyes, I answer him. "My mother."

"What did she say?"

I scoff. "Aside from what a failure and disappointment I am? She let me know how she cancelled the deposit on the apartment because she still has executive power over my bank account since my breakdown last year."

"Hanna," Ellis says, and I hate the disappointment in his voice. I know I shouldn't give her so much power, but what else can I do?

"I have no one else. What am I supposed to do?" I ask, tears brimming my lashes again.

"You have us," Nash says, squeezing me closer.

"You don't need anyone," Ellis adds.

"She's right though. I don't have a job or a future. I threw away my dance career. I shouldn't be allowed to make decisions for myself anymore."

"You know that's not true," he replies against my back.

"I don't know what's true." I'm sobbing now, soaking the pillow again, but this time, I'm not spiraling out of control. I'm safely grounded, tethered to them. "She's been telling me my entire life how I wasn't wanted. She couldn't take me back to Germany because I was born out of wedlock, how my own family would hate me because my skin is a little darker than hers. She used to tell me I had to be a perfect dancer like I had to earn my love, and eventually…it broke me."

Crying into the pillow, I let everything out. I feel only their lips and hands on my body, tender and careful but also assertive and convincing.

And it is convincing. After these strange two weeks, I'm feeling things I never expected to feel. I was never supposed to fall for either of them, and at the very least, I expected sex. But this? This is so much more. It's confusing and terrifying, overwhelming and exciting.

But it can't last.

Nash and I would be dangerous together. With no one around to settle our tempers, everything about our relationship would be toxic. Not to mention, Zara would be hurt. She might not express it, but she's my best friend and Nash is her ex. Or more than that really. They still hold such a big part in each other's lives, and she would never treat me the same way again. It's bad enough what I've already done.

And Ellis? Even if I could somehow live up to his perfection, get through each day knowing I'm not quite worthy of his full attention, I know being with him would break Nash. And that's not fair.

Somehow, even knowing this, I keep a hold of both of them, loving the way it feels in this moment. The safety and peace I feel in my heart is addictive, and I'm not ready to let it go.

I don't think I ever will be.

22

IT'S WELL AFTER THREE IN THE MORNING WHEN SHE FINALLY stops crying, but none of us fall asleep. Instead, we stroke her back, keep her close, plant warm kisses on her body, and never leave her side for a second.

Finally, Ellis gets out of the bed first, disappearing into the bathroom, and I wonder what he's doing until I hear the shower running.

"Come on, baby." He lifts her carefully, cradling her in his arms, and I can't take my eyes off of him. He's so collected. Like he knows exactly what everyone wants or needs at all times. Doesn't he ever second-guess anything? Doesn't he ever worry he's wrong?

He's not in this instance. I follow them into the bathroom, and find him tenderly undressing her from her bathing suit, keeping his eyes on her face as he does. And when he tries to help her into the shower, she reaches for him.

"Stay with me," she whispers.

There's only a moment of hesitation before he peels off his clothes until he's naked climbing into the shower with her. I should feel like I'm imposing on something, but I don't. Instead, I lean against the door frame and watch them through the frosted glass. She's burying her face against him as he wraps his arms around her.

"Nash," she calls.

Ellis peers my way, no expression on his face. He and I still haven't spoken about anything outside of work since yesterday, but I try not to dig up those memories right now. Instead, I shed my clothes quickly and step into the water with them. This shower isn't nearly as big as mine in the main house, so it keeps us close to each other, which is exactly what she needs. Pressed between our bodies, Ellis and I take turns washing her up, taking care of each delicate limb and inch of her body.

After the shower, we take her to the main house to get something to eat. It feels good to feed her, take care of her, give her what she needs. I've never really been in this position before. It's always me being the one getting taken care of.

Then I remember more than once Preston sneaking into Dad's liquor cabinet and getting so hammered he needed me to help him to the toilet, and yeah as weird as it was, I liked taking care of him. I liked being the responsible one.

Hanna sits at the kitchen island, wrapped in blankets, sipping on the tea Ellis made her while I cook up some leftover pasta Thalia left in the fridge. Okay, so I'm not a chef like my dad, but I can at least do this much.

She's gotten some color back in her cheeks. The way she looked when we found her still haunts me. Her skin was almost gray, and her body was contorted in a strange position. There were beads of sweat across her face, but her skin was almost cold. I hated it. I never want to see her like that again.

Every few minutes my eyes meet Ellis's in the kitchen, and I wonder if he's thinking the same thing I am. Hanna cannot go back there. She can't live with that woman again, not when it took one phone call to have her falling to pieces. The emotional damage that woman has inflicted on her own daughter…fuck—it has me fuming.

After next week, she has to stay here. I have to find a way to get her to stay.

The three of us spend the next hour talking and before long we're actually laughing. Hanna is smiling, and it makes me happy to see those pearly whites between her lips.

"Shit, what time is it?" she asks.

"Four-forty-five."

"Damn, the sun will be coming up soon. I'm not even tired." I almost don't want this night to end. It's been so nice.

Then, an idea hits me.

"Come on."

They both look at me skeptically as I slip my shoes on and head for the garage where the keys are kept.

"Where are we going?" she asks, following me to the aircraft parked outside.

I don't answer her as I open the door for her. She stops with Ellis following behind. There's a twinkle in her eye and a subtle smirk on his face.

"Is this safe? It's so dark."

"You trust me, don't you?"

Biting her lip, she finally climbs in. Ellis gives her the front seat next to me while he squeezes into the back. This is the four-seater. Not my favorite, but the other one only fits two and I want the three of us to stay together.

After we all get mic'd and buckled, we take off. Neither of them are new to this experience, but I still love to see the look of excitement on their faces, illuminated only by the soft light from the dash. The horizon is already starting to lighten where the sun is about to rise. Flying along the shoreline I put the horizon on Hanna's side.

She watches out the window as the sun slowly paints the sky orange, chasing out the inky black darkness. Glancing at her, I feel myself falling over again. It feels like Zara all over again…but different. I'm not so desperate anymore. Not so scared this time. I'm sure Hanna and I could work, and we would work well. Everything with her is intense and exciting, and the last time I felt that was with—

My eyes glance back toward his seat. And just like Hanna said that day on the boat, he's watching me. His dark eyes are gazing my way, and I'm hit with guilt again. Guilt for what we did…or maybe for what I did. How I ended things.

Would Hanna still love me if she knew the truth?

Just then, her hand reaches out and she laces her fingers with mine. I glance back at Ellis again, and he sees her hand in mine.

It makes me angry he's not more possessive about it. Why isn't he mad she's touching me…or that I'm touching her? If it were me, and they were holding hands, I'd want to touch them too. If I can't tear them apart, then I'd want to be there with them.

And I do want to be with both of them.
I don't want this week to end.

23

This girl keeps touching him, and it's making me crazy. Sitting at one of our favorite pubs downtown, a couple of girls he seemed to know cozied up in the booth with us pretty quickly after he greeted them.

He's letting her touch him. I can tell, and I think he's doing it to make me crazy.

It's working.

I know Ellis. He could dismiss her easily. I've seen him do it. But instead of telling her to fuck off, he puts his arm around her and glares at me across the table.

I don't want to take anyone back to the apartment

tonight. I just want him. Like we do every fucking night, I want to let him throw me down on the bed or the couch or the kitchen fucking counter and take all of the pleasure he wants to from my body. Instead, he's playing with me.

We haven't had a girl between us in a while. At least a month. And I'm aware that I'm getting dangerously attached to having Ellis to myself. I think he sees it too.

"You seem tense," he says as we walk back from the pub to his apartment, alone. After the third round of beers, he took pity on me and said goodbye to the girls who both looked pathetically disappointed when he did. I enjoyed that part a little too much.

"You were trying to make me jealous," I snap back.

He laughs, and I both love and hate his sardonic tone. I hate when he treats me like a kid, but I also crave that attention. "Maybe I like to see you jealous."

"Well, I don't like it."

"Okay," he replies calmly. "I won't do it again." His arm snakes its way around my waist as we walk, and I tense. Ellis and I have not defined whatever the fuck this is, and the only unspoken rule is that it exists solely within the confines of his apartment. We don't touch each other outside of that space, and we don't tell anyone else about it.

I'm fully aware this won't last long. Sooner or later, this little fling will end. I'm prepared for it, and I'll go back to pussy like I'm supposed to. It's not like this makes me gay, and I have absolutely no plan to come out or pretend that I am. He doesn't bother me about it, so we don't talk about it.

"Why do you like that…to see me jealous?" I ask, pulling away from his public embrace.

He sighs, sounding a little annoyed. "I don't know. I guess I'm a little bit of a masochist."

With a scoff, I glare at him. "That's definitely true."

"You say that like it's a bad thing. I've seen the way you are with women. Don't you think you are too?"

No. I don't like to hurt people. I don't get off on pain. I like the control. But I don't tell him that. Instead, I shrug.

When we reach his apartment, we each take off our shoes and hang our coats on the hook. I'm suddenly not really in the mood to be touched. I'm too restless, too antsy. And in true Ellis style, he picks up on it. Turning toward me, he puts his hands gently on my hips.

"Would it make you feel better if I let you strap me to the bed and paddle my ass?" There's a playful smile on his face, but I know he's not entirely kidding.

"Maybe it would," I reply, testing to see how serious he is.

"I would do that for you," he says, leaning forward to press his lips to my neck. My tension melts a little with the contact.

"You would?"

"Of course."

"But don't you like…to be in charge?"

"Sure, but I also know how good it feels to give up control too. How relaxing it can be to not have to make any decisions. To only feel…even if it's pain."

That doesn't make any fucking sense to me, but as he walks away, I get an image in my mind of him at my mercy, making him do whatever I want, and that shit goes straight to my cock.

"Okay," I say. He turns slowly, a mischievous gleam in his eye.

"Okay…"

"Let's play."

He smiles. "And what would you like me to do?"

Fuck, it feels good already. Just for him to ask me that.

Ellis is usually the one who calls the shots so to have him putting me in charge has me feeling good…but also a little strange.

He walks toward me, pulling his tie loose and letting it hang around his neck. Grabbing the ends, I tug him closer. "Get on your knees."

Dropping to the floor, he stares up at me. Wait, I didn't think this out. I just said the first thing that came to mind, but fuck I love him from this angle. The urge to ask him what he wants is still so strong, but as I rake my fingers through his hair, tugging it back so his jaw pops open, I pull his face toward my crotch.

"Take it out."

He does, softly pulling down my zipper and dropping my pants and boxers to the floor. My cock springs forth, and with my bottom lip pinched between my teeth, I press it toward him, rubbing it against his cheek. It feels humiliating but somehow so damn hot. I keep waiting for him to snap at me or tell me to stop, but he doesn't. He just lets me.

"Tongue out."

As he does, I run my cock along the surface, still holding his hair in my fists. He doesn't close his lips around it but lets me fuck his mouth, reaching as far back as I can until I feel him gag. His eyes water, and I have to pull out before I lose it.

"I want to fuck you," I say in dark tone. "Can I fuck you?" There's no change in his expression, and I feel breathless waiting for his answer. We haven't crossed that line yet. So far, I've been the only one to bottom, but I'd be lying if I said the desire wasn't there.

"Are you asking me or are you telling me?" he replies, and I have to swallow. *Can I tell him to?*

Squaring my shoulders, feeling like I'm doing an Ellis

impersonation, I lean down and press my lips to his mouth. "I'm going to fuck you."

He exhales with a shudder but doesn't respond. He could easily say no if he wanted. We didn't exactly set up a safe word or anything, but we're not so fucking deep into this game he couldn't just say no. I mean in some weird way he's still in charge, isn't he?

This was his idea. He handed me control because he wanted me to feel this. So, it's not really for me…it's for him.

"Yes, sir," he mumbles against my mouth.

With my fingers still against his scalp, I lift him to his feet. My lips find his and I kiss the taste right off his tongue. I love kissing Ellis, the roughness of his mouth, being able to be as hard as I want. As I press him back, we shuffle toward the bedroom, unbuttoning each other's shirts as we move. As we pass the bathroom, I stop. When I see the mirror, I push him toward it.

"Take your pants off and get on the counter."

If I'm going to fuck him, I want to watch myself as I do it.

He does as I tell him, and my mouth goes dry when he sits on the broad white countertop, leaning back against the mirror and staring at me with a hooded gaze. His cock is resting swollen against his leg, and I place myself between his legs, one hand on the mirror behind him as I stroke him slowly.

I'm teasing him, watching his face for signs he's getting close and then letting go just as he does. He grinds his molars and lets out a grunt as I do it for the third time.

"This is for flirting with those girls in front of me."

Leaving him hanging without an orgasm for the third time, I reach into the first drawer and pull out the lube. I'm so fucking glad he made me get tested with him because I can't wait to unload inside of him, feeling nothing between us, just his flesh against mine. First dropping some on my fingers, I watch his face as I reach down and touch him, feeling the tightness give way as I slowly press one finger inside. His lips part as he exhales, and chills erupt along my back.

I can hardly wait to be inside him, but I try to be patient. The longer I wait, the better it's going to feel. Once I work two fingers in, he starts to squirm. Looping my other arm under his leg, I press in firmly, feeling for the spot I know will drive him wild. His body jolts just as I hook my fingers, and I can't take it anymore.

Pulling out, I slather lube on my cock and press myself against his entrance, watching his face as I slip past the opening and sheath myself in his body. His legs wrap instinctively around my hips as he lets out a hearty groan.

I really wanted to take this slow and savor it, but the moment I'm inside him, I lose my control. Thrusting hard in rough strokes, I grip his hip in one hand and his shoulder in the other, losing my mind with how fucking good he feels.

His hands claw at the countertop just as I catch the sight of myself in the mirror. And it catches me off guard how in control I look compared to how out of control I feel.

"Stroke yourself. Come when I do," I tell him, and he does. Watching me while unnatural sounding groans escape his lips, we both fall headfirst into a long intense orgasm it feels as if we share. Catching another glance of my reflection, I find a wave of gratitude flow through me. Collapsing my head on his shoulder, I'm suddenly so thankful I didn't stay on Del Rey. If things hadn't ended with Zara the way they did, I may never have come here. I may never have found him, and although I'm still holding onto this idea I won't stay in this relationship forever, the idea he would leave me first has me feeling suddenly cold and angry.

"Don't leave me," I pant against his chest. The mess smeared against his belly is now smeared against mine, but I don't care. I want it.

He pauses a moment, putting his arms around me.

"Why would I leave you?"

I don't want to answer him because it sounds fucking pathetic to admit, but this is Ellis, and I'm safe with him.

"Because everyone fucking leaves me."

24

I NEED A DRESS FOR THE LAUNCH PARTY. ZARA OFFERED TO let me borrow one, but I sort of feel the need to have my own for this occasion. What's this occasion? I don't know. Feeling worthy of wearing something beautiful maybe. Feeling genuinely loved…well, maybe not *loved*, but adored enough to feel like love.

So, while the guys are in the office, bickering loudly about something, I quietly say goodbye and hitch a ride back to the city with the pilot who transports the staff.

Zara is meeting me at Hawthorne and Davis at noon for lunch and shopping. There's a small coffee shop there where I wait for her as she walks up with the baby in a stroller.

"Sorry, I felt guilty for leaving her again, so I hope you don't mind that I brought her."

I send her a wide smile, pulling her into a warm hug. I love the sudden softness to her cheeks and glow to her skin. In the sleek black stroller, I lift the blanket to see baby Harper sleeping, her big round cheeks pressed against the strap of the buckle.

"Don't you dare apologize. I'm glad you brought her. Nothing wrong with a girls' day."

We make our way down to the first store making small talk. Mostly she asks about how I'm feeling on the island, getting enough peace, not bothered too much by the guys. I try not to look at her as I answer that question. She doesn't need to know everything going on at the island, not yet at least. Eventually, I will have to come clean. She's my best friend.

The first shop we walk into is a boutique, still a bit pricey for my budget, but I still look through the rack. Zara makes quick work of pulling dresses off and handing them to the salesclerk to try on. She's adjusted well to being a billionaire's wife, but I guess anyone would.

Every single one of the dresses is a dud. Just nice, but that's all.

As we leave the first shop and make our way to the next, my phone rings in my purse, and I fish it out to see Nash's name on the screen. Giving Zara a suspicious glance, I stop and hold back for a moment before I answer. "Hello?"

"Find anything?" he asks. His smooth voice sends a warm flush to my belly. I instantly wish I was back at the island.

"Not yet," I answer with a smile. Zara turns around and watches me with a quizzical brow.

"Head over to Joliet's on the south side of Hawthorne."

I stop in my tracks as a scoff escapes my lips. "Very funny. That's a little out of my budget."

"Just go. They're expecting you."

The blood leaves my face as I stare straight ahead. "What did you do?"

"Well, I assume you're going to this launch party as Ellis's date, right?"

"I…uh, I don't know."

"Well, if you go as his date then I want you to be in my dress."

"You can't buy me a dress…"

Stopping myself from saying his name out loud, my eyes flash up to Zara who is now in listening distance and definitely would have heard it. A smirk lifts the corner of her mouth.

"I just did, beautiful. It's under Ellis's name."

"Oh my God…"

"Hanna," he says with authority, and I gulp as I listen to his next words attentively. "You're worth it."

As the line goes dead, a smile cracks across my face.

"What was that?" Zara asks immediately.

"Um…we have to go to Joliet's."

"Joliet's? You have expensive taste all of a sudden."

I clear my throat, biting back a smile. She doesn't ask any more questions as we walk down the street toward the north end. When I walk in, there is a girl standing by the door, jet black hair and translucent, pale skin.

"Ms. Thurber?" she greets me.

"Yes…"

"Mr. Prior called ahead for you. We have a room for

you right over here. Would you like a glass of champagne?"

"Yes, please. For my friend, too," I answer with a smile.

The shop girl gives Zara a polite smile and the stroller a hesitant, but polite smirk. "It's a baby, not an elephant." Zara whispers under her breath as the girl walks away with her nose wrinkled, and we laugh. It's good to see the crass girl I first met is still in there.

Then we walk over to the sitting area where there is a selection of gowns waiting for me. Zara sits on the plush sofa as I run my fingers along the fabric of each dress. Gowns like these don't even have price tags. I can't let him spend this much on me, can I?

"Okay, spill it," she says, checking on Harper who is still sound asleep.

"Spill what?" I reply with my back to her, biting my lip.

"You know exactly what I'm talking about."

"He's just being nice to me. I think he feels bad for me."

"I think you're fucking him," she says, and I see the shop girl's heads snap in our direction. I remind myself she thinks we're talking about Ellis, and I guess we sort of are. Even though it was Nash who put this whole thing together.

I want to be wracked with guilt, but these dresses are… so nice.

"So what if I am?"

"I had a feeling this would happen, and I'm not gonna lie, Hanna. I was sort of hoping it would. He's a catch."

"You're just saying that because he's older than me and rich."

"You make me sound like such a gold digger," she teases me, and I laugh, looking back at her.

"Ma'am, would you like assistance with trying on one

of the gowns?" the girl with the pasty skin asks, walking over to us.

"What exactly did Mr. Prior request?" I ask looking at the dresses all in different shades of ruby, scarlet, and maroon.

"He requested something in red. His exact words were, 'you look beautiful in red'."

A small gasp escapes Zara's lips, and I can't fight the smile on my face. "Thank you. I'll try this one first."

Grabbing the off-the-shoulder gown, I take it into the dressing room, closing the curtain behind me. Taking out my phone, I shoot Nash a quick text.

Red, huh?

The typing bubble pops up.

I expect pictures.
  So does Ellis.

Biting my lip, I set my phone down and strip off my clothes, pulling on the gown. It's gathered on one side of my waist and fits perfectly, hanging off my shoulders. Did he measure me in my sleep or something? My dark hair hangs off to one side, and as I look in the mirror, I try to find the same girl in the reflection I saw in the bathroom the other day. But she's not here. Not in this upscale dressing room. The girl looking back at me isn't so afraid.

Picking up my phone, I take a quick shot in the mirror.

Nash was right. This color looks good on my skin tone, bringing out the warm hues, contrasting the black of my hair.

Then, I shoot the picture in a group text with both of them.

Their responses are immediate.

Nash: Fuck yes.

Ellis: We're not going to make it through the party if you wear that.

Ellis: Try on another one.

Nash: No. Just come home.

I FEEL LIKE A FOOL, grinning like an idiot at my phone.

"WHAT THE FUCK are you doing in there? I want to see," Zara whines.

"Okay, okay." Pulling back the curtain, I walk out to the sitting room, standing in front of the alcove of mirrors to get the full effect.

Zara whistles. "That is hot. He won't be able to keep his hands off you in that."

"He wants me to try the rest of them on."

"I bet he does."

The shop girl brings us both refills of our champagne as I pull the next dress into the dressing room. It's a satin gown with a high slit up the leg. Then a silk, deep cut neckline with bright gemstones like stars on the bust.

.   .   .

Nash: Buy them all.
  Ellis: I like the first one.
  Nash: COME HOME.

I stare at the text for a moment. *Home.* He means his home, doesn't he? It's not my home. I can't let myself think like that.

Coming out of the dressing room in my original clothes, I smile down at Zara, sitting on the plush couch holding baby Harper in her arms. Leaning down, I place a kiss on the baby's head.

"Ready to go?"

"Which one did you decide on?"

"He likes the first one."

"Good choice, Ellis," she replies, putting the baby back in her stroller. "You know, I have to admit," she says. "You two are going to be the hottest couple at the party."

I'm hit with a sudden flush of guilt. "It's really Nash's big night."

At the mention of his name, her head snaps up. "Of course. Does he…have a date?"

Zara asking me about Nash is surreal. If anyone would know what was going on in his life, it would be her.

"Not that I know of," I say carefully without making eye contact. "I think he plans on going with me and Ellis."

"He needs his own date," she replies. My skin is pricking with nerves as I try to act casual.

"You'd be okay with that? Him having a date."

She stops for a second. "Of course. He has to live his own life. I honestly don't know what he's waiting for. Alistair and I thought maybe he met someone in Amsterdam. He seemed really happy for a while."

Turning toward her, I search her expression for any sign she might suspect that person to be Ellis, but then I remember Alistair never even knew the two saw each other there. It makes me sad for a moment that Nash feels the need to keep so many secrets, to hide his own life, so that his own family has no idea when or who he falls in love with.

And I want to tell her so bad. I want to tell her everything she's missing out on with him because he won't open up. Ellis and me and everything, but it's not my place.

It's strange, this soft spot she holds for him. The love that's not quite romantic anymore but not quite friendly either. No one is more protective of Nash than Zara, including his father, but she really has no idea what he's going through right now. Which means she has no idea how to help him.

With that, a sudden wave of protectiveness washes over me, a consuming feeling of *mine*.

AFTER SHOPPING, Zara and I take baby Harper to a late lunch where she lets me hold her and blow raspberries on the fat rolls of her neck, making her giggle loudly on the patio of the bistro. Zara is snapping pictures with her phone of the two of us, and it's really quite nice for a while.

"You sure you don't want kids?" she asks as she prepares a bottle for her.

"I'm sure," I reply, and I am. I've always known that about myself. It's not that I don't like kids or want to be selfish, but I never had a real relationship with my mother, and I want the cycle to end with me. Not to mention, the diaper and bottles and toys aren't really my style.

It looks good on Zara though.

As I pass Harper back to her, she nestles her to her chest, placing love-filled kisses on her forehead as the baby suckles hungrily on the bottle. Within minutes, she's asleep.

After lunch, a familiar black car pulls up outside the bistro. As Nash steps out, I bite back my smile.

"What are you doing here?" I ask.

"Here to take you back. What's taking so long?"

"Are you tracking me now?" I'm not even mad.

"Maybe. Let's go."

"What's the rush?" Zara asks.

He hops the small iron bars separating the restaurant's patio from the sidewalk. Then he leans down and places a kiss on Harper's sleeping head. Something about it sends a rush of butterflies down my spine.

Yeah, this is how women who don't want kids end up pregnant.

"Sit down," I tell him. "We're about to pay the tab."

"You two go ahead. I'm going to let the baby sleep for a while."

"Are you sure?"

"Yeah, go."

I notice the strained expression on her face, the way she's watching Nash, noticing the way his hand rests against my lower back as I stand. When I lean down to plant a kiss on her cheek and thank her for shopping with me, there's something missing from her smile. It's not quite right.

"You should wear that dress tonight," he says as soon as we climb into the car.

"You'll ruin it before the launch."

"That's the idea," he says with a wink.

He can hardly keep his hands off of me on the drive to the helipad. Once he parks the car, leaving it for one of his employees to park, someone takes my dress out of the back and follows us as we cross the cement pad to the aircraft. He takes my hand, looking back with a smile.

Something about that smile. It feels dangerous. It's too rare, too valuable, the kind of smile that makes you want to give everything you own for it. I'd die for that smile.

"I'm surprised you left work long enough to come get me," I say into the headset as we take off toward Del Rey.

He reaches across and squeezes my fingers in his. "For you? Anytime."

"Ellis made you take a break, didn't he?"

He laughs. "How'd you know?"

"Because he cares about you, Nash, and like me, he doesn't want to see you working yourself to death."

Instead of shutting down and snapping at me with something meant to hurt my feelings like he would have two weeks ago, he clenches his jaw and squints his eyes toward the skyline.

"You're not going to argue with me?"

"No," he replies.

"Are you ever going to tell me what happened between you two?"

"We hooked up."

"I realize that, but it doesn't exactly explain why you act like you hate each other now."

"It's complicated."

There's a look of guilt on his face, and we drop the conversation. As the helicopter lands on Del Rey, I spot Ellis standing outside, watching us with one hand in his pocket. Before getting out, Nash reaches across the seat, pulling my face toward him and planting a harsh kiss on my mouth.

I let out a moan as he nibbles affectionately on my lower lip. He's doing it because Ellis is watching, but neither of them really get jealous, so I don't know the point.

As I climb out of the helicopter, Ellis is there to greet me, placing a kiss on my cheek. Ever since my panic attack the other day, they have been especially affectionate. I could get used to this. In fact, I'm afraid I will. No one could live this life and not get attached. But do I deserve this? Is it wrong of me to want this? The love and affection of both of these men?

"Have fun?" he asks as we walk to the house.

"I did." Then, as I turn to Nash who is pulling a long white satin garment bag from the back, I say, "You really shouldn't have bought me that dress. I can't keep it."

"Of course, you can. With the way you looked in this dress, it'd be a crime for anyone else to wear it."

Ellis's hand rests against my hip, holding me close to his side. As I turn to gaze up into his eyes, I get lost in the dark irises. I run my hands through his warm, honey-colored hair. He leans his face down and kisses me on the lips; they're soft and warm. His tongue slips into my mouth and I melt. God, I hope he carries me to his bed right now. It's such a nice day already, and letting Ellis Prior make sweet, slow love to me sounds like pure heaven.

Instead, he pulls away, kissing my nose. "Unfortunately, Nash and I have another business call in an hour, but then we are all yours." He kisses me again.

I pout in return, reluctantly letting him go.

Nash is watching us, his eyes lingering on Ellis a moment longer than on me, and I feel the tension radiating off of him. Every time things start to feel sweet and perfect, the skeletons in their closet are quick to resurface and mess everything up. Nash is insecure about something, and I can't tell if it's guilt or jealousy, but I want him to be able to get over it.

It's almost like they need to just fuck and get it out of their system.

25

Hanna: It's past six.
  Ellis: Don't look at me.
  Nash: Almost done.
  Hanna: You flew me back just to ignore me?
  Nash: I'm hurrying.

A picture pops up in the message. It's a picture of just her legs, long tan and bare as they rest on the mahogany desk in my guest suite. My mouth literally starts to water.

"Can we please wrap this up now?" I ask.

He looks away from his computer for a moment, glancing down at his phone. His eyes widen for a split second. Then they drift up to me.

"She sent this to both of us," I add.

"Is that a good idea…after her panic attack? What if it's too much?"

"That wasn't because of us. The smiles afterward were."

His mouth twists into a knot as he stares down at his phone. I know what he's thinking. He's thinking he really wants to go in there, and he's thinking he wants me in there with him or else he would be fighting me about it. But I see the hesitation, and I can only imagine it's because he's torn between wanting what we had in the hangar and having her love as well.

"It's just for this week, Nash. If you want my word after the launch, I will walk away, I'm giving it to you now."

There's a flinch to his expression as he glances my way. Was that regret?

"Fuck it. We can finish this tomorrow. Let's go." He slams his laptop shut and tidies up his desk before texting her back.

Nash: On our way.

I'M ALREADY LOOSENING my tie as we cross the helipad toward the house. I follow Nash down the hallway that leads to my room and the office at the end. And there she is, in the chair, silhouetted against the setting sun in the picture window. Her feet are still propped on the desk, crossed at the ankles, and she's in nothing but a black bra and panties. Her hair is fixed in a tight bun on the top of her head, and my fingers itch to pull it out, letting it cascade down her back, those tight black curls in my fingers.

"Stop right there," she says as we both reach the door. We freeze in our tracks.

I can see the tic in Nash's jaw, but I can't help the coy smile that plays on my lips. There's a powerful look on Hanna's face, a far cry from the girl who lacked confidence and existed like she was waiting for permission to live. Right now, sitting behind that desk, with lust and excitement in her eyes, she looks ready to take control.

And I'm ready for it.

"I keep thinking about that kiss the other day…" she says before biting her lip.

Nash and I share a look of confusion, glancing at each other before it registers. She's talking about our kiss, and I have to swallow down my excitement.

Even out of the corner of my eye, I can see him clench his fists, ready to argue. He wants to remind her who's in charge, but he's also remembering what pushing Hanna has cost him before. He told her he'd be good. He said he would be better for her, so he's trying.

But also…I know a part of him wants what she's implying.

"I think it will help put me in the mood," she teases, biting back her smile. "So why don't you undress each other here in front of me? I want to watch."

My dick twitches in my pants.

"You think you call the shots, princess?" Nash says, stalking closer. He puts his hands on the desk, leaning toward her and she stops him with her foot on his chest.

"I do call the shots," she replies, and fuck that confident look in her eye drives me wild. I'd gladly lick her shoes if she told me to. I'm at her mercy.

Stepping forward, I come up behind him, wrapping my hands around his waist, reaching for his buttons, slowly undoing one at a time. "There's nothing wrong with submitting once in a while, Nash. You should try taking direction. You don't have to think or fight." Two buttons come off easily before I feel him press backward slightly enough to feel the stiffness in my pants. "Just let someone take control…but it takes trust."

He turns his head to look at me, our faces inches apart, but I don't kiss him. Not yet. She hasn't told us to. Instead, I ease his shirt off his shoulders, looking at Hanna. She licks her lips, watching the shirt glide slowly down his arms.

"Pants," she whispers.

His eyes are on her as my hands find the buckle to his slacks. The room grows silent, the only sound is the clang of his belt. I slide it open, then work to unbutton them. His hands don't leave the desk as I slide them down until he's in nothing but his tight black boxers. My lips hover over his shoulder, breathing in the scent of his cologne.

When he leans back again, his bare back against my shirt and his ass snug against my dick, I plant a kiss on his shoulder. Then, I wait.

"Kiss him," she says in a breathy command.

I don't want to take this too fast, but when he doesn't stop me, I trail my mouth upward, leaving wet kisses along his neck until I reach the lobe of his ear, biting it between my teeth, loving the way he hisses when I do.

Hanna is watching with her lips parted and her breathing heavy. Nash's face turns slowly toward me, until my lips reach his, and he doesn't stop me as I lick into his mouth. I stop, waiting for him to move, and finally he does.

Reaching his mouth toward mine, sucking my lips between his teeth and kissing me with bite.

Turning his body toward me, he fists my loosened tie in his tight grip and pulls me toward him, showing his dominance, and I let him. Nash clings to any sort of control he can when he starts to feel out of control. One of these days, I want to make him truly let go, but not today.

Today, Hanna is in control.

Nash tears off my clothes with about the same patience and finesse as he showed my tie, gripping the fabric and tearing, no care for the buttons or seams.

Our lips don't leave each other's until we're both breathless and in nothing but our underwear. Hanna is now sitting forward, her elbows on the desk as she watches with rapt attention.

"Ellis," she sighs. "Get him ready."

Giving Nash a quick glance, I watch his throat bob as he swallows. Then, without taking his eyes off me, he lifts the waistband of his boxers and lowers them to the floor. He takes his cock in his hand, and looks at me. Licking his lips, and with a lift in the corner of my mouth, I lower myself to my knees and immediately run my tongue along the underside of his cock from his balls to the head. He lets out a hearty groan.

When I draw him into my mouth, Hanna gasps a tiny inhale, so I know she likes what she sees. Then, with my hands on his ass I do as she asked, getting him good and wet for her, making sure not to let him come but teasing him enough to want more.

From the corner of my eye, I see her crawl onto the desk as Nash hauls her closer, kissing her hard. Her bra lands somewhere on the floor behind me, and I hear her moan as he tugs one of her bare breasts into his mouth. As he holds her, I hold him, sucking hard on the head until he's growling and digging his hand in my hair to fuck my mouth harder.

Then, he pulls away quickly, and I know it's because he was about to come. With a shudder, he shakes off the climax that's now subsiding. So, I rise to my feet, stealing Hanna's mouth and kissing her as he latches onto me.

When I reach for her panties, she grabs my wrist, swatting it away. "Nope. I'm not done with you two yet." She hops off the desk, walking over to the bedroom, and we trail after her like bees to honey.

"I did a little digging around the guest house and found a few interesting things. Like this…" she says, holding up a bottle of lube from the side table next to my bed. There is also a small pile of condoms.

Suddenly, my heart feels like lead in my chest as I glance over at Nash.

I had never considered he would have been with any other men since me, and the idea has me feeling suddenly selfish and…sad. I thought he gave up on us because he couldn't be with a man, but maybe it was because he couldn't be with me.

The room grows tense for a moment as I watch her, trying to harden my expression to keep from showing my emotions. Suddenly he's there, standing in front of me, and he fists my hair at the scalp, bringing his face to mine.

"You look jealous. Are you jealous?"

I try to shove him away, but he doesn't move.

"Nash…" Hanna cries from the other side of the room.

"Say it. Say you're jealous," he growls at me.

"I'm not."

He crashes his lips against mine, and I wind my fingers around his throat, shoving him to the bed. I'm tired of this hold he has over me. This constant push and pull, these games we're playing. I'm not going to be the leading role in Nash's denial anymore. If he wanted me, he had the chance, but from now on, it's just physical and just for Hanna.

He wants to rope in my emotions.

He can fuck off.

Sitting on the bed in front of me, he reaches for my cock, and I try to pull away, but the second his hand wraps around me, fighting back is pointless. Instead of pulling back, I push him forward. I hate myself for how much I love the feel of his hand around me.

Before I let things get out of hand, I grab him by the wrist, stopping his motion as I glare up at Hanna. "She didn't say you could do that yet."

There's hesitation on her face, and I can tell she's nervous about the minor scuffle between us.

"What's next, baby?" I ask her.

"Kiss him," she whispers, and I clench my jaw. Hanna wants the problem between us to be fixed with physical touch and affection, but she doesn't know what happened that night. She doesn't know the pain I endured for months…years. How bad Nash broke me.

But I do it for her, convincing myself this can be just sex. I won't get attached. I won't bring my emotions along. So, I lean down, pulling his lips to mine, kissing him without emotion.

But Nash takes. That's what he does. He demands and doesn't ask permission. He takes my mouth without forgiveness, pulling me closer and humming into my mouth, but I pull away before he can take something I'm not ready to hand over.

As we pull away, I see Hanna move away from the nightstand. "I want to see you two together…" she whispers quietly.

Fuck my stupid heart for speeding up. Fuck how bad I want that too.

"Nash?" I ask, looking down at him.

"She calls the shots." He pulls my lips down to his again.

"Get on the bed," I tell him, and he keeps his eyes on me as he shifts backward, and I crawl over him, covering his body with mine. This time, I grasp his hair in my fists, pulling his head back so I can kiss his neck. It's a little too rough, I know that, but I love the way he sounds, fighting the pain of my teeth and five o'clock shadow against the tender skin of his neck.

Hanna crawls onto the bed by his head, watching us quietly, so quietly I almost forget she's there. The room is still dark enough I can only hear her breathing and Nash moaning beneath me. When his hand wraps around our cocks pressed together, I bite down a bit harder. With every ounce of pleasure he brings me, I want him to feel pain. I want him to hurt half as much as I did.

Pulling away, I reach for the lube on the nightstand, and I pop the top. That's when I notice the seal on the top of the bottle. It's unopened. With his eyes on me, I pause.

Then, I glance down at him.

He squirms under me. "What are you waiting for?"

Swallowing down the lump in my throat, I tear the foil off the top and squirt some onto my fingers, then reaching between us to run my fingers around his tight entrance. He shivers as I cover him.

I'm so fucking anxious to be back inside him, but I take my time, prepping him, watching his face as I work in one, then two fingers. Sitting above him, Hanna watches, biting her lip and clenching her thighs together.

I can't take another second, so I reach for the condom.

"I'm negative," he grunts, wrapping his ankles around my waist. "I got tested before you came out."

Glaring down at him, it feels like my heart is pounding a mile a minute. My hand hovers over the foil packets, and I know in my head I shouldn't admit to him I also got tested before my trip. If I tell him I did, he'll know I wanted this.

And suddenly the roles feel reversed. When I first got here, he was the one denying his feelings for me. Now, I'm the one guarding my heart, but I know where he is concerned, I don't make wise choices, and I don't care how much this is going to hurt later.

Looking up at Hanna, she nods.

With that, I press my cock against him, hovering over him as I admit what a fucking idiot I am. "So did I."

Then, I press myself home, inside him, and we both groan. My face contorts, almost in anguish and I rest my forehead against his shoulder, thrusting in hard again. He cries out, his ankles still wrapped around me as he pulls me in again and again.

That's when I lose control. My body moves on its own, and it's like the last three years don't exist, and we're right back where we were. We are together, and tomorrow feels infinite.

My hands roam his body as I fuck him, along his chest, up his biceps, and when I get to his hands, I feel her hands too. Looking up, I see that she's grasping his hand in hers and my fingers mingle with theirs.

When I lift to see her, she bolts forward, kissing me hard. The only sound in the room is flesh pounding flesh and Nash's heavy breathing and loud groans. My hips won't stop thrusting, and when Hanna releases my lips, she leans over to kiss him. As she reaches down to stroke him, I know he'll come fast.

So, I hook an arm under his leg, pounding harder, fucking all of my feelings into him because as far as I know this could be our last time. And I still hate him. I hate him so much for making me feel this way. His skin against mine, bare and beautiful.

With one last heavy thrust, I come hard, letting out a guttural cry as I fill him up. Hanna only has to stroke him a few more times before he shudders underneath me, and I watch as he comes all over his chest.

The three of us are silent for a moment as we catch our breaths. Hanna reaches for a tissue, cleaning up his chest, and I reluctantly pull out, collapsing on top of him.

Hanna lies next to him as I roll away. "That was perfect," she whispers into his neck.

Sitting up with my feet on the floor, I try to remind myself why I'm not getting involved with Nash again. I can't.

"I'm going to go shower," I say, standing up and escaping to the bathroom.

Under the hot spray of water, I let everything roll off my shoulders. I can't let him get to me. I can't.

Soon, the shower door opens and I feel his presence as he steps in. The dual heads give us enough room so we can both shower without touching each other, but he's still right at my back. And it feels like that first shower we shared all over again.

"I didn't fuck anyone else." His voice is low, barely audible over the water. "No guys at least."

"I don't care."

His arms wrap around me from behind, and it feels impossible. Denying him. Protecting myself.

"Yes, you do."

A second later, the shower door opens, and Hanna joins us. Having her with us instantly defuses the tension as she steps against my chest, sandwiching me between them.

Looking down at her, so perfect and beautiful, I feel something with Hanna I don't feel with Nash—safe. This whole time I've been telling myself I can't keep her because he cares too much about her, but I'm finding myself having a hard time imagining a life outside this island. Without either of them.

26

I can't sleep. The launch party is in three days. But that's not why.

Somewhere around midnight, I wake up in Ellis's bed. Hanna is between us with her back to him so they're both facing me. In the darkness, with only the light of the moon entering the bedroom window, I stare at them both.

This week has gone by too fast. We made a deal—after launch, Hanna could return to her life in the city, and Ellis would fly back home and never contact her again. It felt so right a few days ago, but now…it feels wrong. How can I send him away now, especially after last night?

I feel myself pulling him back in, desperate to keep his attention. I can't let Ellis go and maybe I never did.

There's no more sleeping for me tonight so I climb out of bed and pad silently across the house back to my room. Slipping on some sweats and a T-shirt, I leave the house, letting the door close without a sound and crossing the helipad to the office. I could have probably gone down to the gym for a workout. I haven't been down there all week, but there's too much on my mind.

So, I open my email, but there's nothing new. I open the bank account…nothing new. Then, I flip through the documents again, looking for something, anything I can fix or change or make better, but there's nothing.

Somehow, I end up scrolling through my phone. Completely restless, my mind needs something to occupy itself, and I land on my camera roll. Flipping through the past starting from the most recent photos, I scroll through shots of almost nothing. Pictures for work, models, ideas, screenshots. Aside from a few shots I snapped of Harper and before that, the wedding, I have no real memories in my phone.

Until I get to Amsterdam. The trip we took to Brussels. Ellis and I on the train, being tourists in a foreign country. Everything from eating to sleeping…and even fucking in the five-star resorts in high rise buildings in the city center.

I land on one, a selfie he took with my phone. Lying in a white bed with my head against his chest, a smile on his face and a sarcastic scowl on mine. Regardless of how it looks, I was happy. We were happy. Maybe the happiest I've ever been. Trying to remember where my head was then, I can hardly believe for *months* I acted like it was normal…not being with a man, but being *happy*.

He says I never truly accepted it because it was just two weeks after that trip everything fell apart. Okay fell apart is a bad way of saying it. I smashed it all to pieces. I set our relationship on fire, leaving him to watch it burn alone.

There are more pictures of us in Amsterdam before the setting is back to Del Rey.

Zara's smiling face stares back at me in one picture, wet from the pool, sitting between my legs, my hands holding her possessively. I don't look happy in this picture. I look angry, desperate, barely holding on.

In another life, another chance, I could have kept her. I could have been happy. Zara was everything I thought I needed, someone who worshipped me. Never challenged me. Someone who held my hand through my own downfall. Letting her go was one of the few things I did right.

Then why does it still hurt so much?

Before the pictures of her there are pages and pages of blurry memories, regrets, mistakes. Drugs, parties, girls. It's a mess.

Until it's Preston. Pictures from the weekend he died. The catalyst.

The door of the office opens, and I look up to see Hanna tiptoeing across the office in one of my T-shirts. "What are you doing?" she whispers.

"Couldn't sleep."

She sits on the desk in front of me, and I immediately roll my chair putting myself between her legs. My hands run up the soft skin of her thighs as she rakes her fingers through my hair.

"Is this about last night?"

Last night. The first time I slept with Ellis in three years, the best sex I've had in about as long. The way he looked when he thought I had been with other men. The jealousy on his face. And yeah, I bought the lube in a moment of weakness stupidly thinking I could replace him. Thinking I could find someone in the city, accept the truth about myself and pretend it had nothing to do with him.

That bottle never even got close to being opened.

I thought he'd be happy, being together again. I thought that's what he wanted, but he never really shook off the anger at me, and I'm starting to think his little threat the other day about never going back down that road with me was true, and that feels like knives in my chest.

I let out a deep sigh.

"I don't know."

She picks up my phone, seeing the picture of Preston on the screen. Then, she kisses the top of my head and sets it back down. "Do you want to talk about it?"

No, I don't.

But not talking about it has been my MO for as long as I can remember, and look where that's gotten me. Fuck maybe Preston's death wasn't the catalyst after all. Maybe I never had it together even then. Zara admitted she loved me long before the crash, but I had walls up long before she found her way back to Del Rey.

"Ellis and I did a lot more than hook up in Amsterdam," I mutter against the skin of her knee.

"I figured that much out."

"He was the first man…no, the only man I have ever been with. I thought it was just sex, and at first, I think it was."

"Did you love him?"

My throat starts to ache with the emotion I'm holding back. Did I? Do I still?

"Yes," I whisper, shutting my eyes and letting her stroke my head.

"What happened?"

My eyes squeeze closed, painful memories resurfacing. "I fucked up."

I tell her everything. From the first time to the end, the most shame I have ever felt in my life. The point in my story where I hated myself more than ever before.

"Oh, Nash," she whispers, placing her lips on the top of my head.

"What do I do now?" I ask, not even bothering to fight these fucking tears as they land against the skin of her legs.

"What do you want?"

"I don't know." Which is a lie. I know what I want. What I don't know is if asking for what I want is worth the risk of being disappointed, rejected and left with nothing.

"I think you do know."

She pulls my head back, peering down into my eyes. Hanna is so fearless, flawless, and with her I don't feel afraid of what I could become. She makes it so easy to be the man I want to be.

Leaning forward, she kisses my lips.

"What if I want both of you?" I whisper, pulling her to my lap and squeezing her as tight as I can. "I want it to stay like this. I don't want this week to end."

"Neither do I," she whispers, kissing my cheek, her lips trailing over my beard and down to my neck.

"Even after what I just told you? After what I did to him."

"Nash, this is how you are. The harder you love, the more you fight. You made a mistake, but you need to make it right. Apologize to him. Prove to him you're not going to hurt him again."

"Why would he take me back?"

Holding my face in her hands, she kisses me again. "Because he loves you."

27

I HAVE NEVER HAD SO much sex in my life. Even if I could keep my hands off of Ellis, I wouldn't want to.

What started as just once and just to see if I liked it has become an addiction. Ellis's touch consumes me, day and night. After work every day, I go to his apartment where we fuck almost immediately then usually again after dinner and sometime in the middle of the night. Most of the time, I bottom and sometimes, he does. Either way, it's fucking mind-blowing.

There's something about the way he is with me. How it

doesn't feel wrong or strange. Like nothing about me has changed.

It's been over three months since the first time. One Saturday evening, we're lying naked in his bed, both of us putting off ordering something for dinner, and he's lying between my legs, trailing his fingers over the plane of my stomach. If he hadn't just sucked the life out of my cock, it'd be aroused and ready for more.

"I have bad news," he says without looking up at me.

"What?" I'm scrolling mindlessly through my phone, but I set it aside to look down at him. There are a million things he could say right now. Ellis and I never really established the boundaries or labels for whatever this is, but I know he's not fucking anyone else strictly because he is literally always with me.

"My contract with the company is being absolved at the end of the quarter."

"What?" I snap.

"This is what happens. I'm a temporary contractor. These things only last so long. I thought I had until the end of the year, but they want to cut it off in October."

I don't speak because I'm waiting for him to drop the weight he's holding over me, ready to crush me.

"I can do some freelance jobs for now. My work visa isn't up for another year, so I don't need to leave right away."

"What are you trying to say?"

"I'm saying I'm going to stay here for you, you stubborn ass." He places a kiss on my stomach, and I get a sick feeling in my stomach.

"Why would you do that?"

"What do you mean why? Do you want me to leave?" He's getting defensive, and I'm suddenly regretting the way I answered him just now, so I drop it.

"Of course, I don't want you to leave…but I just feel weird, you staying for me."

"I'm staying for us," he mumbles with a little affection lacking in his tone as he climbs off me, grabbing his underwear and getting dressed quickly and walking out of the bedroom and into the kitchen.

Us.

Fuck, I still haven't even told my dad I'm here with him let alone fucking…and what, dating him? What am I supposed to do? Come out? It doesn't feel right. I can't.

I mean…I don't want to do it with anyone else, but that's because I trust Ellis. We're friends. Best friends. My brain does a little dance of denial over and over as it often does when I get lost in my thoughts when my phone rings.

Looking down, I see Zara's picture on the screen.

Fucking great. There's still a little buzz of worry or excitement when she calls. Worry because I don't want her telling me something bad happened between her and my dad, but then there's also excitement because…well, I'm still a fucking idiot after all.

"Hey," I say into the phone.

"I didn't wake you, did I?" she asks, and already I can tell there's some hesitation in her voice. Something's going on.

"No. What's wrong?" I cut to the chase.

"Nothing's wrong."

"You're calling to tell me something, I can tell. Is Dad okay?"

"He's fine, and yeah, I did call to tell you something, but nothing is wrong," she says with tightness in her voice.

"God, don't tell me you're pregnant," I say in a joking manner, but I guess I shouldn't joke about that. Sure, they've been fucking for less than a year, but it doesn't take long to make a baby, and I bet the asshole still has it in him. Zara's only twenty-five, and she'll probably want kids.

"I'm not pregnant."

"Thank God for that."

"Your dad proposed." She says it so bluntly it causes me to freeze. It hits me a little harder than I expect.

"And?"

"And I said yes."

"Fuck, it's a little fast, don't you think?" I snap.

"No, I don't."

"You look like a gold digger."

There's silence on the line, and maybe she's trying to gauge whether or not I'm kidding, and fuck, so am I.

"I knew you were going to be an asshole about it," she mutters. "He didn't want me to call because he knew you were going to be like this."

"Maybe because I fucked you first. Because you were mine first." I'm shouting now, to the point where Ellis is now standing in the doorway, and I wish he'd leave. I already know how he feels about the whole situation with my dad and Zara and his judgment is the last fucking thing I need right now.

"I thought we were over this!" she shouts, and I hear the shake in her voice.

"Oh, trust me, I'm over it. I've moved on, Zara. Very fucking moved on." I throw my phone across the room, but it's not enough.

"You okay?" he asks, staying in the doorway.

"I'm fine," I mutter, getting up and dressing quickly. Why do I give a shit if they're getting married? Good for them. This is what I wanted for her.

It feels like too much too fast. Ellis telling me he's staying for me, and now this. She's marrying him. I'm such a fucking idiot. I told her I loved her, and she's marrying him. She lied to me when she told me she loved me.

A bout of tunnel vision hits me as Ellis steps toward me. "Hey, want a drink?" He touches my arm and I quickly swat him away.

"We're not a fucking couple," I snap, and he flinches, taking his hand away. "You keep acting like this is a relationship or something, and it's not. If your contract is up, then go. I don't care. I'm not asking you to stay for me."

He doesn't say anything. That's the worst fucking part. He just stands there and takes it, letting me pummel him with words that mean nothing to me. Pretending he means nothing to me, but I'm not doing this again. I'm not going to be such a fucking idiot for someone else, spill my heart and say words like "I love you" when the other person doesn't give a shit about me.

"Who was that?" he asks. "Was that her? You're being an asshole to me because your ex-girlfriend called?"

"This is just how I am, Ellis. You should know that by now. I'm not cut out for long-term. And this…" I say gesturing between us. "This shit has reached its expiration date."

"You want to fuck other people? Then fuck other people."

"I used to look up to you. Fuck, I thought you were a God, but now I get it, Ellis. You just need someone to worship you. And you got in my fucking head, had me thinking I liked this shit."

Storming out of the room, my heart is pounding in my ears. Somewhere in the back of my head I'm thinking, this is salvageable. And maybe I don't want it to be salvageable. He's hot on my heels, quick to reply, "You seemed to really like this shit while I was blowing you."

I'm too hot, too angry, too destructive, and I react on

instinct, swinging around and throwing my fist at his face. Making contact, feeling his cheekbone under my fist, breaks me. But not as much as the words that fly out of my mouth. "I'm not a fucking fag like you."

His brown eyes stay trained on me, wide and angry as I tear open the front door and leave his apartment for the last time.

The loneliness drops like a bomb, hitting me hard as soon as I'm outside. But at least it's familiar, comfortable, like coming home and breathing fresh air for the first time. I wasn't happy with him. I was delusional. I can never let my guard like that again.

28

THERE'S NOT A REAL OPPORTUNITY TO TALK TO ELLIS IN the next couple of days. Work consumes us. And he's giving me a cold shoulder, a defense mechanism, which I understand. Hanna and I haven't spoken about what we talked about in my office either.

We both admitted what we wanted out of this, but it feels so hard to admit again. Is this crazy to want to keep them both? Be in some fucked up relationship together?

When I'm with them both, I'm free to be myself. I don't feel so out of control. They give me stability. Ellis takes the control and Hanna takes the pain. But do I offer them anything in return? Are they happy here? And can it last?

Fuck, I don't care.

On the day of the launch, we have to fly into the city to meet with the previous owners, sign some shit and finalize the deal. I hate this part. Fuck, I hate it all. The formalities, the paperwork. I just want to work, make the shit, and watch my company grow, so I guess I should like this more than I do.

What I do like is climbing into the two-seater with Ellis. He's wearing a pair of dark sunglasses, his golden hair combed perfectly to the side, his broad shoulders filling out a dark blue fitted suit. He catches me staring for a moment as we sit in the helicopter before takeoff.

"You look funny flying a helicopter in a suit," he says. "Can't you hire someone to pilot?"

With a smile, I shrug. "Wildes belong in the pilot seat." Then just as I start up the rotors, I glance up. "I can teach you how to fly if you want."

His head turns in my direction, my heart practically deafening me as it beats in my chest. It's the first time we've talked about anything past tonight. There is no tomorrow for us, so I know why he's looking at me like that.

"Yeah, maybe someday."

I don't respond before pulling off. Ellis holds a hand up toward Hanna who is standing on the patio, watching us leave and waving with a sad smile on her face.

The ride is short but silent which makes for awkwardness when I know we both have so many thoughts rolling around in our heads.

"This trip has flown by," he says, staring out the window.

"Yeah, it has."

Awkward silence again.

"I couldn't have done it without you," I say, keeping my voice deep and calm, not letting any of my nerves show.

"Yes, you could have." He looks at me, and it drives me wild.

Suddenly, my heart is pounding. This week is over. We're about to sign the papers and the deal is through. Ellis won't need to stay anymore. He'll leave, and this whole thing will be a memory, just like Amsterdam.

Say something, Nash. Tell him to stay. Tell him you're sorry, you piece of shit.

The words weigh heavy in my gut, so heavy I can't speak them. I can't bring myself to tell Ellis I fucked up, I was a coward, and what I did to him that day was the worst fucking thing I've done in my life, and I don't want Hanna without him.

"You're not going to let her go back to her mother's, are you?" he asks coldly.

"Of course not."

"Good. Convince her to stay on Del Rey for a while. If she could find some work and support herself, she'll find the confidence she needs."

He keeps talking about her like he won't be around… of course because I told him he wouldn't.

It grows silent again, and it feels like the moment has passed so I keep quiet, but I'm dying to tell him to stay. I wish it were that easy. But I'm not stupid, and I know it's not.

We land a few minutes later, and then it's a whirlwind. My dad meets us at the helipad, and the three of us walk together into Wilde Aviation headquarters where we meet with a team of lawyers, the previous owners, and even a few members of the press. My hands are shaking, so I keep them in my pockets, trying to look calm.

I think Ellis picks up on it because he doesn't leave my side, whispering reminders in my ear every few moments, keeping me grounded.

The whole thing goes by so quickly the next moment I blink, Wilde Aviation has acquired an entire corporation and fleet of fixed wing airplanes, including three manufacturing plants, and ten thousand employees.

"You okay?" Ellis asks, his hand on my back.

Stretching my neck in this suit, feeling claustrophobic for a moment, I adjust my jacket. "I'm fine."

I'm ready to get back to the island. The papers have been signed, and everyone is milling around the conference room talking, and it'd be rude for me to leave, so I wait, saying my goodbyes to everyone and putting on a front of complete control, because least of all, I feel Alistair's eyes on me through the whole thing.

He's proud, I can see that, but it doesn't relieve any of the pressure that comes with his scrutiny.

The rest of the day moves in a blur, and it's not until we reach the helicopter that I finally breathe.

"I'm proud of you," my dad says, clapping a hand on my back. "This was a big deal, and you guys did a great job." As he shakes Ellis's hand, I feel my heart rate start to elevate.

"I'll see you tonight at the party," I say to him, desperate to get away.

"See you tonight," he says with hesitation as he climbs into the car, glaring at me through the corner of his eye as he drives away.

"It's hot as fuck out here," I growl, tearing off my jacket.

"Hey, you okay?" Ellis asks as we walk out to the aircraft.

"I just want to go home." This is all happening too fast. We have to be back in a few hours for the party, and then he's leaving, and she's never going to forgive me if I let him leave like this. As we reach the helicopter, I spin around and point a finger at his chest. And of course, I don't say what I really need to say. I take the easy way out.

"She needs you too, you know. I can't help her alone. I'm too busy with work anyway and if she really needs help getting back on her feet without that bitch controlling her, she'll need you too, and you started this whole thing—"

"Nash." His strong hand clasps the back of my neck as he pulls me toward him, placing his forehead against mine. "Calm down. Breathe."

"I'm fine."

"I'll stay to help her if that's what you want. I can stick around for a couple more weeks if that's enough. Just relax."

My hands press against his chest, and I glance to the side, checking for anyone to see us, but there's not a soul around, so I press him against the side of the helicopter, taking his mouth with mine, but he doesn't kiss me back.

My heart lands against the cement as I pull back and look him in the eye. "Fuck, Ellis, give me another chance. Can't we just put that shit behind us?"

His jaw clenches as he stares at me. "I haven't made it this far by making dangerous decisions, Nash, and giving you another chance would be the most dangerous decision I could possibly make. Loving you is dangerous, Nash."

"For Hanna…you know she wants this. She needs both of us."

"You want me to believe you've changed, but if this week has proven anything to me, Nash, it's that you haven't changed at all. You still protect yourself first. You don't give your trust or control to anyone else, and you refuse to be vulnerable. Not even for a fucking second. You want to prove to me you've changed and giving you my heart again won't end the same way it did last time, then go tell your dad right now. Or better yet, tell her. Tell Zara you've moved on and you love someone else."

He pulls his phone out of his pocket and holds it in front of himself. "Here, call her now."

"It's not that easy. I'll tell them but not like this."

"That's right. On your terms, always on your terms."

Pulling his hand off my neck, he moves himself away, and I feel my chest start to seize up at the realization that this is it. I've lost him and I can't get him back. He's right. Ellis is a practical guy. He makes smart decisions, and he doesn't play games. It's one of the things I love about him. He's strong, smart, and confident. That means he doesn't give assholes like me a second chance.

"Come on," he says. "We still have a beautiful woman to show off at a party, and as long as she needs us, I'll be there for her." Then he glares at me. "But this thing between us…it's over."

29

"You cannot go to the party like that," I say to Nash as he steps out of the shower, holding a white towel around his waist.

"Well, I was planning on getting dressed," he answers with a laugh, looking down at his still wet chest. Stepping up to him, I run my hands through his unruly hair.

"I was talking about this."

"Well, it's a little late to go to the barber." He looks into the mirror, and as much as I love the thickness of his beard and the long brown waves that hang in his face, it's not the look of a powerful CEO. It's the look of a young man who works too much and neglects his appearance.

"Well, lucky for you…I'm not too bad with a pair of scissors."

He stares at me skeptically in the mirror. "I don't think so."

"Come on," I say with a roll of my eyes as I pull him toward the kitchen.

A few moments later, I have him sitting on a chair over a layer of towels as I chop inches off the mop on his head. When Ellis enters in his black on black suit, Nash and I both freeze.

"What's going on in here?" he asks like he doesn't look like a God entering the room in that tux.

"Umm…Mr. Wilde needed a little trim. What do you think?"

Stepping back, I take in the handiwork so far. You can actually see Nash's eyes now. I kept it long, just above his ears but cleaned up around the edges.

Ellis approaches, looking down at him. "We'll have to do something about this," he says, stroking the thick hair on Nash's face.

"I can trim my own beard," he mumbles.

Ignoring him, Ellis takes off his jacket and picks the clippers up off the table. Kneeling down in front of Nash, they stare at each other, the intensity palpable as Ellis slips the guard across Nash's beard, trimming it up and straightening the edges. When he's done, he runs his thumb over Nash's lower lip, and suddenly it feels like the oxygen has been stolen from the room. I keep waiting for him to kiss him, but he doesn't. Instead, he stands up and steps away.

The tension between these two has grown since that night in Ellis's room. I had no idea watching them together would have the effect on me it did. And I don't just mean it was the hottest thing I've ever seen in my life, but it tore my heart straight out of my chest. I fell hard for them that night. I never wanted to have them both so much in my life. To be a part of that, a part of their relationship, their love, their life…it's all I want now.

And it consumes me.

But Ellis is still holding Nash at arm's length. He senses what I've sensed in Nash. That until Nash lets go and accepts this part of himself, truly giving himself over to someone else, it will never be safe to really love him.

I know it too, but it's too late for me.

I'm a good deal more reckless than Ellis. He will remain guarded, but I'm throwing myself headfirst into what will probably be the biggest heartbreak of my life.

"Shouldn't you be getting yourself ready?" Ellis asks, looking at me. I'm in nothing but a robe, but my hair and makeup are already done.

"All I have to do is slip my dress on."

"Can I help?" he asks with a coy smile.

"I think I can handle it."

"I'll go wash all this hair off." Nash interrupts us before disappearing down the hall, leaving Ellis and me alone in the kitchen. As I start cleaning up, I feel him approach me from behind. Wrapping his arms around my waist, I turn and gaze up into his eyes. I'm hit with a wave of sadness thinking about him leaving, especially after knowing how badly Nash wants him to stay. How much we both want him to stay. But I won't say the words I know need to come from Nash.

"Did something happen between you two?" I ask.

"Nothing at all."

It's a cold, emotionless answer, and I know it's not one-hundred-percent true.

"Listen, Hanna. I don't want you going back to living with your mother. You should stay here until you can get back on your own two feet, okay?"

"And what about you?" I ask. "Where will you be?"

There's a hint of sadness in his eyes. "You know I can't stay."

I know the reason he can't stay is because of the man in the shower now. Dammit, Nash. Just be honest with him. Apologize. Tell him how you really feel.

"I wish you would," I whisper as he leans down, placing his lips against mine. I try to absorb his kiss, his taste, everything about him. Ellis feels so perfect for me it breaks my heart knowing he can't be mine because our hearts both belong to the same person.

"You know if you need me, I'll do anything. You know that, right?"

Letting out a breath, I nod.

"You're staying until tomorrow at least, right?" I need one more night with Ellis, one more night with both of them. One more night of us.

His eyes brighten with a smile. "Of course."

A few moments later, Nash emerges from his room. He's in a dark blue suit with black accents. His beard is clean, and his hair has been fixed to the side with some product. He looks good enough to eat, and I'm already anxious to bring them both back here tonight. I wish the party was over already.

How the fuck did I get so lucky? This is too much for one woman.

There's an almost silent groan from Ellis's chest as we watch Nash cross the window toward the door.

"Okay, okay, my turn," I say, skipping out the door, toward the guest house. After slipping into the dress and fixing my makeup where Ellis kissed me, I stare at myself in the mirror. I can't be the only one who notices the way I fill out this dress more than I once filled my ballet costumes or how I find myself smiling by default instead of forcing it.

I mean, it's no revelation I'm happier on this private island with two hot rich men, but it's about so much more than that. It's about being seen, listened to, loved. But I can't really stay here, can I? What kind of life would that be?

And if Ellis leaves…me and Nash alone?

To be honest, I'm scared, but I can't think about that now.

Right now, things are good.

Walking across the long drive toward the waiting helicopter, the two men standing there both turn back and watch me as I approach. I can't wait to be near them, in their arms.

Neither of them move as I get closer until Nash steps forward, putting an elbow into Ellis's chest as if to beat him to me. Wrapping his arms around my waist, he moves in for a kiss.

"No, you'll mess up my lipstick!" I whine, pushing him away.

"Oh, I'm messing up that lipstick at some point tonight."

He settles for a pinch of my ass as I move toward the door of the helicopter. Ellis holds it open and helps me in.

As we enter the party, I stand between the two of them, not taking sides or leaning toward one more than the other. As far as everyone is concerned, I'm here with Ellis, but I want to be between them…figuratively and literally.

"You have no idea how much I want to claim you as mine right now," Nash whispers into my ear as we stop by the door.

"Play nice. Don't you think I'm thinking the same thing? Every girl in this room is drooling over you in that tux."

"Well, there's only one I'm going home with."

I hum as he touches my back, and I smile up at him. Ellis takes my hand, pulling me toward him as Nash gives his attention to a man reaching out to shake his hand.

"Jealous?" I whisper as we move together through the crowd.

"You're turning me into an animal in that dress."

"That's the point," I mumble.

Ellis and I linger on the sidelines as Nash is absorbed by the crowd, greeting everyone and giving them each his best fake smile. It feels strange to leave him alone. I wish I could be at his side so he wouldn't have to be alone. One glance up at Ellis, and I see the same look in his eyes.

Just then, I spot Zara and Alistair across the room, so I pull Ellis in their direction.

"Holy shit, Hanna. You look phenomenal!" Zara says as she leans in for a hug.

"Stop. So do you," I reply, and she does. She's so petite and cute in black next to Alistair who is sporting a deep gray suit.

The launch party drags, and we hardly see Nash all night. Ellis keeps me close to his side all night, giving harsh glares to men who stare at me a second too long.

"You're being strangely possessive tonight," I whisper as he hands me a flute of champagne.

"I know what these men are thinking when they glare at you like they own you, and it's making me irritable."

"What about that one?" I ask, nodding to Nash. "He's been watching me all night too."

Ellis smiles into his drink, which makes me laugh.

"I like you when you're jealous," I say, leaning close,

but not too close. "Always so calm and collected, it makes me want to flirt with everyone in this room just to rile you up."

"You do and you'll be regretting it later."

My cheeks flush hot. "Is that a threat…or a promise?"

A moment later, feeling restless and well, bored, I get an idea. "What do you say we rile him up a little? Give him something interesting to look at?"

"What do you have in mind?"

Taking his hand, I slip away taking him with me as I exit the conference room.

"Did he see us leave together?" I ask.

"Naturally."

With a smile, I lead Ellis down the long open corridor. It's a large building, and I've been here a couple of times before, and I know there's another banquet hall on the other side of the stairs.

The sound of the party fades behind us as we walk. I shoot him a mischievous smile as I turn into the silent dark hallway just past the stairs, pulling him in with me.

As soon as we are alone in the empty room, his hands are around my waist.

"He's not going to like this," he whispers, pushing me against the wall.

His lips land against my neck, his smooth beard against my collarbone as he kisses me.

"That's the idea," I gasp as his hand slips under the slit of my dress, growling as he finds the moist lace of my panties. As Ellis drops to his knees, shoving my dress up to my waist, I pull my phone out of the deep pocket of the dress. I nearly drop it as he buries his nose between my legs and inhales like it's his favorite drug.

I let out a moan as he slips the fabric to the side and

runs his tongue along the moisture, devouring me frantically like he's in a hurry to get me screaming his name.

A muffled cry escapes my lips because he most definitely is going to get me there in record time. "Fuck, Ellis."

With one hand clutching the hair on the back of his head and my phone in the other, I turn on the camera and snap a picture at the exact moment a quick and intense orgasm shudders through me. The flash lights up the room and I open my eyes to find a picture of me, seedy and dark, Ellis's face smashed into my pussy and a look of pure ecstasy on my face.

That will do just fine, I think as I send it to Nash in our group text message.

"Did you send it?" he asks as he stands up.

"We will have hell to pay," I answer with a laugh.

"I can't wait."

30

I'M LITERALLY IN THE MIDDLE OF A CONVERSATION WITH MY new head engineer in the fixed wing program when my phone buzzes. I know what it is before I even glance discreetly at the screen.

Those mother fuckers.

The picture is dark and red, her dress around her waist and Ellis face-first in my favorite cunt. All while I'm stuck here talking to a bunch of assholes I don't want to be talking to.

When I look up, Ellis walks in, stealing the air from the room as he so often does. And the asshole has the nerve to wipe the corner of his mouth with his thumb as he stares right into my eyes.

A second later, Hanna is by his side, clinging to his arm, and I can't help myself. Hooking my finger at her, I keep a professional facade up as I beckon her over. I'm tired of her putting so much space between us. The engineer's wife is droning on about something I'm not even paying attention to as Hanna reaches my side.

"Well, I don't believe we've met," her husband says, looking at Hanna. I want to fire his ass immediately for the stupid smile on his face.

Instead, I hide the fact I'd much rather everyone in this fucking room vacate except for two specific people.

"I'm sorry. Please let me introduce my friend, Ms. Hanna Thurber. Ms. Thurber was the principal dancer for the city's ballet company."

His wife gasps. "Oh my gosh, I recognize you."

Hanna immediately clenches up next to me, which is a pity considering she's probably just a couple of minutes post orgasm. But I can imagine after her public breakdown last year, being recognized isn't always the reaction she's looking for.

"We saw you in Swan Lake years ago. You were…well, you were phenomenal."

Hanna's grip on my arm relaxes, and a wave of pride rushes through me as I stare at her.

"That was my first professional production," she replies, biting back her smile.

"I'll never forget that ballet," the woman says, almost looking emotional. "It was by far my favorite."

"Mine too," Hanna replies.

"Are you still with the company? I'd love to see you dance again."

Hanna handles this with so much grace, it's unbelievable. With a pleasant smile and a look of gratitude, she simply replies, "I'm actually retired. But I'm honored to hear you say that."

"Well, good for you," the woman replies.

They talk a moment longer about ballet, and if Hanna wasn't the center of attention, I would end this conversation quickly, but I don't want to steal this from her.

My dad has other plans because just then he steps up to the podium and calls my name, asking me to say a few words.

Fuck, I hate this part.

But I manage it without looking like a complete idiot. Standing at the front of the room, next to him, I do my best to address everyone, but I only see two people.

The rest of the party wraps up quickly, and I lose track of Hanna for a moment as we say our goodbyes, and I'm crossing the room in a hurry before I feel a hand on my arm. Spinning around, I come face to face with Zara.

"Hey!" she says, stopping me as my eyes still dance around the room. "I haven't been able to say anything to you all night."

"Oh, sorry. It was busy."

She's being strange, looking at me with skepticism as she forces a smile. I know her well enough to know her real ones to know that's not it.

Her hand lands on my arm. "You know we're proud of you, right?"

I scoff, rolling my eyes. "Don't say it like that. It's weird."

There's a hint of humor in her eyes. "Well, whatever. You know what I mean."

I try to relax for a moment, stopping my search for Hanna as I let myself talk to Zara for a moment. "You look beautiful tonight." And she does with a new glow in her cheeks and sleek black dress I keep my eyes from glancing down.

"I'm sorry you had to third wheel it with them," she says carefully.

Shrugging in response, I run my hands through my hair, messing up the product that held it in place. "It's fine. Not like I have time to find a date."

"You should find time, Nash. I hate thinking about you out there by yourself all the time."

Fuck, this is awkward. Why is she telling me this? Because she feels bad for leaving me alone? I wish she wouldn't. With what I have planned this evening, I'm very glad my dad and Zara moved out.

"Are you sure there isn't anyone…"

My eyes widen as I glare at her. "What? No."

"You could tell me…if there was."

"Why are you being so fucking weird. I told you there was no one."

"Jesus, calm down," she says, putting her hands up. "I just…noticed your attention across the room all night." Her eyes glance over my shoulder, focusing on something, and as I turn, my gaze lands on Ellis standing with my dad, and my breath starts to stutter in my chest.

What the fuck is she implying? She couldn't possibly know… How could she?

"I don't know what you're talking about," I snap. I want to say something about how he's my friend or make up *some* excuse as to why I did keep staring at him all night because fuck, look at him. It's almost hard to focus on him, like the way he looks in that suit literally hurts my eyes. But no. I'm not even going to acknowledge what she's implying.

"Okay…" she says carefully. "Not that there's anything wrong—"

"Zara, stop." It comes out too harsh, and we definitely catch the attention of a few people around us, so I do my best to recompose myself, smiling politely.

"It's been a long day. I'm out of here."

Before I can leave, she grabs me and pulls me into a hug. I can't help myself from wrapping my arms around her waist and squeezing her closer. Everything that used to bond us still does. Her sister and my brother still died in that crash together, so nothing that happened after changes how we feel about each other now.

But I realize as we separate, I'm not hiding things as well as I thought I was. And that only makes me irritable. When I try to keep people out, they still find their way in.

Pushing the thought away, I grab the two only people I care about right now and practically drag them out into the night.

Climbing into the helicopter that night, as soon as the doors shut, I let out a gruff exhale. Reaching across the seat, I grab Hanna by the back of the neck and crash my mouth against hers, smearing her perfect red lipstick across her face as I kiss her deeply.

I can feel Ellis's eyes on us from the backseat. He deserves so much worse after that stunt they pulled at the party.

"Just take me home," she whispers as soon as I let her up for air. My dick is already hard in my pants as I start up the aircraft. This flight is going to be way too fucking long.

She squirms in her seat the entire way, and no one says a word. I feel his eyes on me as I fly, but I can't look at him. There's too much tension in our glances. Too many things left unsaid. Too many thoughts about what Zara said.

Once we land, I tear off my mic and pull her face back

to mine, devouring her mouth. The electricity between us burns, and I'm waiting to explode. My hands are ravenous, unbuckling quickly and pulling her dress down until I have a handful of her breast against my palm, giving her a harsh squeeze.

I can't stop kissing her, practically pulling her into my lap as I get a taste of every part of her body I can reach.

"Should we make him watch?" I ask, my lips against her neck. Ellis is still sitting behind us, watching with that lust-filled gaze. "After that little stunt you two pulled at the party."

She smiles. "I think he likes to watch."

"Did that feel good? His face between your legs, making you come with his tongue?" I ask, slipping down the zipper of her dress fast enough to make her gasp. It feels a shame to nearly tear it, but I'm desperate to have her naked.

"Yes," she breathes.

"Were you thinking about me when he did it?"

"Yes."

Once she shimmies the red fabric down her body, I slide my hand into the front of her lace panties, gliding easily through the moisture pooling there. I'm having a very hard time taking my time right now. I mean, we can't even wait until we're out of the aircraft. But it's been a stressful day, and I'm tense, ready to explode. Ellis seems to pick up on this as he opens his door on my side, climbing out and opening my door next.

"I get the feeling Nash is a little tense tonight," he says. Looking me in the eye, he says in his deep authoritative voice. "He's been thinking about those beautiful red lips of yours around his cock all night, haven't you?"

She bites her lip at him as she shifts in her seat until she's kneeling. When her hands touch my belt, I shudder.

Having their attention on me, both of them, I feel like I'm flying, weightless. As she unfastens my pants, Ellis slowly pulls my tie from my neck, gazing into my eyes. Just as she places her lips against my cock, he slams his lips against mine, kissing me harshly.

I am consumed, drowning in this pleasure.

His mouth on my mouth, hers on my cock. He pulls at the buttons of my shirt, and I'm breathless, gasping for air, and all I can think is how I never want this to end. This feeling right now could last me the rest of my life, and I'd finally be happy, at peace. And not just the pleasure, but the comfort. They are my safety net.

As she hums around me, I push her away quickly, afraid I'll come too fast. In a frantic rush to get him as naked as I am, I tear at his buttons while she trails her lips up my stomach and everywhere but directly on my dick, which only drives me crazier.

Ellis is still standing in the open doorway while Hanna and I are still squeezed into the helicopter, putting his cock at the perfect angle for me. Once I have his pants undone, I eagerly reach into his boxers to wrap my hand around him, loving the way he moans my name as I do.

With his hand around my neck, he pulls me out of the cockpit, and we help her out after us, but we still don't make it to the house. Standing outside next to the helicopter in scraps of clothes and mostly naked, we resume our kissing, his lips on mine, then hers on his and then I lose track of whose hands are where.

"I think it's his turn, Hanna," I whisper before kissing him again. She drops to her knees in front of him and takes him into her mouth, eliciting a low growl from his chest. Pulling away, I watch as he bites his lip, and I run my thumb across the bottom one, licking a line from his chin to his ear. His fingers press harshly into my back.

"So tense," he whispers as his hand engulfs my cock. "Why do you keep stopping us? Let it go."

"But—"

She must have heard him because she turns right back toward me, swallowing me down in one strong pull, and I feel myself seizing up.

He moves away from my front to hold me from behind. I feel the warmth of his kiss against my neck as his hand roams my chest. Looping an arm around my waist and one around my head, he pulls my weight onto his chest.

"Just let go, Nash. We've got you."

Hanna's mouth pumps harder, and I lose all control. Ellis's erection presses firmly against my back as I let out a heavy groan, coming hard into Hanna's mouth.

I feel her throat working as she swallows it down, slowing her motion and running her hands up my thighs. I feel like heavy mud, lax in Ellis's arms.

"Fuck…" I say as he runs his hands across my chest.

"Feel better?" he whispers in my ear.

Opening my eyes, I stare straight ahead. Hanna stands up, and immediately kisses Ellis over my shoulder. Pulling away from his lips, the three of us pressed together and impossibly close, smiles suddenly warm on each of our faces.

"Why don't we go inside?" Ellis says, nudging us toward the house. Leaving our discarded clothes on the ground, we walk together toward the patio door.

Once inside, I can't let go of Hanna, thinking of how beautiful she was swallowing it down the way she did.

"You two, go to the bedroom. I'll be there in a moment," he says from the bar.

He doesn't have to tell us twice. It's only a moment after we get to the room when Ellis follows us in, handing me a glass of the whiskey we drank the night in the pool.

"You have a seat right there. Relax."

With a glance toward the chair in the corner, I do as he says. I'm in nothing but my pants, still undone and hanging open.

Then, I watch as Ellis finishes the job of taking off his clothes. He turns toward Hanna, and I enjoy the point of view for a moment, being the one watching, getting to be the outsider, but not feeling like the outsider.

Ellis leans down, hooking his hands under her thighs as he lifts and wraps her legs around his waist. She lets out a playful laugh as she kisses him, and I can't help but smile. This feels so good, being with them like this.

He takes her to the bed, and my dick starts to rouse already as he tosses her onto the mattress, climbing over her like a prowling animal. He stretches his body over hers, and I watch as he presses kisses down her chest until he licks and nips at the tawny buds of her breasts. She moans, groaning even louder as his fingers drift to the apex of her thighs. Her back arches as he presses one inside her, then her head turns and she stares at me, the sweet sounds of her pleasure through her lips as our eyes meet.

I tug my bottom lip between my teeth as he enters her with force. It feels like he's entering me at the same time, and my breath hitches in my chest as he slides as far in as he'll go. She lets out a throaty cry, grabbing for his back, the bed sheets, the headboard as he thrusts harder and harder.

Before long, my cock is ready for another round, but I'm not ready yet. I like watching. I like the way my chest grows hot seeing them together, and it's not jealousy. It's...pride. I feel so intensely for each of them that seeing them together feels like my heart is about to explode in my chest.

Hanna's breathing gets higher and more shallow, her

legs clinging to him as I know she's about to come, but he doesn't stop. He notices it too, picking up his pace and keeping up his exact cadence until she's shivering and screaming.

He kisses her hard as she comes, and I feel like I might explode right along with her. But judging by the way he's still moving, I know he's not done yet, which is good. Because I'm not done either.

Coming up for air, Ellis leans back long enough to stare down at her, brushing her hair out of her face and looking at me with a sly smile.

"I think he's ready to jump back in."

"About time," she whispers with a wicked grin as they roll over so she's on top, riding him slowly as she watches me. Getting up from my chair, I palm myself, walking toward them. Running my hands along her scalp, I grasp a handful of hair and pull her face toward me. Tangling her lips with mine, I kiss her hard, feeling her whimper into my mouth as Ellis jerks his hips upward.

I drift my hand down her spine, trailing slowly over her ass and pressing one finger over the soft entrance there. Her eyes widen as she bites her lip. When she doesn't say anything, I kiss her again and then move away toward the side table to retrieve the lube still in there.

My eyes meet his as I climb onto the bed behind her. Cool drops of lube land against the surface of my cock as I slick myself up, a shiver running up my spine watching her hips tilt for me.

"You ready?" I whisper against her back.

"Yes, please," she whines, drawing it out.

After taking a moment to prep the puckered hole, slipping a finger inside and hearing her moan, I add a second and love the way it makes her hips move faster. Then, I press the head of my cock to the tightness, pressing in, sheathed in warmth and suddenly it's like I've never felt closer to two people in my life.

The three of us cry out together. I barely move at all as Hanna rides our dicks together. She clings to Ellis with one hand and me with the other, and my eyes keep finding his as she draws herself closer and closer to another climax.

Liquid heat travels up my spine, our breaths mingling like watercolors, the three of us so blended, we're bleeding into each other, colliding into one. No longer three separate people at all. I feel him and I feel her and soon I can't tell who I am in this mixture. Soon it's just us.

She lets out a strangled cry, her nails digging into my hand as I feel Ellis's hips jerk up with the spasms of his orgasm. Hanna shudders, her legs shaking around him, and I drive into her, possessive and wild.

This is the part I love, how it feels to fall, throwing myself off the edge and spilling everything I have into her. There's a strong, broad hand clutching my leg as I let go, and it stays there throughout the entire release until I'm panting and sweaty, leaning on her but being held up by him.

Together, Hanna and I collapse, settling each of us on either side of Ellis's pounding heart. We lie there for a moment, catching our breaths and letting our heart rates settle into a normal rhythm. It's silent—a comfortable silence where none of us feel the need to speak. I feel his hand against mine as I turn onto my side.

"I don't want this week to end," she says, gasping for air.

"Hm," Ellis replies, kissing her on the forehead.

"It doesn't need to," I add.

He's still facing her, and there's fear racing down my spine as I remember what he said earlier. This is really over with him. I fucked him over too bad.

"So, what if we stay?" he asks, turning toward me. "What will you say to people when they ask about us?"

I swallow. "I'll tell them it's none of their fucking business."

"That's what I'm afraid of. You're still holding on to so much fear, Nash. You refuse to be vulnerable. So afraid of what others might think about you if they knew the truth."

"I don't care what people think."

"No, but you know letting others in means there's nothing standing between you and happiness. But you can't let yourself be happy, Nash. I don't understand why."

"I am happy," I whisper, turning onto my stomach and touching his lips. Hanna is resting her head on his chest and just looking at both of them, I feel like this thing in my chest might explode.

I can accept this. I can tell the whole fucking world I love these two people and not give a shit what they say. Fuck, I'll tell them all right now. Then…then we can just be us. Free and happy and it will all be fine.

"I'm happy too," she whispers, resting her eyes and reaching for my hand.

"Are you happy?" I whisper to him, lost in his gaze.

His jaw clenches and he lets out a heavy breath. Squeezing Hanna a little closer, he says, "I'm afraid so."

Leaning forward, I press my mouth to his, breathing in the same air and letting my tongue slip through to taste him. After slowly pulling myself away, I keep my eyes on him as I rest my head on the pillow.

I can let myself be happy. If it means keeping things the way they are right now at this exact moment, I can.

31

It's still dark out when I wake up. The bed is warm, almost too warm with bodies tangled next to me. The only sound is the A/C running, mingled with the heavy breathing of the two other people in my bed. My back is to Hanna, and when I turn over, I notice the way she's resting comfortably in his arms. Her head is on his chest, the tight black curls of her hair cascading across his arm, and I reach out to play with the softness.

My mind replays what she said last night. She wants it to stay like this, the three of us. And yeah, I want that too, but that's a stupid thing to want, isn't it? It's unrealistic, not to mention the attention we'd get. And least of all…my dad and Zara would lose their shit. It's not that I care what they think about my life now…but fuck, do I?

Fuck, then Zara's words pierce every single thought and panic worms its way in. Does she already know there's something going on with me and Ellis? This whole time I thought I was keeping a wall up, and I wasn't. I'm not being careful enough…reckless. I'm being reckless. Just like after Preston died.

And if I give in to this idea…letting Hanna and Ellis into my life. No one will think it'll last. They'll see how reckless I am, foolish, trying to replace Zara or what the three of us had. I'll look like a fucking idiot.

I can't lay here and stare at them anymore. The longer I do, the longer it starts to look like a very similar situation from three years ago, lying with Zara between us, her leaning a little closer to him. And look how that turned out.

Climbing out of bed, I walk to the bathroom, shutting myself in before I turn on the lights. The man in the mirror makes me stop. My hair is a little shorter, my beard trimmed tight. And as hard as I try to find the CEO, the man, the one who has everything together, someone like Ellis, the more frustrated I become because the guy in the mirror is still the same fuck-up who lost the only girl he ever loved to his fucking dad.

I was supposed to have it together when I went to Amsterdam, but I didn't have shit together. It was just the beginning of a slowly escalating tailspin that has now grown completely out of control. If the mess I was in before Zara came to Del Rey was bad, what is this I'm in now? There is a man and woman in my bed, and they want me to be in a relationship with *them*.

I'm a goddamn joke.

Clutching the end of the countertop between my

fingers, I take heavy slow breaths, trying to calm the manic rattling in my brain. But the voices are persistent and too fucking loud.

I'm out of control, again. I'm fucking everything up again. I own a goddamn company and I'm acting like a child.

I should have died in that crash with Preston. Or worse…I should have saved him.

If I hadn't been so selfish, so lazy, so cold and terrible, I would have made that flight with my brother, and I would have stopped him from ever flying in the bad weather that day.

Preston is dead because of me.

There's a torrent in my brain at the exact moment Ellis opens the door, and it's really just bad fucking timing.

"What happened?" he asks, deadpanned and aware, as if he knows what's going on inside my head, as if he has any fucking clue.

"Nothing," I mumble, shutting down, immediately closing up so he can't see what's behind the mask.

I step away from the counter, pushing past him toward the bedroom in a desperate attempt to flee. I need to walk away, brood alone until this terrible episode passes, and I can breathe again. But no, he pushes because that's what Ellis does.

He prods and demands and controls, leaving no room to breathe or fidget or lie. And as he grabs my arm, giving me an expression that looks almost like worry, I sneer at him.

His fingers release my arm immediately, so I guess the anger in my face was enough.

"Talk to me," he says, his deep voice carrying through the silence.

Storming out of the bedroom in my underwear, I head

straight for the bar. A drink will calm my nerves, quicker than anything else I have on hand. I sure could go for a joint right now, but I haven't kept that shit in the house in years. So straight vodka will have to do.

"Should I be worried?" he asks as he steps up behind me. He's so fucking calm, and I have the naivety to love that about him. I used to emulate him, but I should have known I'm nothing like Ellis.

So, when I realized I couldn't be him, I settled for fucking him. Or rather letting him fuck me which I guess is a more appropriate way of putting it.

Pathetic.

"Nash, talk to me, please."

"I can't do this," I say before throwing back the luke-warm vodka letting it roll down my throat like lava.

"And by this…you mean—"

"This," I bark, gesturing between us. "I can't keep lying to myself. Besides, I don't have time for a relationship with one person, let alone two. And do you have any idea what the media would do with me if they found out. What it would do to my company?"

"I won't talk down to you, Nash or treat you like you don't know what you're talking about, so I won't comment on the business part of what you just said, but if we're going to go round and round about you 'pretending' to be something you're not, then you're right. *This* isn't going to work." He gestures between us and it stings. A lot more than I expect it to.

A few hours ago, we were connecting. We were in some fucked-out bliss, but right now, I'm ruining it. I'm burning it to the ground before it even had a chance to start, and I hate myself for it. But it's not like I can tear down this wall of anger now. The vulnerable, scared version of myself beneath it is pathetic, and I don't want his sympathy or his pity. I'd rather he just fucking leave.

"Just out of curiosity, what happened between last night and just now? Why do you flip so fast from looking at me like you love me to showing me all the hatred you really feel?"

I swallow at those words. Love and hate.

"I just realized this whole time I've been trying to get back what I had with Zara and somehow settled on a cheaper version by fucking both of their best friends."

His nostrils flare, and the first thing he does, which I give him credit for, is turn back to make sure Hanna is not within earshot to hear what I just said. Then, he charges straight for me, and at first, I think he's going to hit me, and I almost wish he would. But he doesn't. Instead, with wild anger in his eyes, he presses me against the bar, his hand firm and broad on my chest.

"I hate myself for letting you in again, but I don't hate you. Because you're so fucking broken you make it impossible to hate you. And you think you're hiding how scared you are, but I see it. I always saw it. It's the part I fell in love with...both times. And this time, I had myself fooled you would let go, maybe for her, maybe because she was a soft place to land and if I had both of you, I could finally let myself love you again without being scared you would do to me what you did last time. Because I don't think you realized what you did to me, Nash. I don't think you saw how bad that killed me. And I can see by the look in your eye now this isn't what you really want. What you really want is to have someone who will protect you when you finally let go of all of this anger and misery you've trapped yourself in. I tried to be that person for you...fuck, I wanted it so bad, but I can't keep letting you break my heart just to protect yours.

"So, you can feed me all the bullshit you want about Zara and your dad and continue blaming the world for your issues, but I won't be around for it anymore."

This close, I can see the moisture in his eyes, the raw emotion because Ellis is always so pure. There are no lies or deceptions with him. So, when his eyes brim with tears, falling over his cheeks, I feel them like stones in my heart.

"Goodbye, Nash."

And just like that, his hand leaves my chest and the warmth of his body pressed so closely to mine is gone.

I did it. I did what I set out to do which was keep my heart guarded and my head focused on work and the things that really matter. And when he packs his bags and stands by the helicopter a few hours later ready to catch a ride back to the city for good, I remind myself this is what I wanted. What I need.

For the fucking life of me, I can't remember why.

Something about how pathetic I am and how I don't have time for relationships, but it all feels so forced now. My wall is fading away, so when I watch Hanna squeeze him with her face shoved against his chest, her back shuddering with sobs, I lose the will to fight anymore. She goes to her room where she stays for the rest of the day.

And Ellis gets on the helicopter, and he lets it take him far from here. I pushed him to do that. I might as well be the one in the cockpit flying the helicopter separating us.

32

I should have known it was all a dream. Did I really expect this island paradise to be real or for any of it to actually work out?

For a moment, I did. For a few brief seconds, I actually believed good things would just fall into my lap, but that's not how it works.

Since the only reasonable place for me to live outside of Del Rey is my mother's house, I decide to stay behind when Ellis leaves. Hugging him goodbye, seeing the despair and anger on his face still haunts me. He looks broken, and I don't blame him.

Nash Wilde breaks people. It's what he does. I had all

the red flags, and I knew enough about him before coming here, but he got under my skin. When he took down the mask, I saw the vulnerable boy beneath, and I gave in to my urge to heal and nurture him. What I really ended up doing was falling in love with him, with us, with everything, and it was stupid.

So fucking stupid.

Because Nash's walls are back up, and Ellis is gone.

EVERY DAY this week I've spent on the mainland, in the city, doing everything that needs to be done in order for me to start over. A new apartment, not as nice or as expensive as the last one. Renting of course because trying to put a down payment is clearly out of the question.

The second order of business, and this one took a lot less time than I expected it to, was finding work, real work. Zara offered me a teaching position at the studio, and this time I actually took it even though it won't pay the bills by itself, which brought me to *La Folie*, an upscale bistro on the main drag of the city where the manager took one look at me and offered me an immediate interview.

After a couple of days, I was offered a position as a server, and swallowing my pride, I took it. Almost immediately, I felt a little freer. I'm starting a new life, which means dreams won't fall into my lap. If I'm going to do this, I'm going to have to climb my way there.

The last thing on my list is in a manilla envelope sitting on my lap on the metro ride across town. The entire ride over, I write verses in my head, trying to calm my erratic brain. Of course, every line, thought, and feeling is of them. Nash's sea blue eyes and how they seem even bluer when he's wet. The way the sun reflects off Ellis's hair. How I can recognize each of their kisses even with my eyes closed. And the strange way being with them together was so different than being with them each alone.

Even after everything, the thought of them—of us together, calms me.

Getting off at the familiar old exit, I feel my skin start to crawl. I almost back out, almost letting the voices change my mind, and the closer I get the more nervous I get.

I need another voice to drown them out so before I turn my last corner, I stop and pull out my phone.

He answers on the first ring.

"Hanna," he says, his deep voice sending warm waves of pleasure through my body.

"Ellis."

"Are you okay?"

"I'm about to see her. Take her the papers."

He lets out a heavy sigh that sounds like relief. "I'm proud of you. You can do this."

"Thank you," I whisper, feeling the rising emotion in my throat.

"Want me to stay on the phone? I will." He sounds different, softer somehow.

"No. I just wanted to hear your voice before I go in there."

"I'm right here," he says, and I wish that were true. I wish he was right here, next to me, holding my hand, being the strength I need, the man I need. But we both know that's not an option. For one, he's still too hung up on Nash. I don't think he realizes how much he let on, how hard he fell, and how much it showed.

The other reason we could never truly be together is because we're both hopelessly stupid and our dating would only hurt the one person who hurt us most. How ridiculous is that? But Nash would always be there. He would be in every conversation, every intimate moment, every kiss, every memory. Just like he's in this conversation right now. Ellis wants to ask about Nash, but he can't. He can't ask about him, because that would let on how bad he's hurting. His pride won't let him. So, I tell him anyway.

"I'm moving out next week. I don't think he'll notice. He does nothing but work now."

"I don't care," Ellis says, cutting me off. It's just for show. I think knowing how bad Nash is will make him feel better about how bad he is.

"The other day I noticed him in his office at three in the morning. I don't know if he never went to sleep or if he woke up that early."

"Hanna."

"And when I did see him this morning, he looked like shit."

Ellis lets out a heavy sigh. After a few moments of silence, he says, "Let's have lunch next week. After you move in. I'll come over."

My throat feels tight as I nod, knowing he can't see me. "Okay. That would be nice."

"I have to get back to work, but call me after you talk to her. And Hanna…"

"Yeah?"

"You'll always have me."

My breath hitches, forgetting to take a breath for a moment as I let his voice and those words sink in. How long will this hurt? How long will I feel like this and is keeping Ellis in my life, knowing I will never be enough, really the best idea?

But who else would understand this feeling more than him? Not even Zara can sympathize. She got her happy ending. She was able to choose one.

"We'll always have each other," I add. "Just two idiots who fell in love with the same person."

I RING THE DOORBELL, which feels strange considering it's my house. She's not expecting me, and after the harsh phone conversation we had a couple of weeks ago, she's probably still angry at me. When she answers the door to our three-story row house, her face behind the screen sends a chill up my spine.

A look of disappointment washes over her. "Took you long enough. I assume you want to move home now? Your rich boyfriend finally kicked you out?"

Just ignore her. She's trying to discourage you to withhold power over you. Don't let her.

The voice in my head sounds like Ellis. And I pretend he's here, standing behind me, encouraging me to do what I need to do.

Without any greeting or response, I start. "I'm not going to come in or move home. I'm just going to say my piece and hand you this."

"What the hell is this?" she asks, pushing open the door and reaching for the envelope.

"It's a restraining order."

Her face falls, and for a minute, my heart breaks. What am I doing? She's my mother, my own flesh and blood.

You're doing this for yourself. You deserve this. I remind myself.

"Hanna," she gasps. The worst part is she never saw this coming, and not because it's a complete shock but because she never thought I'd have it in me to stand up to her.

"You've spent my entire life manipulating me, using me, and treating me like I was less than you. I've removed you from my bank account and according to this court order, you cannot contact me or come within a hundred feet of me."

She's speechless, staring at the envelope, waiting for any of this to make sense.

"I'm doing this for myself, because my entire life I've grown up believing the only way to earn your love is with ballet, to impress the world, to make up for the fact that twenty-nine years ago you made a mistake. You've made me pay for your mistakes, treating me as if I was a mistake, and because of that I will never know my own father or have a real family. For my entire life, I believed your lies about me. Every single one of them."

Her disbelief is turning to anger, and she glares up at me. "You think you can live without me?"

"I know I can," I say, interrupting her.

"You have always been so impulsive, Hanna. Who is talking you into this? What kinds of friends are you with who would tell you to do this to your own mother?"

Ignore her. Block out every word.

"This was my choice. I don't need anyone to take care of me, least of all you."

Turning around, with shaking hands, I start to walk away. She's still going on behind me, berating me, and there are still unspoken words on my tongue, but none of it matters. I wanted to tell her this doesn't have to last forever and that I want a real relationship with her, but she's too busy talking to listen. And I'm too busy moving on with my life.

33

"Are you sure there's nothing you need, sir?"

Turning back toward the girl standing in the doorway, a pleasant, doe-eyed look on her face, I smile and reply, "No, thank you, Valerie. You can go."

It's only two-thirty in the afternoon, and I see the way she chews her lip apologetically, as if she's sorry a killer blowjob can't solve my problems. I wish it could.

She waves goodbye and disappears through the apartment just when I hear the phone rings, and she answers it.

"One moment, please."

Her heels click across the marble as she comes into my office. "Sir, there's a Mr. Wilde downstairs to see you."

My heart wants to pound right out of my chest. I have half the mind to ask which Mr. Wilde she's talking about, but I don't because I know. It's not Nash.

"Send him up."

A few minutes later, the elevator door chimes and Nash's father steps into my office, a careful tight-lipped smile on his face. It's a polite, disingenuous smirk reserved for business or uncomfortable conversations. I can already see where this is going.

"I hope you don't mind me dropping in. We were in town so Zara could get something for her studio, and I took the opportunity to see you. Since we didn't really get to say goodbye."

Ah, yes. There was no warning when I left Del Rey. I boarded a flight off the island and never looked back.

"I'm glad you did," I answer cordially as I cross the room to shake his hand. There's a strange look in his eye, something uncomfortable, like he wants to say something. "Have a seat," I say gesturing to the chair in front of my desk.

"I want to thank you for helping Nash," he says, drumming his fingers on the arm of the chair.

"You don't have to thank me. I was just doing my job." I try to force a smile, but it's too hard, so I give up.

It's quiet for a moment, him just staring at me, and I try to remember we're old friends. But inside my head all I can think is Nash has his lips and jawline, and I miss Nash so much I could throw this fucking desk across the room. But I bite down those feelings.

"You did more than your job though, didn't you?"

I let out a breathy chuckle. "What do you mean?"

"I'm sorry for being so forward, but I know my son better than he thinks I do, and I saw the way he looked at you."

My mouth goes dry, and I maintain my composure, trying to act natural.

"He always looked up to you, maybe more than he looked up to me. And during this acquisition, I noticed the way he gravitated toward you, always looking for your approval, your…praise."

Forcing myself to swallow, I keep my face blank, and my eyes trained on him.

"I didn't know if you were aware of Nash's feelings toward you or if that was something you reciprocated, and I know he must have made your life hell this summer. Maybe…maybe longer."

I clear my throat, leaning forward just to shift out of the statue-like position I was sitting in. "Alistair, it's not my business to tell you anything about Nash that he's not ready for you to know."

"I'm not asking about him. I'm asking about you."

"Are you asking if I have…feelings for your son?"

"Yes."

I take three long breaths before I nod. "Yes, I do."

He rubs his face, letting out a heavy sigh before biting his bottom lip tightly. "Zara picked up on it before me. I think it was at lunch that day on the island. I was so blind, so focused on work and trying to find ways to cure him of his constant anger, but she noticed you. And it was the day of the acquisition that finally confirmed it for me."

I'm still frozen in place, like facing down a wild animal I don't want to scare. Alistair could be ready to break, yell and scream at me, maybe even hit me. It's his son, someone I knew as a child, and I've just admitted to romantic feelings for him. He doesn't know the half of it, but I'm guessing he can figure out the rest.

"I can assure you Nash and I…" I stumble on my

words, finding them hard to get out. "We have nothing between us. I'm not going back to Del Rey."

"Can I ask why it didn't work out?"

Three more long breaths I use to steady myself. "I don't think your son wants to be happy, Alistair. I don't know if he knows how."

"Do you blame me for what happened?" he asks and I know he's referring to his relationship with Zara.

"It's none of my business."

"Yes, it is. You were with him shortly after, weren't you? In Amsterdam? See, I told you I know more than he thinks I do. Of course, I thought it was just friendship."

Shifting in my chair, I reply, "Yes, I was. And no, I don't blame you."

"Zara says he still blames himself for what happened to Preston. Maybe that's why he won't let himself be happy. But I know my son, and I know if he has no anger to shield himself with, then he has nothing. He will choose misery and loneliness over vulnerability every day."

"I know he does," I say shaking my head and clenching my leg between my fingers.

"He really did give you hell, didn't he?"

I don't answer. Because what I want to say is Nash didn't give me hell. What he gave me was the complete opposite. He gave me a new perspective, something to fight for, a chance for something real, a hard-won love that didn't come easy but was worth every second.

Instead, I nod my head and try to keep my expression casual.

"Well, I'm sorry. I wish I knew how to help him, but he's twenty-eight years old. And I really hoped if Zara couldn't, you could."

I feel the blood drain from my face. "Is that…" I stand

up, unable to stay sitting as this suddenly registers. "Is that why you called? That's why you hired me?"

Now it's my turn to want to punch him. A white heat courses through my veins. The pain I'm feeling right now, this re-opened wound, is because Alistair wanted to throw someone else into the fire for his son?

He stands up, too calm for my level of anger. "Before you get upset, I called you because I remembered you were the only man my son looked up to more than me. I also knew he had a lot of anger and feelings he had still to let go of, and I knew you were the right person to help him. I'm sorry it didn't work out, but you have to understand he's my son, the only one I have left. I just don't want to see him hurting anymore."

He starts to leave, but I blurt out exactly what I'm thinking before he can disappear. "But you arc the reason he's hurting."

Alistair stops, flinching as if I hit him, but I shake my head. "I don't mean what happened with Zara. I mean… talk to your son. He's so afraid of being vulnerable because he doesn't know how. He's afraid if he ever lets down his guard, he'll disappoint you."

I'm not hoping this will fix Nash and everything will work out. There is so much more Nash needs before I would even consider going back into that mess, but I sincerely hope Alistair listens to me. I hope Nash doesn't live with this pain forever.

"Thanks," he mumbles before sending me a casual wave and walking out of the room.

34

Hanna doesn't come out of her guest house, at least not to see me. When my dad's helicopter lands on the tarmac, she emerges, and I have a feeling it might be because this is her last day here. Like the last pile of dirt on my coffin.

This is really it for me. If I couldn't make it work by now, there's no hope for me. Maybe Ellis was right. Maybe I don't know how to be happy. Maybe I don't want to be.

Sitting alone in my office on a Saturday, I watch as Zara greets Hanna, and it's not as happy as it was a couple of weeks ago. Everyone looks a little sadder these days, or maybe that's just me.

Then I watch as my dad pulls Harper's little baby carrier out of the back and takes her toward the house. My house.

You'd think living on an island would mean peace and privacy, but that doesn't seem to be the case at all. Instead, I have them in my business literally all the time. When the girls glance toward the office, I don't move. After a few seconds, they follow Alistair to the house. No one comes to get me, which is better. With any luck, I can avoid them all day.

Hanna will leave, and I don't have to bother with good-byes or the feelings that come along with them.

There's only a few minutes alone before I watch my father cross the grounds toward the office. As he pulls open the door, I do my best to look busy in hopes he won't stay long.

"You don't think I've tried to avoid life with work before?" he asks as he slips through the door.

"I'm not avoiding anything."

"Oh, because you don't have a life?" he asks.

"Something like that."

He's walking casually around the office, and I fight against the tic in my jaw as I wait for him to leave. "I saw Ellis yesterday," he says and it's probably the only thing he could say that could actually make me falter. And he definitely catches the way my eyes flash up to his face.

The office falls silent as we glare at each other. "He thought maybe it would be wise of me to listen to you. That maybe you want to talk to me."

I scoff. I'm not a fucking teenager, and I have nothing to say to him. So, I shake my head and give my attention back to my emails.

His gaze freezes on my face, and the tension strings out between us, making it hard to breathe. Finally, he settles against the desk and rubs a hand over his face. When I glance up at him, I'm nearly broken by the despondent expression on his face, with wide, tired eyes and a turned down mouth.

"You gotta give me something here, Nash. It's been five fucking years I've been trying everything I can think of to help you, and I already lost one kid. I can't lose another. Just come back to me."

Moisture pools in his eyes, and I swallow the knives in my throat.

"If you're looking for permission to be happy, to move on, you don't need it. You don't need to keep punishing yourself for what happened to Preston. If you want someone to blame, then for fuck's sake, blame me, son. Just…just stop torturing yourself."

Something breaks, and my chest quakes as I try to breathe through it. Then, the words just come out because if I just say them, then I can't take them back and I can stop holding them in and letting them fester.

"I was with Ellis in Amsterdam. For nine months, we were together…as in…he was my boyfriend. And I—" Fuck, this is hard. "I didn't tell you. But I was in love with him."

"Was?"

The tears pooling in my eyes slip out with the next blink, falling across my face and landing like bombs against the desk.

"I am. I do love him. I guess that makes me bisexual, so there you go. I mean, I am. I'm bisexual. I don't know why that was so hard to accept. But it's out now."

"Do you feel better?" he asks.

With the next exhale, my shoulders slide a little lower and the pain in my chest eases like I can breathe at last. "Yeah."

He breathes too, and I finally get the nerve to look at him. There's always an eerie feeling when I'm alone with my dad, like Preston—no, Preston's death, is there with us, between us, filling every molecule of space in the room. We can hardly see past it, but right now, he's looking at me, and it's just us. Cleared space and room to breathe.

"Good," he replies. "Are you going to call him?"

I laugh. "No. He'll probably never talk to me again."

"Worth a try. Have you tried groveling? It worked for me."

With a subtle sad smile, I shake my head. "I don't know if there's a punishment on earth that would make up for how I treated him."

He's glaring down at me with his arms crossed. "And do I want to know how Hanna fits into this equation?"

With that, I laugh in earnest. I'm not even going to answer that question, not yet at least. He doesn't push me more about it, but after a few minutes, I do finally shut the laptop and follow him out of the office toward the house.

As we step outside, he grabs my arm and pulls me toward him, wrapping his arms around me. I don't remember the last time I hugged my dad, but I don't fight as he squeezes hard. It makes me wonder why I couldn't just tell him this sooner.

After a few minutes, he lets go and we walk together toward the patio where the girls are sitting. My eyes meet Hanna's right away, and I think she knows.

A small smile lifts the corners of her lips, but I try not to let myself hope for much. She's still leaving, and Ellis is already gone.

This little moment with my dad was great, but it was far too late for me this time.

· · ·

EVERYTHING with my dad has left me feeling raw and exhausted, so after we finish lunch, I get up from the table and head inside. I just need a break from people and penetrating eyes for a moment. Standing in the kitchen, trying to decide if I need a drink with alcohol or caffeine, I hear a small cry coming from the living room, so I walk over to inspect. Harper is awake in her little car seat, clawing helplessly for a pacifier that fell out of her mouth. The buckles take me a moment to get undone, but once I do, I pull her gently out of the seat.

Her sweet blue eyes latch onto me immediately, staring up at me with her little mouth open.

"Don't look at me like that," I say to her. "I'm not the cool, fun brother. I'm the mean one."

A smile spreads across her face, putting deep dimples in her pudgy cheeks.

Jesus, she's fucking cute.

She starts rooting around for something, so I put the pacifier in her mouth and carry her in one arm to the kitchen. "The question, little sister, is vodka or coffee? What do you think?"

She's going to town on that pacifier, and I laugh. "Yeah, coffee." It's not easy, but I manage to get the machine loaded with one hand, and she hardly moves, watching every single thing I do like it's the greatest thing she's ever seen.

While I wait for the machine to brew, I look up and notice there are a pair of mismatched eyes gazing through the window, watching me. It makes my chest ache. I wish she'd stay, but I know I have no right to even ask her to. I said I was going to be better for her, and somehow, I ended up being worse.

"Harper, never believe a man when he says he'll change."

She coos against her pacifier, and when I look up again, Hanna is staring away from me, a contemplative look on her face. Then the patio door opens, and Zara walks in, looking at us with a tight smile.

"I'm fighting the urge to take a picture right now."

"Thank you for that." I love pictures of Harper, but memories of this day, no thanks.

Keeping Harper in my arm, I pour myself a cup of coffee, and when I look back at Zara, she looks almost impressed. Sitting at the counter across from me, she smiles.

"Want one?"

"Sure," she replies, so I pass her the one I just poured.

It's only comfortably silent for a moment before she starts with the questions.

"Have a good talk with your dad?"

I roll my eyes. "Yeah, he can get you all caught up later." I desperately don't need to go through that whole thing again. It was awful enough once.

"I think I'm just about caught up," she says while walking to the fridge to pull out the coffee creamer she uses.

"Think so?"

"Don't forget I know you, Nash Wilde. I used to know you better than anyone else, but I don't think I get to say that anymore."

I catch the way her eyes glance out to the patio, and my mouth goes dry. Here we go.

"If you think I'm mad, I promise I'm not."

"I thought you'd hate us together."

As she sits back on the stool, she looks at me for a moment before leaning forward and saying, "Don't be mad at me for what I'm about to say. You're holding my baby.

But Nash, I never wanted you with Hanna…to protect Hanna."

Ouch. I probably deserved that.

And as I bring the cup to my lips, blowing on the hot coffee, I don't argue.

"I was that bad, huh?"

"You were that broken. I expected you to come back from Amsterdam a stronger, happier version of yourself, but you were more broken than when I first came to Del Rey. You just hid it differently. I knew something happened there, and I assumed it was my fault. I was afraid your dad and I got married too quickly, and it didn't take much digging on your dad's part to figure it out."

"What do you mean figure it out?" I ask.

"He had some friends there. He made a few calls, found out you were spending all of your free time with Ellis Prior. He just didn't understand the scope of it yet, but I had my ideas…"

What the…fuck?

"Why didn't anyone say something to me?"

"Talk to you? We could hardly get you to look up from your phone for three years straight. Alistair assumed once you got the company back, you'd have something to distract you. He just wanted you to be okay. And when it was very clear you weren't…he called him."

Shit, it all makes sense now. When my dad called him, I assumed it was because he didn't trust me to handle it on my own. Naturally, he had to fucking meddle in my personal life.

"Granted, he thought you were just friends, but at lunch that day, it was very clear to me it was more than that. Then I went shopping with Hanna…and that's when I realized shit was a lot more complicated out here than I thought."

"Fuck," I mutter, leaning against the counter. Glancing down at Harper still in my arms, and I realize she fell asleep, snoring peacefully in my arms.

Zara gets up from her stool, walking over to place her lips against the baby's head. When she looks up at me, she ruffles my hair. "We don't care who you love, Nash. We just want you to be happy. Then maybe you can have something like this for yourself."

She carefully rolls Harper out of my arms and carries her over to her car seat, laying her down with care. I'm left reeling in the kitchen, feeling a little side-swiped by this news that not only did my dad know about Ellis and me in Amsterdam but he wanted him out here to try and make me happy…again.

This is the second time he's done this. I just wish I knew why the fuck it doesn't ever seem to work.

AFTER SAYING goodbye to my dad and Zara, I go to my room to hide. I don't want to be around when Hanna leaves. I've faced enough failure today. I just need to be alone with it for a while. But it's only a few minutes after I drift off to sleep that I feel someone's weight settle on my bed.

When I open my eyes, I stare at her as she crawls across the mattress and rests on the pillow next to me.

"I thought you were leaving."

"I can't. Not with us like this."

I let out a sigh. "You don't have to feel bad. Just go."

"They already left. You're stuck with me. For a few more days at least."

It's silent between us as she watches me with sadness in her eyes. Then she tells me about her apartment and giving the restraining order to her mom and her new job at the restaurant. It feels good…to see her moving on. Living her own life.

"Are you going to see him?" I ask, not because I'm jealous but because I'm just curious. It's weird that I hope she is. It's bittersweet, but I want them to be happy, even if that's without me.

"Not like that."

"Why not?"

She looks at me like I should know the answer to that question. Rolling onto her back, she drapes an arm over her head. I have to fight the urge to touch her. I want to kiss her so bad it hurts.

"Because he may never be over you enough to date, and he'll never be over you enough to date me."

"That's not true," I say, leaning on my elbow.

"You think this is what I want? I wish I were wrong, Nash, but he will never be able to look at me without seeing you."

"Fuck," I say with an exhale, reclining against the headboard. "What am I supposed to do?"

"Well, have you tried apologizing?"

"For what? Being an asshole? You think after the *two* times I have fucked him over, saying sorry will make any difference? Would you believe me if I told you I'd really change this time? That I wouldn't fall apart and go back to my old fucked-up ways next time shit gets hard?"

"But why don't you lean on us? Open up. Tell us when you're stuck in your head. Stop punishing us for loving you?"

Raking my fingers through my hair, I let out a loud groan. "I know that now. I'm trying. I promise, but a lot of good that does me now. He would never believe me if I told him that."

"You should at least try. He might do it against his

better judgement, but I believe he would take you back, Nash."

"Hanna," I say, looking at her. "I would let him do whatever he wanted to me to make that true. If he wanted me to get on my knees and beg I would. I'd let him…"

My voice trails, my mind latching onto an idea.

"What?" she asks.

I hate to get my hopes up, but my mind immediately goes back to a moment three years ago when it felt like Ellis offered me everything I ever wanted. Control over him, the opportunity to make him completely mine.

It was a moment so simple yet so powerful, to be handed his trust so complicitly. Am I crazy to think if I offered him that right now, he'd consider taking me back? Isn't that what he always wanted, my complete trust. To have me so vulnerable in his hands that he could own me without question.

There's only one way to find out.

35

My hands are shaking as we get out of the car in front of his building. In classic Ellis style, it's sleek, expensive, but not intimidating. Stopping in front of the door, I start to panic. Maybe this is a bad idea. What if he has someone over? What if he's already moved on? What if…it doesn't work?

No, it has to work. This is all I have left. I have no idea where to go after this if it doesn't.

Hanna sends the doorman a charming smile and tells him we're here to see Mr. Prior on business. His eyes linger on her a moment too long as he makes a call up to the apartment, and I stand there shaking in my shoes. When he tells Ellis over the phone it's Ms. Thurber, he smiles. Leaving my name out is a good idea.

"Penthouse," the doorman says, pointing to the metallic, shining door of the elevator.

With one push of the button, we're headed up. Hanna clings to my arm. "It's going to be okay."

Then the door chimes, opening to a grand entryway that leads to a large living room on the left and a marble white kitchen on the right. He's waltzing toward us from a room off the side I recognize as his office when he sees me and freezes.

"What the hell is this?" he asks.

In my periphery, I see her bite her lip. "Go on, Nash."

Here I fucking go.

"I know you don't give a shit about apologies at this point—"

"You'd be right." His jaw clenches.

Clearing my throat, I continue. "I'm not here begging for you to take me back or to forgive me. I'm here because I think I know what I need, and you're the only person I trust to give it to me."

His brow raises in curiosity, and I'm sure I have his attention now.

"I remember that night…with Lilac and I remember something she said about being submissive, about giving up control, how freeing it is, and I need that, Ellis."

With a gentle squint in his eye, he steps forward. "I'm not going to force you into submission so you can feel better—"

"I'm giving it to you," I say, stopping him. "I trust you."

Silence fills the room like a dark cloud, and I can see in his eyes he wants this. Maybe it's what he's always wanted but was too afraid to ask for.

His hands tighten into fists with his arms crossed over his chest, the thick veins of his forearms popping as he clenches. He's thinking about it, imagining me vulnerable and powerless. He wants to break me. I just hope he wants to build me back up afterward.

His eyes drift to Hanna who is standing next to me, and without looking at her, I know she softens under his gaze.

"It's not that easy," he says, more to her than to me. At least he's apologetic about it. As if he wishes he could offer her a better solution and the guilt I feel for being the person, the problem, the broken cog in this machine, stings like acid.

"I know it's not," I reply, stepping forward. "But since when did we ever take the easy route? And I'm not asking you to take it easy on me. I'm asking you to give me what you've wanted to since we met. You've known this about me the whole time, haven't you? You could see what I couldn't. I was meant to do this. It's what I've always needed when I was so convinced I needed to be the one in control. Ever since my brother died in the crash I should have prevented, I've been in a tailspin, thinking I only needed to regain control. But you knew…what I really needed was to give it up. Let go."

He stares at me a moment, his chest moving with his heavy breath, his pulse pounding in his neck. Then he steps forward, his body almost touching mine as his dark stare penetrates all the confidence I walked in here with.

"You remember the safe word?"

I swallow. "Trust."

"I'm going to crack you open, tear away every single layer, until all that is left is you. Just Nash."

"I'm ready."

His thumb touches my chin, and instantly the contact

makes me melt, missing him so much I could cry for him to do it again, even if it hurts. Then he runs it down along my jaw toward my neck as his hand encircles my throat.

"Hanna, are you staying or going?"

She steps up next to me. "I'm staying."

"It might get intense. You won't like it," he says and suddenly I get nervous for her. A cool pit of fear settles in my bones. Hanna nurtures, she worries, she cares. This will be too much for her to watch, and as much as I want her here for the aftercare part, I don't know if she can handle everything leading up to it.

"You should go," I tell her, but she only shakes her head, a quiver to her lip already.

"It's all of us or nothing at all."

His hand slips from my throat and he walks away toward the hallway leading to the back of the apartment. His place is large, expansive, with thick white marble floors and floor-to-ceiling windows.

Following close behind him, my shoulders begin to tighten along with the heavy knot in my gut. He goes straight for the large bedroom at the end of the hall, and I know immediately by the scent of him as we pass through the doorway it's his room. The bed, with its black bedding, is large and neatly made. The instant memories of Amsterdam hit me hard.

He passes through the space for the large walk-in closet he enters and turns for the drawers along the back. After opening one, he begins pulling things out and turns to set them on the bed. I recognize them immediately: the rope, the blindfold, the paddle, the flogger, and last, he adds something else.

My pulse quickens.

"Take your clothes off," he says in a low, authoritative tone.

Without hesitation, I pull off my shirt, folding it and setting it on the dresser against the wall. Hanna finds a spot in the opposite corner, watching as I peel off the rest of my clothes until I'm down to my boxers.

Ellis walks slowly over to me with a familiar black piece of silk running sensually between his fingers. "On your knees," he says, tilting his head back and glaring down his nose at me. "You might have asked me for this, but that's all the say you're going to have from here on out. I know what's best for you, and I'll be the one giving it to you. You don't ask and you don't argue. Understood?"

"Yeah," I answer in a shaky breath as I lower to my knees. Ellis bends at the hips, gripping my hair tight in his fist and pulling my head back so I can look at him.

"What was that?"

"Yes, sir."

"You can make this difficult, and that's fine. I like a little fight, but I have a feeling you're not going to like this so much."

He drapes the black silk over my eyes and the world goes dark.

"Arms up," he says coldly. There's a subtle boredom in his tone as if he's uninterested in this, and I know he's doing it on purpose. To deny me his attention and interest is its own form of torture.

Obediently, I raise my arms, and I feel the cool leather of the cuffs as he snaps them around each wrist. Pulling a little harsher than he might pull anyone else, he hoists me to my feet and leads me across the room. When I feel the bed against my legs, I freeze.

"Climb up, on your knees."

Doing as he says, I get on the bed and wait for his next instruction when I feel him walk away, no longer hearing his breath or smelling his scent. Somewhere in the room,

Hanna is sitting silently watching, and I wish I could look at her, touch her, feel her comfort, know she's not too scared.

When Ellis returns, I feel something large and soft against my legs. It comes up to my hip bones, and when he hinges me forward, I realize it's a wedge ramp, putting my ass up in the air as I rest my forehead on the smaller wedge attached to the opposite side. It's a form of humiliation, having my ass in the air, and I breathe through it.

He's making me vulnerable, and I knew going into this he could do just about anything, and after everything I've put him through, I prepared myself for him being harsh. He knows my wounds and now he can throw all the salt he wants in them. I just fucking hope it pays off in the end.

Suddenly my arms are pulled tight over my head and I hear the snaps as he attaches each one to his bed post, so my top half is completely stretched out across his bed with my ass high for him. When his hand rests possessively on my back, I flinch.

"A little jumpy," he growls. Then he's close to my ear, and I shiver as he whispers, "I knew you'd hate this, but this isn't for you. It's for me."

He runs his strong hands along the muscles of my back, and it's a contradiction to his harsh tone. They are soothing, like his touch speaks a different language than his words, and I melt into the contact. Even as he peels down my boxers, leaving me completely exposed, my semi-hard dick presses against the velvet texture of the ramp. There's a cool breeze on my balls as Ellis nudges me to spread my knees. Stretching the skin, I know this is about to hurt like a bitch.

"We'll start off slow with just the paddle. You will count. Eight for the first round."

When his hand leaves my back, it's silent, and I stiffen, trying to breathe. "Yes, sir," I mumble.

Suddenly, the paddle lands hard against my backside, reverberating through my spine in a sharp crack and I let out a grunt. The pain hits me by surprise. My breathing picks up as I start to panic, clenching around the tight knot of nerves in my stomach.

"Nash." His voice carries loud and angry through the sound of my heart pounding in my chest.

"One," I groan.

It lands again, this time on the opposite side feeling even harder. Mother fucker said he was going to start off slow. Like hell that's starting slow. Struggling against the restraints, I clench my jaw wanting to yell at him, tell him to start easy like he said he would.

"This is the last time I'll remind you to count before I add another eight, and I won't go easy after that."

"Two!" I shout through gritted teeth.

The next three smacks against my ass feel like fire licking through my flesh, but I breathe through it all, counting as he told me to, but it's not until the seventh and eighth hit I start to feel the muscles in my arms soften like butter.

He runs his hands across my ass, and I hiss in response to his touch.

"Oh baby, that was nothing. Don't you want more?"

Fuck him if he thinks he's gotten even close to breaking me.

"You're going to have to do better than that," I snap which earns me a harsh pinch of my sensitive flesh. I let out a muffled string of obscenities.

"Don't make me gag you," he says, dragging his nails across my sore ass.

Squeezing my eyes shut, I breathe through the urge to

talk back, but I know he'll keep his word if I do, and that nasty thing crammed between my teeth is the last fucking thing I want, so I bite my tongue.

His hands drift upward, across the tense muscles of my back, along my sides until he's squeezing my shoulders and neck.

"What are you holding onto?" he says, but this time he's speaking in the familiar Ellis voice, not the low, controlling tone. Like he's stepping out of character, and it hits me a little harder. Knowing he's in there. Knowing he cares.

I don't answer him. Instead, I mumble into the velvet. "Again please."

He lets out a sigh and his hands leave my back. When I hear him pick something off the bed, I prepare myself for another paddling.

"Eight again. Don't forget to count."

As the thick strands of leather land hard and sharp across my back, I let out a yelp and fidget against the restraints again.

"Fuck!" I cry out because the pain doesn't fade away. It gets stronger, spreading across my back like he's pouring boiling water on my flesh.

When it lands again even harder, I lose the ability to breathe.

"Count and start at one," his voice booms through the panic echoing through my skull.

What the fuck? How did Lilac put up with this? I'm not a fucking pussy, but right now, I'm realizing I had no goddamn clue what that girl was feeling.

My mind is racing, trying to catch up with itself when he hits me again, and I scream.

"You are still on one, and if I were you, I wouldn't forget to count."

"One," I gasp.

He sounds so fucking angry, I cower to it. It's like I'm a ten-year-old kid again, staring up at a man who represented everything I wanted to be. Confident, smart, rich, good looking. I wanted to be him so bad, I built my life around that desire. And now he's angry at me, landing another soul crushing hit against my back. Something in me breaks like a tiny crack in the dam.

"Two," I mumble out, my mouth wet and breathless.

He's not taking it easy on me. Every harsh crack of that flogger against my back is like knocking another peg out, and instead of fighting the pain, I let it flow through me.

And it's burning down everything.

My groans turn into shouts, but I keep up my counting. I hardly notice when we get to eight and I'm sweating all over the ramp, breathing through something even more painful than what he's doing to my back. It's a stabbing wound in my chest, and it's making it hard to breathe.

"Still holding on. Maybe we should stop. I don't think you can handle any more."

"No!" I burst out. "No…I can handle it."

"Eight more," he says, and I whimper, already anticipating the pain, which comes down hard, and I can't tell if my back is sore or numb, but the sting feels more like a shallow stabbing pain.

He doesn't let up, and I start to realize what we started with was easy compared to this, but with each lash, I drift farther and farther from this moment, from this pain and the voice in my head. They send me deeper and deeper, flushing away the thoughts that plague my soul.

I don't know how I remember to count, but I do, and he keeps it up.

I cease to exist by the fourth.

And on the sixth, I see Preston's face, and a dry sob escapes my lips.

The seventh and eighth go by in a blur, my face contorted in anguish as I'm wracked with pain, shivering as it becomes a part of me, like a hot blanket soaking into my skin, easing away everything else.

"That's better," he says, pulling my hair out of my face, but I can't see him with the blindfold still on. I take in a shaky breath when Ellis touches my back. "So beautiful seeing the way you give in, let it replace every thought in your head. We're so close, aren't we?"

I can't answer him. I'm still in a fuzzy blur of pain and peace, but I know what's coming, so I feel myself bracing again.

"Eight more."

There's a small gasp across the room, and my ears perk up. I forgot she was here, and suddenly my attention is on Hanna, knowing she's seeing me like this, afraid for me.

"Hanna wants to know you're okay. Tell her. Tell her how much you need it."

"I'm okay," I whisper, my voice shaky, but fuck, I wish I could touch her. Feel her skin under my fingers, crawl into a warm space where there is no more pain. "I need this."

Ellis slaps my ass and I wince. "You came here and asked for this. Remember that because what you felt so far is nothing compared to what you're about to feel. We'll let Hanna count these ones out."

Suddenly, it's like a lightning strike against my back, and I open my mouth to yell but there is no sound. I know it's the crop now, that thin piece of leather that delivers the sharpest pain against my already sore back.

As the pain skitters across my body like fire ants, I struggle against the restraints again. Somewhere in the last thirty lashes, my cock has gotten unbelievably hard.

Shoved against the ramp, I settle myself from struggling since the friction would easily have me coming all over this thing.

"One," Hanna says, her voice tight and low, like she's trying to hide something. Is she crying for me? God, I want to look at her.

He strikes again and again and again. Hanna's voice grows tighter, a slight shake and gasp with each syllable.

I don't know much anymore, but I know I'm sobbing again. I know the end is near, and I know everything inside me is raw. The dam is broken, my pain and emotions spilling out through the now gaping cracks.

What's the strangest by the seventh crack is how I feel almost closer to him. He's inflicting my pain, but I welcome it. I love it. And I know he's letting up. That is until he gets to eight, and he delivers the hit against my back that makes me scream the loudest, my howling cries drawn out as I melt against the bed.

The tension in my arms eases as I feel someone loosen the restraints and then my wrists are pulled out of the cuffs. Still, I'm shaking, crying like a child, and I don't know if it's because of Preston, or Zara, or Hanna, or Ellis. Or just for myself. My spent anger and years lost to regret. The pain I inflicted on others now directed back at me.

The night I found Zara at the strip club and treated her so badly, forcing her into something she didn't want.

The night I forced myself on Hanna, wanting her to hate me for it.

The night I broke everything between me and Ellis like it was a person I could murder, like the monster I am.

For all of those things, I drown in my pain and my tears.

Suddenly, I'm being lifted, my back held against his

body, warm hands on my chest and lips against my shoulders.

Fuck me, please. My mind chants as my rock hard length rubs against the soft friction of the pillow, but mostly I want him inside me. I *need* him inside me. To truly own me, use me, take his pleasure from my body.

"Fuck me." The words slip from my mouth, and with the blindfold still around my eyes, I feel him there, his cock already slick and hard against my entrance. He enters me easily, my body pliant and open for him, but his thrust is harsh. Then he grunts low and gravelly into my ear, and I swim in the sounds of his pleasure.

Clutching his arms, he holds me up when I notice the sudden absence of the ramp that was pressed against my legs. Then, she's there. I feel her warm, naked body against my chest, and I don't know whose hands I'm feeling, but I know they're there. I'm consumed by them.

My arms wrap tightly around Hanna, needing her close, burying myself in her until I'm bathed in her warmth.

All I know is them, their cries of pleasure filling my ears and my mind. Pressed between the beating of their hearts, we move to the same rhythm, like waves crashing together against the shore. And when I feel them climax around me, I let the tide take me too.

I come, and come, and come until there is nothing left of me.

My ears begin to ring, my body buzzing like the static of a radio as I collapse.

"You're okay. We've got you."

Instead of wanting to escape, feeling like it's wrong to be so vulnerable, I let them have this raw, unguarded version of me.

"It's okay, Nash," she whispers, her lips pressed against my neck.

"Let it out." His voice comes from the opposite side.

All of the emotion bubbling, spilling, hemorrhaging from my insides, runs like a river over everything between us. And there is no stopping it.

"I'm so sorry," I sob. "I'm sorry for everything I did to you. You're the last ones I ever wanted to hurt, and I hurt you so bad."

They squeeze me tighter. Then the blindfold is pulled back and I squeeze my eyes closed, but the room is dim, almost pitch black. Still, I can see them. Hanna is quick to wipe my tears while Ellis brushes my hair out of my face. "There you are," he whispers.

"I love you," I say before I can stop myself. Before the fear crawls back in to censor me from saying the things I should have said a long time ago, and I hope they know I mean the both of them. I love the way things are right now when we don't need to define anything or fear anything and we are truly free.

Free to fall.

36

AM I A FOOL TO TAKE HIM BACK? MAYBE, BUT THERE IS something invisible stringing us together. Something unbreakable, and I can either live in agony, knowing I'll never be truly free of Nash Wilde, or I can spend every moment of my life reeling him back in every time a part of him retreats like he did before.

If I have to lay him out like I did today, I will. I won't say I didn't love it, watching him break, lashing him with every ounce of hurt he embedded in me.

I climb out of bed, unable to sleep and walk silently to the kitchen. Pulling a glass from the cabinet, I opt for water instead of whiskey. A clear head is probably the best way to go here.

It's only a few minutes until I see his silhouette walking quietly through the apartment. He stops on the opposite side of the island, watching me cautiously. Even in the dark, I can see the heavy bags under his eyes. If I had to guess when the last time Nash truly let go and cried the way he did tonight, I'd guess it was easily five or more years and definitely not so openly. I could see the adrenaline coursing through him, and I know the way he's feeling now. Renewed, but exhausted.

Without a word, I push the glass of water across the countertop, encouraging him to drink. I made sure he hydrated before he fell asleep and even forced him to eat something, but he sobered up with hesitation. Not ready to face reality I assume.

He takes the glass and drinks, setting it down when it's empty, so I refill it, taking a sip of my own. It's silent a moment before he finally mumbles a soft, "thank you."

"I didn't do it for you," I reply. It's only partly true. I did it for all of us.

"I know."

"How are you feeling?" I ask, leaning against the counter with my arms crossed. My body language says I'm not opening myself back up to him, and yeah, a part of me wants to see what version of Nash I'm getting today before I let him in. In my head I know it doesn't matter. I'm helpless against him either way.

"Good…great."

"That's good."

Silence again. And with every passing second the tension grows. Finally unable to take another second, he steps forward, bracing his hand on the granite between us.

"I know I'm fucked up, Ellis. I know I can be difficult

and nothing I do is ever right, and there is no excuse in the world for how I treated you. Not my brother, not my dad, not Zara. And I'm not promising I won't ever hurt you again because one night of getting my back thrashed to death won't fix everything, but I promise I'll try."

Looking at him in the dim light with the shadows over his apologetic eyes, I fight the urge to gather this broken, sad boy into my arms and kiss away every ounce of pain and fear because I want him to know this love is hard fought and hard won.

But I can't make him suffer for it anymore.

"Come here."

He rounds the island quickly and lands hard against my chest as I wrap my arms around him, holding him close. He breathes heavily into my neck, and I feel the pounding of his heart against mine. There is nothing between us now. No regrets or secrets or lies.

We stand there a moment, not speaking. Not moving.

Not until we hear the sound of footsteps approaching. Hanna runs her hands softly against my back, and Nash and I both move to pull her in at the same time. Squeezed between us, we breathe the same air, sharing one space.

"This is nice," she whispers. And it is.

Conventional? No.

But we're all broken down so far that it takes more than one person to complete us. This relationship wouldn't stand if even one person were to leave it. But it's what makes us stronger together.

"Who's hungry?" I ask as I pull away.

"I'm starving," Nash groans. The two of them cuddle on the couch while I make a midnight breakfast.

As we gather around the table to eat, things are comfortable. The only sound that fills the room is our breathing, the delicate clang of our forks against the plates, and after the intense, emotionally draining day we've had, the quiet is welcome.

"I heard my dad paid you a visit," Nash says in a soft tone.

"He did." I watch his expression. The sudden reminder of Alistair in my office makes me nervous. If Nash is going to fight opening up to his family, then I'll know we still have a long way to go.

"I told him everything," he says. "I, um, came out."

I have to swallow the bite of food in my mouth before I let myself smile, just a lopsided grin as my eyes travel up to his face.

"And?"

"And they already knew." An easy laugh spills out of his mouth, and if his cheeks weren't already red from the crying he did earlier, I think he'd be blushing.

"I bet it still felt good," I reply.

His blue eyes shine as he focuses on me. Nodding, he says, "It did."

Through the entirety of our relationship, Nash held onto a sense of fear and shame, unable to accept what he is, a bisexual man. It was all just a part of his armor, and I know that now, but it feels so fucking good to see him shed that facade. To be truly free.

Hanna clears her throat, dabbing her lips with her napkin. "I need to do a little coming out of my own," she says, looking at Nash.

We both turn to work her with furrowed brows.

"I have to tell Zara about us." She looks genuinely nervous, biting the inside of her lip and letting out a heavy exhale.

"Oh, she already knows," Nash says with a wince.

Hanna's eyes widen as her gaze bounces between me and him.

"She does?"

"Yeah. She said something to me while we were inside today, or yesterday. I don't even know what day it is, but she brought it up, and she's not mad."

"Not mad at you," she says with a scoff.

"Or you." He places his hand on hers and looks her in the eye. "Honestly, I think she would have tried to set us up if I hadn't been such an asshole. Zara has been through hell too, Hanna. She wants for you the same thing she found."

"A rich man with a private island?" Hanna adds with a wide smile, leaning her head on her hand propped up on the table.

I find myself laughing and reaching across the table to touch her. After everything, it's so nice to be able to crack jokes and smile with them. It feels like the days on Del Rey when it all started with the three of us.

"Speaking of my private island," he says, touching her elbow.

"I'm not moving there," she replies quickly. "I still need to do things on my own for a while. I have my apartment, a new job—" She puts up her hand when she notices him about to argue. "I know I don't need either of them if I'm going to be with you...and you." Her gaze travels my way, but I don't argue with her. Giving her a gentle smile, I squeeze her hand.

"We know you do. But we can still make this work," I say.

Nash looks nervous, breathing heavily with his hooded eyes focused on her. There's not a doubt in my mind he's afraid of losing her—and me—because neither of us need him, not in that way. So, I ease his discomfort.

"Just because we're not living on Del Rey with you, doesn't mean we're not with you."

"I'm in this one-hundred percent," Hanna adds.

"So am I." My opposite hand reaches for him, and our fingers meet, latching onto each other like they were meant to.

"One-hundred percent," he says.

"Let's go back to bed," Hanna whispers after a moment, but Nash is still frozen like stone, looking deep in thought.

"I'm going to move to the mainland." His words settle like a heavy fog, silencing us all for a moment. Hanna and I glance at each other, and I know she's thinking the same thing I am. This is big.

Nash has lived on that island for almost his entire life. It was the physical barrier between him and the rest of the world, and it was the setting for every moment of trauma he's experienced. Him wanting to leave it is a sign he's ready to make real changes.

"Are you sure?" she says in a low whisper. She looks hopeful, and I admit I am too.

"Yeah. Can I stay with you?" he asks her and her eyebrows nearly hit her hairline.

"You want to move from your mansion on an island to my shitty apartment?"

"I really do." There's not a hint of humor or sarcasm in his expression, and I have to bite back a smile that wants to reach my ears.

"Nash…"

"If we're going to do this, I want it to be real. Living on Del Rey is like living in a fantasy. I want the two of you to be my life, not a dream."

Tears brim in Hanna's eyes as she stares at him. "Okay," she manages to mumble.

"Okay," I echo.

"Are you moving in with me too?" she asks with a laugh as a tear rolls down her cheeks.

With a heavy chuckle, I reach over and wipe it from her face. "I'm going to be really fucking jealous if you two get to live together without me. One-hundred percent, remember?"

The table breaks out in laughter, the three of us high on this future we're building. And although I have no plans to sell my apartment for now, I love the vision of the three of us living perfectly ordinary lives together.

"Okay, can we please go back to bed now?" she asks.

"Fuck yes," he answers quickly as he jumps from his seat and pulls her into his arms. She wraps her legs around him, and he carries her toward the bedroom.

Watching them together, I realize there are no guarantees, and we have no way of knowing if this will work forever. But if things had never fallen apart between Nash and me in Amsterdam, we never would have found her, and I believe it all happened for a reason.

Sometimes things have to be broken before they can be truly whole again.

EPILOGUE

AFTER A LONG DAY of walking around the city, I sleep so deeply, wrapped in warmth with hands and legs and bodies in my space, I don't dream a thing. And when I peel my eyes open in the morning, Ellis is spooning me, his arm draped over my waist.

The first thing I feel is his morning wood pressed snugly between the cheeks of my ass, and on instinct, I shift my hips back. A warm thrill shoots through my body and my already stiff cock twitches with anticipation.

Ellis groans, grinding against me. Then his lips find the

lobe of my ear, and he bites down, making me even harder.

Fuck, I love this. We used to start so many days this way in Amsterdam before and they were so fucking wonderful I don't know how I went so long without being fucked first thing in the morning.

"I wonder if we can do it without waking her up," he whispers as I feel the warm tip of him at my entrance. My hands fumble for the lube on the table, and he takes it while still nibbling on my neck.

"I think she likes being woken up this way," I reply, my voice still groggy with sleep.

He eases in, and I gasp, arching my back to give him easier access.

"God, you feel so good, Nash. This won't take me long at all," he whispers, reaching for my cock. With my hand over his, he thrusts slow and deep, and my body is on fire, red hot flames reaching the very tips of my toes.

His husky grunts of pleasure in my ear push me closer to the edge.

"Fuck," I gasp as he jolts forward, fucking me in deep, smooth movements. It's the precipice of pain and pleasure, touching that most sensitive spot inside me, the one that makes my dick throb and my heart stutter in my chest.

"Oh God…" His deep voice echoes through every bone in my body as he shakes and shudders, his release spilling inside me.

When his hand leaves my dick and latches onto my throat, I want to tell him I'm his. I'm all fucking his. He can do whatever he wants with me. When he's fucking me, I don't need a goddamn thing, except for maybe the woman next to him, the one who treats my soul with such tenderness I would die a thousand times to be better for her.

"She's still fucking asleep," he says in my ear, and we both laugh, catching our breaths at the same time.

"No, I'm not," she groans. "You two don't fuck as quietly as you think you do."

Ellis climbs out of bed and walks to the bathroom, and I roll over, gathering her tiny body in my arms. "What's wrong? Jealous?"

Trailing my fingers down her stomach, I reach into her panties and run them through her warm folds. "Nothing gets you hotter than hearing us fuck, does it?" I murmur against her neck, running my tongue up to her lips as she moans through me plunging my digits into her warmth.

I love watching her moan and writhe underneath me. And yeah, sometimes I like to wrap my hands around that little neck of hers, her eyes filling with fear and arousal as I fuck her, claiming her and her beautiful pussy as mine. That's what she comes to me for. She knows if she wants it sweet, she can go to Ellis. He might be hard on me, but never on her. That's my job.

When I hear the shower running, I know he can't hear anymore, so I tear off her underwear, making her yelp. Then she looks up at me with her lip pinched between her teeth.

Flipping her roughly to her knees, I work my way into her from behind, and she lets out a gasp, clawing at the headboard. Once I'm buried as far as I can go, I slam into her again and again, slow but deliberate.

"Harder," she pants, and I grip harshly onto her hips and give her exactly what she wants.

Holding out until I feel her tense and shivering is hard considering Ellis got me all warmed up, but her climax finally sets me free, and I slam in one last time, holding her hips hard against me as I spill myself inside of her.

We fall to the pillows together before she crawls over and rests her head against my chest.

"What do you want to do today, beautiful?"

"We still haven't seen the Rijksmuseum. Or Anne Frank's house."

"It's up to you," I mumble against her hair. Just then, Ellis steps out of the bathroom, towel drying his hair without a shred of clothes on, and Hanna and I both stare in interest.

"We could also stay in the hotel all day," I say before she playfully slaps my chest and climbs out of the bed.

"There is such a thing as too much sex."

Ellis and I glare skeptically at each other in a shared expression of disapproval. She kisses him quickly before scurrying to the bathroom, holding her legs close together to keep everything I just spilled in her from running down her leg. It makes me laugh as I lie on the bed with my arm folded behind my head.

"What are you smiling about?" Ellis asks while getting dressed.

Why wouldn't I be? It's been a year since we made our way back together. It was never easy, especially at first as we tried to let Hanna make her own way in the city, working long hours, scraping together her tips to make ends meet, knowing full well neither Ellis nor I would let her go one second without everything she needed. But we tried not to help too much. He had to stop me from anonymously dropping two-thousand dollar tips on her checks or paying her rent for the year.

"She needs this," he told me. And I understood. Like me needing to be whipped within an inch of my life sometimes, submitting everything to him because it's what I needed to let go.

Those first few months in the apartment were my

favorite. She furnished it with her savings, and we ate dinners Ellis would cook at a tiny secondhand table in the kitchen, and every single moment was perfect. Those days were the real start to our life, humble and beautiful in its imperfection.

Letting people know about our relationship wasn't as hard as I thought it would be. The people who mattered the most, like Dad and Zara, didn't even act surprised when we told them. Like everything else, they knew long before we ever made it official, and aside from Zara threatening my life if I didn't treat Hanna like the goddess she is, I think it went over pretty well. It was important to all of us that everyone understood this wasn't a fling or a kinky arrangement. These two people are my forever—all or none. One-hundred percent.

And it wasn't until we decided to let go of Del Rey a couple of months ago they finally understood. We bought a big house on the mainland, something that fit all three of us. Something closer so Hanna could keep working and Ellis could get his space when he needed it.

It was hard at first. Letting go of that house, the memories there, but I don't belong on an island anymore. I am not an island. I am grounded, setting down roots and happy for the first time in my life.

But now I wake up each morning between the two of them, and I don't know where we'll go from here.

"You need to get out of bed, Nash Wilde," Hanna scolds me as she walks out wrapped in a towel. Her hair is piled up on her head in a messy bun, and when she pulls out the clip, it cascades down her back, and I want to touch it, bury my face in it and breathe her in.

"We should get married," I blurt out, a smile still stretched across my face. They both freeze in response, glaring first at each other before looking at me.

"I'm not talking about a wedding or anything. Fuck we don't even need the certificate, I just want you to take my name."

"Me?" Hanna says, touching her chest.

"Both of you."

Ellis smirks. "And what makes you think we would take your name?"

"Because everyone wants to be a Wilde," I answer with a laugh.

"I will," Hanna says with confidence. "I don't want my name anymore anyway." Her smile falters for a second, and I know bringing up her mother is still a sore subject. After moving on with her life last year, her mother hasn't reached out even once, even after Hanna tried to contact her. I know she's hurt by their distance, but it only makes me want to smother her with love even more. We are a family now, so she doesn't need her. She has us.

"We could hyphenate," she says, pulling on her bra.

Ellis and I both scowl at the same time.

"No, let's take Wilde. I'll change my name."

For a moment, I don't move, letting his words sink in. I won't say I was joking, but I'll admit it was hopeful banter. There's nothing I want more than to make this thing between us concrete. It's already real, unshakable and forever, but to have it on paper, knowing he is mine and hers and we are each other's without shame… I almost can't believe it.

"You mean that?" I ask.

Just as he finishes dressing, he sits on the bed next to me. "Of course. Why wouldn't I?"

The reasons running through my mind are weak compared to the look he's giving me now. Because I've broken his heart twice. Because it's unconventional, taboo, wrong. Because I'm *not good enough for you.* But those are the voices in my head, and his voice is louder.

"Let's do it. As soon as we get home." Leaning down, he plants a kiss on my lips like this is casual conversation, like getting a dog or buying a car.

"Okay," I reply.

"Seriously, though. I'm starving and I want waffles, so get your ass up, Nash!" Hanna yells, throwing a pillow at me.

I can't peel the smile off my face as I jump up and run to the bathroom. The mirror grabs my attention as I turn on the shower, and I see a happy man looking back. It's a new reflection, and it's taking some getting used to. It was a long road to get here, and I hate to think about how easily I could have missed this. I could have done a million things differently that would have led to any other outcome, most likely me growing up miserable and alone, punishing myself for not being in a crash I had no way of preventing. Holding onto the guilt like it was my life raft.

But the only thing I'm holding onto now are the two people in the other room, the one who nurtures me and the one who challenges me. And as long as I have them, I'm free.

ACKNOWLEDGMENTS

Thank you for reading Free Fall. I wrote this book for you, my readers. I knew you would love Nash even when I was writing Gravity, but to be honest, I never really planned to finish his story. But you inspired me, and I'm so glad you did.

I have loved every minute of writing this book. It was the most difficult story I've ever told, and even I didn't expect where Nash would go with this one. What a ride it was. I'm going to miss Del Rey and the Wildes more than you'll ever know. Thank you, thank you, thank you.

Once again, my team is owed a million thanks for everything they have done to help me make this book a reality.

Suzanne, you know how nervous I was about this book. I would have never had the courage to tackle it if it wasn't for your confidence and support. You're the greatest.

Amanda, thanks for loving our boys as much as I do.

Adrian, always and forever, my alpha. I love you.

Rachel, thanks for reminding me to go big!

My amazing PA, Lori Alexander. My #1.

My publicist, Amanda Anderson, and the amazing team at Wildfire Marketing.

All the thanks in the world to the rest of my awesome team:

My ARC team of readers and bloggers. I appreciate you every single time.

Michelle Lancaster for the stunning cover photo.

Give Me Books promotions.

My editor, Amy Briggs of Briggs Consulting.

My proofreader, Gem's Precise Proofreads.

Kate Farlow of Y'all That Graphic for the graphic designs.

And last but definitely NOT least, All of my Sweets in Sara's Sweets for being the best fans in the world.

Dangerous

Defiant

ABOUT THE AUTHOR

Sara Cate writes forbidden romance with lots of angst, a little age gap, and heaps of steam. Living in Nashville with her husband and kids, Sara spends most of her time reading, writing, or baking.

You can find more information about her at
www.saracatebooks.com

Printed in Great Britain
by Amazon

86807104R00196